The heavy door was jerked from Ricky's grip

It slammed against the side of the pod with a clang. At the same time, a huge tentacle shot inside, wrapped around Ryan's waist and yanked him off his feet.

As Ricky lunged to grab him, Ryan caught the edge of the door frame with his hand as he was hauled through. But no sooner had he latched on to it than the free-swinging portal swung back on its hinges and smashed into him.

Already exhausted, Ryan couldn't hold on any longer. His fingers slipped off the metal lip, and he was pulled out into the dark and stormy night.

**Other titles in the
Deathlands saga:**

JAMES AXLER

DEATH LANDS.

Dark Fathoms

A GOLD EAGLE BOOK FROM

W♦RLDWIDE.

TORONTO • NEW YORK • LONDON
AMSTERDAM • PARIS • SYDNEY • HAMBURG
STOCKHOLM • ATHENS • TOKYO • MILAN
MADRID • WARSAW • BUDAPEST • AUCKLAND

Recycling programs
for this product may
not exist in your area.

First edition September 2013

ISBN-13: 978-0-373-62622-9

DARK FATHOMS

Printed in U.S.A.

Only God Almighty and naval research can save us from the perils of the sea.
        —U.S. Senator John William Warner (ret.)

THE DEATHLANDS SAGA

This world is their legacy, a world born in the violent nuclear spasm of 2001 that was the bitter outcome of a struggle for global dominance.

There is no real escape from this shockscape where life always hangs in the balance, vulnerable to newly demonic nature, barbarism, lawlessness.

But they are the warrior survivalists, and they endure—in the way of the lion, the hawk and the tiger, true to nature's heart despite its ruination.

Ryan Cawdor: The privileged son of an East Coast baron. Acquainted with betrayal from a tender age, he is a master of the hard realities.

Krysty Wroth: Harmony ville's own Titian-haired beauty, a woman with the strength of tempered steel. Her premonitions and Gaia powers have been fostered by her Mother Sonja.

J. B. Dix, the Armorer: Weapons master and Ryan's close ally, he, too, honed his skills traversing the Deathlands with the legendary Trader.

Doctor Theophilus Tanner: Torn from his family and a gentler life in 1896, Doc has been thrown into a future he couldn't have imagined.

Dr. Mildred Wyeth: Her father was killed by the Ku Klux Klan, but her fate is not much lighter. Restored from pre-dark cryogenic suspension, she brings twentieth-century healing skills to a nightmare.

Jak Lauren: A true child of the wastelands, reared on adversity, loss and danger, the albino teenager is a fierce fighter and loyal friend.

Dean Cawdor: Ryan's young son by Sharona accepts the only world he knows, and yet he is the seedling bearing the promise of tomorrow.

In a world where all was lost, they are humanity's last hope....

Prologue

Poseidon Base—a top secret location
in the Pacific Ocean
0729 hours
January 20, 2001

The blaring Klaxon jolted Lieutenant Commander Martin Yates, United States Navy, out of a sound sleep and into instant alert. He'd swung out of his bunk in his cramped quarters and was in his boots and pulling on his one-piece, navy blue jumpsuit almost before he'd registered what was happening.

Another drill?

As he finished dressing, he listened to whatever announcement was being broadcast along with the wailing alarm.

"—all personnel are to report to their emergency duty stations. This is not a drill, repeat, this is not a drill. All personnel are to report to their emergency duty stations—"

Yates's pulse quickened as the words sank in. What the hell was going on? He touched the photo of his wife, Maryann, and his five-year-old daughter, Raina—both living topside in Annapolis, Maryland—for luck. Then he walked to his door, which opened at his approach, and joined the steady stream of men and women hurrying to their various stations in the red-lit corridors.

No one ran, no one talked, everyone moved swiftly and with purpose. But as Yates merged with the tide of humanity, he saw something he had never seen in their faces before—fear.

As he strode to the main command and control center, Yates ran through what might have gone wrong. The all-hands alert wasn't for an equipment malfunction—that was a different announcement altogether. Neither was it for a crew accident; again, that was a different alert. As he hit the elevator for the bridge, his efficient mind came to the only logical conclusion, which matched the growing unease in his stomach.

Something had happened on the surface.

He blinked as the small elevator began its rise to the command center, then pushed that thought away. Without facts, he could not analyze the situation. And there was no way to react until he learned what he—what the entire sixty-seven-person crew—had to deal with.

A soft, pleasant female voice announced, "Command center." The doors slid open.

"Executive officer on deck!" The previous watch commander, Chief Warrant Officer Rodney Spielman, came to attention and snapped off a crisp salute, but none of the other men and women at their various duty stations did. Yates's eyebrows rose when he glanced around for the captain but didn't see him anywhere. He also noticed that the metal shutters were all down over the thick, panoramic windows that allowed them to see outside. He returned the CWO's salute—noting that he'd never seen the other man so pale—and the transfer of command was complete.

As he expected, every person was alert at his or her station, ready for whatever was about to come down the pike. He allowed himself the barest of smiles at their efficiency—the pride of the U.S. Navy manned Poseidon Base, and it showed in the adeptness of his crew. He ordered the Klaxon turned off, although they still remained at emergency lighting for now.

"What's the situation?" he asked Spielman.

"Sir, at 0726 hours we received a Priority One signal from NORAD." Spielman lowered his voice. "It said that Washington, D.C., has been hit by an as-yet-undetermined number of nuclear weapons."

Yates blinked as his subordinate's words sank in. He never realistically thought he'd live to see a nuclear strike on American soil. "Washington…how?"

"We do not have that information at this time, sir."

"But—today's the inauguration…" His family… Maryann and Raina had been planning to attend the swearing-in ceremony, weather permitting. But Annapolis, less than ten miles away from Washington, D.C., would be suffering from the aftermath regardless, especially the fallout, depending on wind direction. Even as the realization that his wife and daughter were most likely dead threatened to overwhelm him, Yates kept his anguish off his face and simply nodded. Now was not the time…

"Yes, sir. We have not confirmed this report yet, but are requesting more information. However, it was immediately followed by the announcement that all U.S. military forces are currently at DEFCON 1, and all personnel not in front-line positions are to await further instructions. Since then, communication has been…sporadic, at best, sir." The CWO paused. "Standard emergency protocols are being followed—all outside excursions have been recalled or canceled, and all personnel are at general quarters, awaiting further orders."

When the CWO finished, Yates took a deep breath

as he absorbed the fundamental alteration of his entire
world in the last sixty seconds. Even though he was
dying to learn more about what was happening thousands of feet above them—in particular, to his family—
he knew his first priority was to ensure the protection
of the men and women under the Old Man's—his—
command. Yates exhaled slowly, tasting the faint me-
tallic bite in the recycled air that he'd never gotten used
to in the six months he'd been here. Then he got down
to business.

"In the event that this is a real scenario, what is the
station's condition?" he asked.

"All oxygen scrubbers are working at full capacity,
and spares are in stock. Assuming that rescue will not
be possible for several months—" the look on Spielman's face matched the thought in Martin's mind, *if ever*
"—we are able to exist down here for the next twelve
to eighteen months."

Yates grunted. "Well, at least we'll be able to breathe
for that long. How about our stores?"

"Stores are at 98.5 percent capacity, as we've just
been resupplied for our next ninety-day duty stretch.
When those are gone, we should be able to survive in-
definitely on what we can harvest from the ocean, including kelp and algae, which will now move several
notches up the priority list."

Yates nodded. "Yeah, well, Rainer and his staff
were wondering how long it would take to achieve their
benchmarks. I guess they're going to find out on a very
accelerated timeline. What about potable water?"

"The desalinization system is operating at 99.7 percent efficiency. We are working to keep all storage tanks
at maximum levels. It's chemical showers for everyone
for the foreseeable future, at least until we know how

things are going to shake out topside. Sir…" Spielman paused. "Permission to speak freely?"

"Go ahead."

"Given what's happening, shouldn't we order a general evacuation of the base while we still can?"

Yates wet his lips. "The thought had crossed my mind, as well, but ironically, we're all probably safer here than anywhere else. Besides, where would we go—Hawaii? The Philippines? Japan? We'd just end up stranded there, most likely, and after this I doubt that Americans are going to be hugely popular in what's left of the world, no matter who started it."

Spielman nodded. He and Martin had served together at several Navy facilities around the world, and their thought processes complemented each other perfectly. It was one of the reasons they worked so well together. "Figured that's what you'd say. Just wanted to double-check my math."

"Understandable, given the circumstances." Yates looked around again, making sure no one was eavesdropping on their conversation. "Okay. What about AIDAN?"

A frown crossed the CWO's face. "That's the other weird thing. The moment we got the message, Kasperic said AIDAN received a burst of information that it's been processing for the past several minutes. Any attempts to access the information or query AIDAN regarding the information get no reply."

Yates's eyebrow arched. "Does he think it's been hacked?"

"No, the sender was Department of Defense and legit." Spielman thought for a second. "He did say that it came from some sort of project or division with an unusual name—Project Cerberus? A division of something called the Totality Concept? Sound familiar?"

Martin shook his head. "No idea, although if it is black box, that doesn't sound good. Think it has anything to do with Pod Seven?"

Spielman stared at him. "Uncle Sam doesn't pay me enough to think *anything* about Pod Seven, sir."

"Affirmative on that. Let Kasperic know I want to know the second there's any change in AIDAN."

"Already done."

"Excellent." Yates looked around again, then eyed his CWO. "Now I gotta ask—where the hell's the Old Man?"

Spielman shrugged. "He was notified when the message came in, and said that you were on your way up here. I don't think he's left his quarters since."

Yates pursed his lips as he digested that information. It was very likely that the Old Man was reviewing the sealed orders that were included as standard protocol in every U.S. Navy facility, every ship, every submarine. Even in experimental ones such as this.

"Incoming message, Commander!" a nearby officer said as a printer began to chatter.

"I'll take that." Yates walked to the printer to pick up the page and read the message himself—primarily because he wanted to give the rest of the crew members a focal point to take their minds off their worries and fears. Oh, he had them, too, but a commander was always supposed to be above that.

The typed words he read on the flimsy paper chilled his blood.

TOP SECRET—CLASSIFICATION ULTRA BLUE
    EYES ONLY
    FROM NORAD:

UNITED STATES ATTACKED WITH NUCLEAR WEAPONS BY USSR. AS OF 1210 HOURS E.S.T.

CONFIRMED THAT PRESIDENT-ELECT AND VICE PRESIDENT-ELECT HAVE BOTH BEEN KILLED IN FIRST STRIKE THAT DESTROYED WASHINGTON D.C.

AS PER DOD ORDERS, ASSASSINATION PROTOCOLS HAVE GONE INTO EFFECT.

FULL COUNTER-STRIKE MEASURES ARE BEING LAUNCHED AT ALL LEVELS.

ALL RANKING NAVY OFFICERS WITH TS CLEARANCE ARE TO OPEN THEIR SEALED ORDERS IMMEDIATELY AND TAKE ALL NECESSARY ACTIONS.

FURTHER INSTRUCTIONS WILL BE FORTHCOMING.

"Jesus Christ, it really is World War III, isn't it, sir?" Spielman asked.

"Looks like it." He glanced at the man sitting beside him at the console, who had tears running down his cheeks. "Get hold of yourself, Lieutenant, or you will be relieved of duty!"

"Aye, sir." The young man wiped his cheeks. "Sorry, sir."

Yates straightened to address the rest of the command staff, all of whom were now staring at him. He took a deep breath.

"As of—" he glanced at his watch "—twenty-five minutes ago, the United States was attacked in a nuclear first strike on Washington, D.C., by the USSR. The president-elect and vice president-elect have both been killed. We are now at DEFCON 1. A full counter-strike is being launched as I speak."

"What about us?" one of the engineers asked.

"Right now, you all are to remain at general quarters until further orders are issued," Yates replied. "I am going to conference with Captain Lucas immediately to discuss what our next steps are going to be. I will return to inform all of you, as well as the rest of the crew, shortly. Until then, this information is to not leave the bridge."

He was about to head to the Old Man's quarters, but was intercepted by Spielman. "Kasperic's asking for you—he said AIDAN is back online."

"He'll have to wait until I've talked to the Old Man—" Martin began.

"Kasperic said you should stop by the control room immediately. His exact words."

Yates's stomach clenched even further at the message. "Tell him I'm on my way." The elevator doors opened and he stepped inside.

The ride down was agonizingly long. Yates felt his tears building but wiped them away. He needed to be strong for everyone else here. Again, he pushed all thoughts of the world above, even his family, out of his mind.

There would be plenty of time to grieve later.

The doors opened and Yates was surprised to see Chief Engineer Rolf Kasperic waiting for him. A short man, he had curly red hair and a smattering of freckles across his cheeks, making him look younger than his thirty-four years. The man was a computer engineer without peer. Yates had never seen the look on his face before—one of puzzlement. Regardless, the other man came to attention and saluted him as Yates stepped out of the elevator.

"Status report, Chief?"

"AIDAN came back online at 0729, and…it's doing something I've never seen before."

"Any intel on the burst packet it received?" Yates asked.

Kasperic shook his head. "Negative. Whatever was contained in that transmission, it's not telling."

"This just gets better and better." Yates's stomach clenched a little tighter. He'd never been comfortable with entrusting so much of Poseidon Base's systems to AIDAN, and now that it seemed there might be a problem his comfort level was dropping even further.

"I thought that maybe with your clearance, you might be able to get farther with it, sir," Kasperic continued.

"Only one way to find out." He gestured for the stocky engineer to proceed. "Lead on."

Along the way, he filled Kasperic in on what they knew. The engineer shook his head philosophically. Along with the majority of the crew, he had no immediate family topside. "That's a damn shame. Bet it has something to do with AIDAN's weird behavior, though."

"No bet, Chief—I'm already in too deep to you as it is." With his steel-trap mind, Kasperic played a vicious game of Texas Hold'em and had fleeced the other officers out of thousands of dollars.

They reached the door simply marked AIDAN. Yates slid his ID into the slot next to it, then supplied a voice sample and thumbprint identification. The door slid open, revealing a shadowed room with a plain desk, a monitor and a microphone.

Yates walked inside the antiseptically clean space and took a seat in the chair. Pulling the microphone close to his mouth, he spoke into it. "AIDAN, this is Lieutenant Commander Yates."

"Good morning, Lieutenant Commander."

The calm, synthesized reply came from speakers mounted on the walls. Yates repressed his constant shudder at hearing the voice—he'd seen *2001: A Space Odyssey* enough times to be leery of communicating with any AI program.

"Good morning. I want to know the contents of the data burst transmission you received earlier this morning."

"I have received several such transmissions so far this morning, Commander. I am afraid that you will have to be more specific."

Yates leaned back to Kasperic. "What time did you log that one as received?"

"At 0718, sir."

"The transmission received at 0718 hours."

"I am afraid that I cannot disclose the contents of said transmission, Commander."

"AIDAN, this is an executive command level order. I, Executive Officer Martin Yates, ID number 55625533461, authorize you to disclose all material pertinent to my command immediately."

There was a pause of about a second. "Under the new regulations and protocols I have received from the Totality Concept, I am afraid that your clearance is not high enough to order the release of that information, Commander. May I suggest that you confer with Captain Lucas? He may be of some assistance regarding this situation."

AIDAN had never refused a direct order before. Cold sweat broke out on the back of Yates's neck as he looked up at Kasperic. "What the fuck is going on?"

Lips pursed, the engineer gave the answer both men hated most. "I don't know, sir. Should I try a controlled shutdown?"

"Not yet—there's no telling what new instructions AIDAN has received. Who knows what sort of response a perceived aggressive move could provoke? Do you know anything about whatever this Totality Concept is?" At Kasperic's slow headshake, Yates stood and nodded at the door. "Let me talk to the Old Man first."

Once they were both outside, and the door was securely closed, Yates put his mouth close to the other man's ear. "Do you have any back doors into AIDAN's programming?"

"Off the record, sir, I've tried exploring its architecture, but haven't had much luck," Kasperic replied. "Whoever constructed it protected it six ways from Sunday. Truth be told, I'm not really sure what a lot of its programming *is*."

"Yup, better and better by the minute," Yates grumbled. "All right. Just monitor it until I talk to Lucas. Call me if there's any change, no matter how small."

"Aye-aye, sir."

Yates didn't wait for the salute, but took off running down the hallway toward the captain's quarters. As he did, he felt a tremor shake the corridor, hard enough to jolt him off his stride. The engineers had built the complex to survive a 9.0 earthquake, but Yates had hoped he would never be in here if one hit.

He reached the captain's quarters and pressed the button to hail the occupant. "Captain, it's Lieutenant Commander Yates."

"Enter," a haggard voice replied over the speaker.

Yates stepped inside, wrinkling his nose at the smell of unwashed clothes and body odor in the darkened sleeping quarters. "Sir?"

"Office."

The captain's quarters consisted of a small, two-room

suite, with a tiny office barely big enough for two people off the main room. Yates walked over, stepping over a wrinkled dress uniform as he did. When he reached the doorway, his eyes widened. "Captain?"

Captain Roger Lucas, U.S. Navy, looked like a pile of wet shit that had been poured into his jumpsuit. His eyes were bloodshot, salt-and-pepper stubble dotted his chin, and his short hair stood up in odd clumps, as if he hadn't washed in days. Wrinkles seamed his cheeks and forehead, making him look as if he'd aged a decade in a day.

The office around him was just as messy, with papers and other debris strewed everywhere.

"Sit down, Commander." Lucas reached down to the floor next to him and came back up with a bottle. "Drink?"

"I'm on duty, sir." As he took the other small chair, Yates noticed that the small safe to the right of the captain's chair was open and frowned. Lucas shouldn't have both keys. Military protocol dictated that the top two commanding officers each have one of the two keys that would open the safe containing any classified or top secret orders.

"Relax, it's just you and me here." He waved dismissively at the back wall. Yates turned to it to see the captain's dress uniform hat hanging over where an electronic eye would normally survey the room. But AIDAN hadn't notified anyone of this breach in protocol. The fear in Yates's stomach coalesced into a cold, hard knot of terror.

"All right, pour me two fingers." Hoping the acceptance would relax his superior officer, Yates took the plastic cup and knocked back a healthy swallow. He remained silent for a moment, feeling the whiskey burn down his throat and bloom into warm fire in his belly.

"Thank you, sir." He waved at the safe and the papers on the desk. "I assume you've received the message from headquarters."

"Of course. Don't look so shocked—a good captain always has ways of circumventing his officers."

"Yes, sir—"

"Jesus Christ, Marty, didn't I tell you not to take this post?" Lucas interrupted.

"Yes, sir, you did—but it was the right choice for me. There was no way of knowing what was going to happen up there...was there?"

The captain shook his head. "There are always ways...nothing concrete, mind you, but...there are ways. Putting the right intel together...even gut feelings count." Lucas picked up his cup and swirled the liquid inside around. "Me, I just had a fucking feeling about this. I went in with my eyes open, but you—" He picked up his cup and drained it, then poured more whiskey. "You shoulda been on the surface, with your family, instead of down here."

"With respect, sir, if I had been, then I would be dead, as well, instead of here, able to assist with rescue efforts and the rebuilding of our country—"

Lucas barked out a short, harsh laugh. "'Assist with rescue and rebuild'? That's what you think you're gonna do once the shit storm stops raining down?" He tossed the slim packet of information at his XO. "Take a look at what's in store for you, me, and everyone else in this godforsaken place." He tipped his cup back, draining it.

Yates read the top secret documents, his mouth dropping open at their contents. When he was finished, he looked back up at his commanding officer. "They can't be serious—"

"Bet yer ass they are," Lucas replied, his voice slurring. "Protocols're already in place. That goddamned computer will prevent any attempt to evacuate the facilities. I guess they're supposed to bring new blood in through Pod Seven or some such bullshit. *Now* do you see why I told you to turn this post down?"

"But…" Yates waved the sheaf of papers around. "This—this is monstrous. They cannot possibly expect us to follow this—"

"Oh, but they do, my dear lieutenant commander." Shaking his head, Lucas rummaged among the papers on his desk. "Fortunately, I will not be around to see that happen…"

He came up with what he was looking for—a black, snub-nosed revolver.

Yates gaped at it—firearms were strictly prohibited, due to Poseidon Base's very nature. "Sir, what are you—"

"The bad news, XO, is that *you* will be. I hereby relieve myself of command."

With that, Captain Lucas put the barrel of the pistol in his mouth and pulled the trigger.

Chapter One

Apex predators had an instinctual knowledge of their general surroundings at all times. Simply put, they just knew whether they were safe or in danger. If they sensed a threat nearby, they might not know exactly what hazard they were facing, but forewarned was still forearmed.

Such was the case when Ryan Cawdor opened his single blue eye and saw the ceiling of the mat-trans chamber above him. Blinking a few times while he took stock of himself, he realized that he felt as if he'd just run twenty miles through stickie country. His lungs labored every time he drew a breath, as if they weren't able to draw enough oxygen.

He moved his head enough to take in the rest of the group, mainly to make sure everyone had come through in one piece. While Ryan had lost count of the mat-trans jumps he'd made, he still didn't trust the predark technology. Like much of life in the Deathlands, it was a necessary evil as far as he was concerned.

He looked down to find his fingers already curled around the grip of his SIG Sauer P226. Sometimes Ryan thought he'd spent more time alive with a blaster or other weapon in his hand than not. This, however, definitely felt like one of those times he needed to have a blaster ready to fire.

To his right was the beautiful, flame-haired Krysty Wroth, his longtime lover. Apparently her own keen senses were also alerted to danger. He had never seen her hair, which often moved of its own accord, depending on her mood, curled so tightly into a ball at the back of her head and neck.

Gratified, but not surprised that his instincts were correct, Ryan turned his head to the left, where his oldest friend and comrade-in-arms, J. B. Dix, lay. Short and sallow, the man known as the Armorer looked as if he had just set his beloved, battered fedora beside him, folded his hands on his chest and lain down for a short nap. Between them, the two men had raised more hell, found more trouble, and chilled more bastards, stupes, evil men and other creatures throughout the Deathlands over the years than either could count.

As if sensing Ryan's stare, J.B.'s eyes popped open. The first thing he did was to check that his Mini-Uzi submachine gun was right next to him. Then he removed his wire-rimmed glasses from a pocket and hooked them over his ears.

"Trouble?" he asked, just loud enough to be heard.

"Mebbe." Ryan sat up, wincing as the aftereffects of the jump strobed flashes of light behind his eye, accompanied by sharp stabs of pain in his temples. Still, his gaze roved the mat-trans unit, checking the rest of his companions.

Next to J.B. was a stocky black woman, her hair plaited into short, beaded braids. She moaned as well after their jump across thousands of miles in a blink of an eye. "Just when I think I'm getting used to these damn jumps, they find a new way to turn my head inside out."

Dr. Mildred Wyeth had been thawed back to life in the dark jungles of the long-ago state of Minnesota, and had accompanied the companions ever since. A skilled medical doctor and crack pistol shot, she was a walking repository of information about the twentieth century—a time so different that it might as well have been prehistoric for Ryan and the rest of the group.

Lying on his side a few feet away and curled into a tight ball was Jak Lauren. A true albino, his stark-white hair was oddly muted in the light of the chamber, and his red eyes were squeezed tightly shut.

"You all right, Jak?" Ryan asked.

A low groan was the teenager's only reply. Slowly, he uncurled his skinny body, clad in a camouflage-pattern jacket with shards of glass and metal sewn into it, black fatigue pants, and well-worn combat boots that matched those on J.B.'s and Ryan's feet. Even unwell, Ryan saw the young man check the massive .357 Colt Python tucked into his belt. "Feels…wrong here—"

A snort then a gasp interrupted him. Those noises were followed by a shout from the tall, skinny man with a lined face who was lying next to Jak. Dressed in cracked knee boots, stained black pants and a frock coat, his shoulder-length, silver-white hair splayed around his head as he shook it back and forth.

"No, Emily…dear Emily, do not…do not follow me!"

"Fireblast, he's having a nightmare again," Ryan said. "Mildred, would you check him?"

She was already at his side, nudging him gently. "Doc…wake up, Doc!"

"Wh-what?" With a stutter and a shake, Doc Tanner's pale blue eyes fluttered open. He looked around wildly for a moment, then his gaze fell upon Mildred and he calmed. "Ah, young lady, you must be here to take my breakfast order. Two eggs poached, several slices of bacon, well-done, sourdough toast, and the hottest pot of Earl Grey you can find. Hurry along, now."

Mildred's brown eyes narrowed as she stood. "I don't

know where you *think* you are, Doc, but I'm the last person you should be asking to fetch your breakfast." She turned and walked back to J.B. without another word.

Meanwhile, Doc stared at the rest of the group with a bewildered expression on his lined face. "Dear me, this is not the Paxton Hotel. And you are most certainly not the ladies and gentlemen I enjoyed a most excellent repast with last night…I beg you all, kindly inform me as to where I am and how I came to be here among you?"

"Shit," Jak said before turning and spitting at a corner of the room. "Doc's off rocker again."

"Got a few hours, Doc?" J.B. asked before heading over to take a look at the door.

"*Mierda!* Is he…all right?" Ricky Morales, the most recent addition to their group, asked while cradling his stocky, thick-barreled De Lisle carbine in his arms. About the same age as Jak, he'd joined their group after a perilous adventure in what had once been the island nation of Puerto Rico. A tinkerer by nature and an avid gunsmith, he fit in well with the rest of the group, particularly J.B. Ricky was traveling with them hoping to find his sister, who'd been captured by slavers and taken to the mainland. Although he'd been with the group for several weeks, he had mostly seen Doc at his best.

"Yeah, he'll snap out of it in time," Ryan replied, striding over to the old man, who had drawn his knees up to his chest and was looking around fearfully. "Some jumps're worse than others, that's all."

The truth, of course, was frightfully more complicated. Like Mildred, the man known as Doc had arrived in the Deathlands out of the past. How he had gotten here, however, was the very stuff nightmares were made of. The only survivor of the time-traveling experiments done by government whitecoats in the late twentieth century, Doc had been trawled forward from 1896 to the 1990s. When his behavior had become too difficult to handle, the scientists had cruelly sent him forward in time—into the Deathlands. The chron jumps, not to mention the trauma of losing his family, had scrambled his mind. Most days Doc Tanner was a lucid and valuable companion; some days, after a jump, he would be in a daze, stuck in the past.

Ryan knelt beside the old man, taking his face by the chin and moving it over until he was staring into the other man's lost gaze. "Doc, you know me, and you know the others. We're in a mat-trans chamber, like we've been many times before." Where his tone had been relatively gentle before, now Ryan put steel-hard command into his voice. "Now you've got exactly one minute to get together, 'cause we're moving out!"

Dr. Theophilus Algernon Tanner blinked once, then again, then twisted his face out of Ryan's grip. "A simple 'we're leaving,' would suffice, my dear Ryan. There's no need to coddle me like a wayward child."

"Glad that's settled, then." Ryan rose and looked at the rest of the group. "Time to go."

Pushing himself to his feet with the sound of his old knees popping, Doc looked around the room as if seeing it for the first time. "By the Three Kennedys, this does not look like a well-maintained facility. Is it just me, or is it hot in here?"

"Not you, Doc," Jak replied. "Air's…different. Not bad, not good."

"Tastes like home," Ricky said. "Got salt in it."

"Yeah, and what's with these walls?" Mildred asked, waving at the armaglass slabs that ringed the mat-trans chamber. Usually they were some uniform color, from bright yellow to deep red and all colors in between.

These walls might have been a bright green at one time, but looked altogether different now. Dull and cloudy, each one was edged in black, as if they had been scorched by something on the other side. All in all, they didn't inspire a lot of confidence in Ryan about what they were going to find in the anteroom.

He eyed the door, which J.B. was already standing next to. "Only one way to find out. Fingers on triggers, people, we're going out on triple red."

Chapter Two

The mat-trans door was balky beyond belief, and it took
the effort of Ryan, J.B., Jak and Ricky to force it open
just enough for them to slip through. Darkness and silence lay beyond the narrow opening.

"Dark night! A plas-ex charge would have been easier." J.B. grunted, wiping sweat from his brow and re-
settling his fedora on his head.

"No power out here," Krysty said, wrinkling her nose.
"I can smell smoke pretty clearly, though. Looks like
this may have been a one-way trip."

"Let's not abandon the wag till we see what shape it's
in first," Ryan replied.

"Or 'abandon all hope, ye who enter here,'" Doc said,
making the others—except for Mildred—turn to him
with puzzled frowns.

"Jak, you're on point." Blaster at the ready, Ryan nodded the young man forward. The albino's uncanny night
vision made him the perfect choice to scope out the
room. With a nod, the skinny, fox-faced teen vanished
into the blackness, a throwing blade held between two
fingers, his own blaster drawn just in case he encountered something resistant to his leaf-bladed stickers.

Everyone fell silent, waiting for the young man to
return. Ricky fingered his blaster as he peered into the
darkness. After a bit of initial wariness, the two teens

had formed a strong bond, second only to Ricky's admiration of J.B. "Sure he's all right out there?"

As if in answer, there was a loud *click,* followed by several isolated fluorescent lights blinking on.

"There's your answer," Ryan said as he stepped into the room and looked around. There was no anteroom. J.B. and the others were right behind him, fanning out to cover the room.

"Place looks shit," Jak said from the other end.

His assessment wasn't very far off the mark. They looked directly into a control room. Every control console for the complicated, delicate computers that ran the mat-trans was encrusted with deposits of some kind of white, crystalline powder. Several sparked and popped in the silence, trickles of gray smoke drifting lazily into the thick air.

"Looks like...smells like—" Mildred wet a finger and touched the powder, then brought it to her mouth. "Salt. Must be near an ocean. The question is, which one?"

"You agree about the condition, Doc?" Ryan asked, eyeing a discolored sign on the wall that told him this place was something called Pod Seven, part of something called Poseidon Base. The name tickled his memory for some reason, but he couldn't put a finger on it.

Shaking his head, Ryan returned to the issue at hand. Every mat-trans unit had a Last Destination setting that could take them back to the redoubt they'd used to jump here. If that didn't work, however, then they were stuck.

The old man wandered among the stations, running a wrinkled hand along them. "What? Oh, yes, Ryan, this mat-trans will not be transporting us or anyone else out of this room ever again. The damage by the encrusted salt is complete. Indeed, by allowing us to complete the jump in relative safety, Providence has shone her eternal countenance on us once again."

"That's comforting," Mildred said, her gaze on the door at the far side of the room.

"What'd he say?" Ricky whispered to Jak.

"Old buzzard said we're lucky," the white-haired youth replied.

"Map here." J.B. was examining the plastic-enclosed diagram on the wall. "This was built apart from the rest of the complex. Only way out—"

A burst of static from a speaker on the wall interrupted him. The sudden noise made everyone draw or aim their blasters at the noise before realizing what was going on.

"Welc—Posei—on Base for O—ic res—New arriv—cede to main lev—orientat—uty assign—" The garbled message repeated itself again, the bursts of static making the words nearly impossible to make out. As the message ended, the speaker popped and hissed, a small wisp of smoke drifting out of its casing. As if dying with it, one of the lights flared and died, as well, allowing the shadows in the room to approach a bit closer.

"Sounds like a welcome message," Ryan said, checking the action on his blaster. "Might mean a welcoming party's also on its way."

"This just gets better and better," J.B. said, also eyeing the door at the end. "Shall we?"

Ryan and he walked to the door, with the others split and behind them: Mildred, Ricky and Doc behind the Armorer; Krysty and Jak behind Ryan. No one had put their blasters away yet.

Usually a keypad was positioned beside each exit door, but this control room didn't have one. The one-eyed man checked with J.B., who was holding his Mini-

Uzi like he'd been born with it. He nodded at Ryan, who hit the door lever, ready to kill anything that moved on the other side or shut the door in the event of something they couldn't contain, like water, or poison gas or who knew what else.

The door reacted with the same obstinacy as the mat-trans portal, only getting about halfway open before shuddering to a halt. Ryan had been unconsciously holding his breath, ready to throw the lever again if anything came at them, but the corridor beyond seemed as silent and dead as the rest of the redoubt so far.

No, not quite. The air outside seemed even heavier and still, as if it hadn't stirred in many, many decades. Ryan could also see thick rimes of salt on the wall next to the door. Usually, the air-conditioning systems in these complexes kept the air clean and relatively comfortable. The fact that the fans didn't seem to be working hinted at a redoubt that was on its last legs.

All the more reason, Ryan thought, to find a way out triple quick.

"Let's go." The one-eyed man led the way, but hadn't gone a half dozen steps before stopping again, staring down the corridor as the motion-sensitive lights came on.

"Fireblast."

The corridor sloped down—into a mass of still, black water.

"Like I said, better and better," the Armorer muttered.

"Jak, you're up again," Ryan said, not taking his eye off the placid surface. Jak was already shucking out of his boots and jacket.

"Can I go?" Ricky asked. "My father taught me how to swim very fast."

J.B. tapped his eyes. "I'm sure he did, but Jak's got better dark vision, which he'll need."

"Plus, we'll be able to see his hair as he goes down. If it looks like he's in trouble, we'll be able to reach him faster," Mildred said.

A foot-long Bowie knife clamped in his teeth, Jak waded slowly into the water. The others covered the still pool as he moved, ready to chill anything that might try to take a bite out of him.

"Warm—like blood," he grunted around the blade. He waited for a few seconds, gulping huge breaths to help him stay underwater longer. If anything was going to come out and investigate him, it would be now, but the water remained still. With one more step, the teen dived cleanly in, barely making a splash as he swam into the darkness. Within seconds, he vanished into the murk.

Silence fell among the rest of the group. Ricky, however, posed the question on everyone's mind. "What happens if Jak doesn't find a way out?"

Ryan and J.B. exchanged wry glances. "It's never happened before, Ricky. We've always found a way—"

"Over, under, around or through," J.B. interrupted.

"Yes, but what if we can't do any of those things?" the teen persisted.

"Then you got a choice, Ricky—fast or slow," Ryan said. He paused, waiting for the kid to realize what he was saying.

Ricky's face wrinkled in puzzlement. "I don't understand."

"You can either put a blaster in your mouth and punch your ticket for the last train west yourself," Ryan said. "Or you can wait here to starve to death."

"Actually, you'd suffocate long before that happened," Mildred said with a frown at Ryan.

"Truth is truth, Mildred," Ryan replied, not minding

her glare in the least. "Ricky made his choice when he came with us. Every choice has consequences."

"Like ours to trust our lives in those cantankerous contraptions every time," Doc said, jerking his thumb back at the mat-trans chamber. "Upon my soul, it is a wonder that we have not awoken one time to find our atoms scattered throughout the universe—"

"Hold up, Doc. I see something," Ryan said from the edge of the water. "Jak's coming back."

The white blur grew rapidly into the pale form of the young man, arms and legs churning the water for all he was worth.

"Coming in hot—" was all J.B. had time to say before the albino broke the surface of the water, rearing out as he sucked in a great gulp of air. A line of bright pink circles ran diagonally across his chest.

"Jak, what's—" Ryan started to ask, but stopped as three gray tentacles, as thick around as his waist, burst out of the water behind him.

Chapter Three

One of the waving tentacles lashed at Jak, snaring him around the waist and tightening. The other two moved toward him, as well. "Fucker!" the youth gritted as he stabbed into the crushing appendage with his Bowie knife.

"Nukefire!" Drawing his panga, Ryan splashed into the water to try to distract one of the other tentacles. He heard the peculiar cough of Ricky's carbine behind him, and the tentacle nearest him spurted black ichor as a hole appeared in it about a foot from the tip. It drew back.

"Watch your fire!" he shouted.

Jak, meanwhile, had been grabbed by another tentacle, and was being drawn below the water, his face growing even paler than normal as the constricting limb crushed the air out of his lungs. Despite that, he still slashed at the tentacle around his waist.

Ryan took one more step and lunged out of the water. As he came back down, he swept the panga in a savage slash, putting all of his two hundred pounds behind the blow.

The razor-sharp steel sliced deeply into the same tentacle Jak was working on, nearly severing it. Ryan pulled the blade out and swung again, cutting through the rubbery flesh and chopping the young man free. The wounded appendage drew back, black fluid spraying everywhere as it writhed about. Tearing off the rest of the limb, Ryan threw it into the water, hoping the other two would be distracted by the movement.

They weren't.

The one around Jak's arm tightened its grip, making him grunt in pain even as he kept stabbing the ropy, boneless appendage. The one with the hole in it went for Ryan, who was now standing chest-deep in the water.

Instead of dodging, he brought the panga around again in a ferocious swing. The blade hit the tentacle again, but bounced off the rubbery skin. It shot past him, and Ryan turned to see J.B. standing a few feet away, a combat-type knife in one hand, his Mini-Uzi in the other.

"Get Jak!" the Armorer yelled as the tentacle kept coming for him.

Ryan turned back and grabbed Jak's trapped arm, pulling it toward him as hard as he could. He stretched the tentacle out, too, but Ryan felt it only go a certain distance before it stopped, as if it was affixed to something big—really big.

"Ow—what you doing, dammit?" Jak asked.

"Hold still!" Ryan said through gritted teeth. Raising the panga again, he brought it down in a swift slice, severing the end completely. Jak fell toward him as the rest of the writhing appendage shot backward and disappeared into the water.

A burst of automatic weapon fire made Ryan turn just enough to see J.B. holding a three-foot-long segment of gray, suckered limb still squirming on his blade. His Mini-Uzi was smoking, making it obvious how the Armorer had dealt with his attacker.

"Ace on the line—" Ryan began just as he felt something snake between his legs and curl around one ankle. Before he could move, he was jerked off his feet and into the water.

He did have the presence of mind to draw a breath right before he went under. He jackknifed to saw at the tentacle that was trying to drag him into deeper water and drown him. While he fought to loosen its crushing grip, he looked around to see how close he was coming to whatever the relentless arms were attached to. But they disappeared into the black water, which was just as well. Ryan wasn't in the mood to find out what was on the other end.

A glance up showed the light and the rest of his companions receding. Ryan just kept cutting at the tentacle, which kept tightening its grip. A flash of white streaked by him, and Ryan saw Jak dive down and begin sawing at the tentacle with his Bowie knife. Between the two, they cut off the suckered appendage and headed back to the surface.

Ryan's lungs were bursting as he got closer, and the thick, salty air had never tasted so good. Jak and he both splashed out of the water as fast as they could, with J.B., Ricky, and both women covering their retreat until everyone was back at the doorway to the mat-trans control room.

"You get…a look…at what those were attached to… Jak?" Ryan asked between pants for air.

The albino shook his head, spraying drops of water everywhere. "No. Came out big, dark hole in wall. Got outta there." He swept his hair out of his eyes. "Corridor continued past, but mutie waiting to grab anything swimming by."

"And good Homer thought the many-armed Scylla merely a figment of his imagination," Doc mused. "Or perhaps it was based merely on a purported sighting of a giant squid, whose tentacles would surely pluck unlucky crewman from the decks to be drawn into its gaping, beaked maw and devoured while still alive."

"Either way, we got a bitch of a problem on our hands," Mildred said as she took a look at Jak's chest. "You didn't feel any kind of stabbing or needle-like pains, did you?"

Jak shook his head again. "Nope. Just thought bastard gonna crush ribs."

"You'll live," she said before straightening to regard the others. "Well, whether it's wounded or not, I sure as hell don't want to face that thing on its own turf with only a knife to fend it off."

Ryan nodded. "Ace on the line on that. No way are we facing that thing down there." He looked at J.B. "Blast it?"

The Armorer nodded as he pulled a lump of plas-ex from one pocket of his battered leather jacket and a small, waterproof detonator from another. "Should have just enough. Besides, the shock wave ought to stun it no matter what." Having prepped the charge, he looked around. "I need something to weigh it down."

"Perhaps this would do, John Barrymore?" Doc had gone back into the control room and came back wheeling a salt-encrusted chair in front of him.

"Yeah." J.B. pressed the plas-ex firmly onto the seat, activated the timer, then nodded at Ryan. "Do it."

Picking up the chair, Ryan hurled it as close to where the ceiling met the water as he could. It hit the water with a splash, and although he couldn't be sure, Ryan thought he saw a tentacle curl just high enough to grab it.

"Any luck, it'll bring it right back to wherever it's hiding," Krysty said with a shudder.

"That's the idea. Let's head back inside," Ryan suggested, and everyone was more than willing to follow his advice, spreading out from the half-open door on the other side.

"Crouch down, ears and eyes shut, mouth open," Ryan told Ricky. "The blast may be underwater, but just in case…"

"How long did you set it for?" Ricky asked as he cupped his hands over his ears.

"Figured thirty seconds—" J.B. was interrupted by a dull report that sounded far way. Ryan stuck his head out in time to see a huge bubble of water burst on the pool, with several small waves lapping at the shore.

"Time to go." Once again he led the group to the edge of the water. "Damn, I sure wish we had a light."

"If wishes were horses, then all beggars would ride," Mildred said as she waded past him. "Never liked the water in the first place, damn sure like it even less now. Let's just get this over with."

Ryan thought he saw her shudder a bit, but it was gone so quickly he wasn't sure.

"Agreed, Mildred, most definitely agreed." Doc had drawn his rapier from its walking-stick scabbard, tucking it into his belt before wading out, as well.

The rest of them followed, all gulping great breaths of air to fill their lungs.

"Which side, Jak?" Ryan asked, but the albino was already swimming to the right.

"Fucker was over there," he said pointing at the left wall.

"Hopefully there's nothing on this side," Ricky said, his words hanging in the silence.

"All right, everyone follow the wall single file, and go as far as you can," Ryan said. "We'll count up on the other side."

With that, Jak slid into the water, followed by Doc, Mildred, J.B., Ricky, and then Krysty. Ryan slid into the water last, taking one final huge breath of air and clamping his panga in his teeth before descending under the surface.

The light from the corridor penetrated only a couple of feet, so it wasn't long before he was swimming in pure blackness. Ryan experimentally waved a hand in front of his face, but saw nothing. If it hadn't been for the motion of the others in the water, he never would have known they were there.

Weighed down by his weapons and clothes, Ryan realized he was on the bottom of the corridor. He began moving along the wall, keeping his right hand pressed against it at all times, and his left out to the side, in case the tentacles came back.

The next couple of minutes were among the hardest in his life. Ryan had been in plenty of ass-puckering situations before, but this—holding his breath underwater, in complete darkness, with the possibility of some kind of huge, aggressive mutie creature nearby that he and the rest of the group had little chance against—was a new situation. On top of all that, there was the strong possibility that this tunnel would end in another rock wall, or just keep going on and on underwater until they all drowned.

His lungs began straining for oxygen, and Ryan gave it another few paces before pushing off the bottom and swimming for the surface. As he went, he thought he could see the dim glow of light above him, and increased his speed. He also felt some kind of disturbance in the water, someone thrashing around nearby. Ryan kept heading up, but as he did, he looked around, checking for tentacles coming after him or anyone else.

Just when his lungs had reached the bursting point, his head broke the surface, and Ryan took a huge gulp of fresher-tasting air. Shaking his head to get the water and his black hair out of his eyes, he heard splashing nearby, and looked around to see what the hell was going on.

He immediately counted six other heads either in the water or heading to the edge of the water. Krysty and Jak stood waist-deep in the pool, looking back at the others. Krysty in particular looked as though she was about to head back into the water. Ricky was also joining them, with Doc paddling a few yards behind him. That left only J.B. and Mildred. As Ryan glanced over, he heard a panicked shriek.

"Let me go, dammit!"

"Stop thrashing. You're going to drown us both."

Ryan looked over to see J.B. struggling with Mildred. Her eyes were wide and staring in the gloom, and she was taking huge, panting gulps of air. She was also trying to climb on top of J.B., who had his hands full keeping her restrained while also making sure he didn't drown at her hands.

Ryan launched himself toward the pair with powerful strokes. But even as he did, J.B. drew his hand back and slapped Mildred across the face, the smack echoing across the water. Her head snapped back, and she quieted immediately, turning to stare at him with shocked eyes. The Armorer didn't say a word, just began towing her to the edge of the pool. He glanced at Ryan as he did, and the one-eyed man immediately changed course to join the rest, hanging back to make sure they weren't attacked from behind.

Once everyone was out of the water, Ryan took a moment to make sure their position was secure. They were at the other end of the corridor, with a large door a few yards away. This part appeared to be just as deserted as where they'd come from. There didn't seem to be any immediate danger, but he leaned against the wall in a position where he could see both the water and the door with relative ease. He didn't say anything about what had happened, figuring it would come out in its own time. For once, both Jak and Ricky were also content to follow his lead.

Finally, J.B., who didn't take his eyes or hands off Mildred until they were out of the water, asked, "You okay?"

She rubbed her cheek, then looked up at him with a hint of a grateful smile and nodded. "Yeah. You did the right thing, as much as it galls me to admit it. I—I just panicked."

J.B. blinked. "Easy enough to do, with all that water."

"I flat-out panicked. I'm sorry about that, everyone. I could've messed things up even worse."

"The most important thing is that everyone's all right," Krysty replied. "With Gaia's blessing, I hope we don't ever have to do anything like that again." She caught Ryan's eye. "I could sense whatever it was on the other side of the passage. The blast had stunned it, but it was still very much alive. Alive…and very, very large."

"Coulda told that," Jak said.

"That's enough excitement for one day," Ryan said. "Let's hope there's something better on the other side of this door."

Chapter Four

While Mildred regained her composure, Ryan took a look at the door.

At first glance, it appeared to be a standard redoubt blast door, but it wasn't constructed of the usual titanium steel. When Ryan tapped it with the handle of his panga, it rang like ceramic, making him frown. To one side of the door was a control panel that featured a small monitor above the standard keypad along with a keycard slot. It was all dark, however, and no amount of button-pressing could make any part of it light up.

A boot heel scuffed the floor behind him, and Ryan turned to see a bedraggled, dripping-wet Doc standing a foot away. He seemed completely recovered from the disorientation he'd experienced in the mat-trans. Even their swim through the darkness hadn't seemed to affect him, and now he flashed his oddly perfect teeth in a genial grin.

"Have you figured out the proper method of ingress yet?"

Ryan turned back to eye the door with a sour expression. "Not quite. The controls are broken, so we either have to find some backup system, or we're going to have to blow it, which won't be good for any of us in this enclosed space."

"Indeed." Doc had resheathed his sword, and now tapped the bottom of the cane on the floor. "Mayhap I

could be of some small assistance in this matter? Based
on what we have seen and experienced so far, I have been
formulating a hypothesis about our current location. If
you will allow me?"

Ryan stepped aside. "It's all yours, Doc."

The old man stepped forward and examined the door
carefully, then the dead control panel. He looked at the
ceiling, then at the wall above the panel, then at the
wall below.

By now, Ryan had been joined by Jak and Ricky. The
three all watched Doc move about with various expres-
sions of puzzlement on their faces.

"¿Qué está haciendo?" Ricky asked. "What's he
doing?"

Ryan had been asking himself the same question for
the past minute. "I have no idea."

Now Doc bent and tapped the wall beneath the panel
with the silver lion's head of his cane. The section of
wall thudded dully under his blows. Then he straightened. Drawing his foot back, he lashed out at the piece of
wall under the control panel, the impact echoing through
the corridor.

Nothing happened.

Muttering to himself, Doc cocked his leg and kicked
at the wall again. This time, a section popped out, just
enough to be visible against the rest. Dropping to his
knees, Doc inserted his fingernails into the crack and
slowly wrenched the panel open, revealing a short lever.
But instead of looking pleased, he got to his feet, accompanied by the pops of his ancient knees, with a worried
expression on his face while he recovered from the exertion.

"That's…what I was…looking for…mechanical backup…lever…to open…the door," the old man said be-

tween pants of air. "Usually…not this…well hidden, however."

"Great. So, what's the problem?" Ryan asked.

He pointed at the lever. "Let us see what's on the other side of this door first, and then I will tell you." Drawing his LeMat blaster, he moved out of the way. "You will have to pump it up and down to raise the door."

With a shrug, Ryan made sure J.B. and Mildred were ready to go first, then he knelt in front of the lever. Grabbing it, he pulled it up, having to use all of his strength. "Damn! I sure hope this bastard lever gets easier."

"They operate on a hydraulic principle, so yes, it should get easier with each pump," Doc replied. "It is just that having not been utilized in more than a century has rendered it a mite balky. Much like myself sometimes."

"Got…that right…Doc." Ryan shoved the lever down again, then repeated the process. After five or six times, he heard a creak from inside the wall, followed by the door shaking as it began to move. Increasing the tempo of his lever-pumping, each up-and-down motion raised the door another inch or two. When the door cleared the floor, a thin wash of brackish, greenish-brown water sluiced in around their boots.

"Gaia! What's that smell?" Krysty asked, drawing her Smith & Wesson 640 revolver.

Mildred drew her own blaster with one hand while covering her mouth and nose with the other. "Damn! Not even the autumn pig slaughter smelled as bad as this."

Doc, meanwhile, stood resolute in the other corner, swordstick in one hand, the LeMat held by his side in his other. "'Will all great Neptune's ocean wash this blood clean from my hand? No, this my hand will rather the multitudinous seas incarnadine, making the green one red.'"

"What you sayin'?" Jak asked, as he squatted to peek under the door.

"I am saying, dear Jak, that we may be in far, far greater danger than I had initially suspected," Doc replied.

"Fuck," the albino teen said. "Always talk lot, but say nothing. Place stinks."

"Anyone see any movement inside?" Ryan asked, still pumping the lever.

"Nothing yet," J.B. said, his Mini-Uzi at the ready. "Just that incredible stench."

As Ryan continued to raise the door, he got a whiff of it, too, a powerful miasma of rottenness carried along with a hot blast of air. Whether it was flesh, vegetable or something else, he wasn't sure.

When the door had been raised to waist height, he stopped and stood, drawing his SIG Sauer. "Triple red, everyone."

With that, he took a peek. When he was satisfied with what he saw, Ryan bent under the door and stepped inside, splashing through the filthy water, causing the automatic lights to flash weakly on.

Instead of a corridor, however, he stood in an airlock, with a similar door at the other end. Although the smell was stronger in here, there was nothing rotting that would have made it. The door had a small window in it. Ryan moved to check it while J.B. examined the keypad.

Doc took in the door with an unusual expression on his face. "Yes…yes," he muttered. "This would certainly be needed."

"See anything, lover?" Krysty asked, her blaster held down by her side.

"Nothing but dark. How's the pad look, J.B.?"

"Troublesome," the shorter man replied. "Good news

is, this pad seems to be working. Bad news is that since this is an airlock, that door—" he pointed at the one they'd just come through "—needs to be closed before we can open this one. Assuming this slot here runs off some kind of access card, we need to figure out how to bypass it—if we can."

"Bypass?" Ricky asked.

"Yeah," the Armorer answered. "Some doors we've come across open and close using sec cards—little flat pieces of plastic that serve as electronic keys. Shove one in a slot, and if it matches the built-in code the pad recognizes, the door opens."

"And if it doesn't?"

"In this base, I'd say more likely than not we're in a world of hurt," Ryan answered. "So, how do we get it open?"

"I'd think there's a manual level on this side that'd lower that one," J.B. replied. "See if you can find it, Doc. I'm going to keep working on this."

"I can help." Ricky stood at the bespectacled man's shoulder.

"We'll see, Ricky." J.B. said.

"I have located the manual lever for the first door, John Barrymore. Do you wish it closed?" Doc asked.

J.B. glanced at Ryan, who shrugged. "Might as well. Nothing to go back to there."

Doc began struggling with the lever, which was stuck just as badly as the other one. Catching Jak's eye, Ryan nodded him toward the old man. The albino walked over to him. "Move, Doc. I try."

Doc did so, and Jak began to pump the lever, allowing the door to slowly begin descending. Meanwhile, J.B. and Ricky were still puzzling over the keypad.

"Other airlocks I've seen have an emergency open

mechanism. I'm hoping this one does, too." J.B. waited until the far door had closed completely. "Yeah, there it is."

The typical request for an entry code appeared. J.B. hit the three-five-two sequence, but couldn't do anything when the prompt requested a card be inserted. Instead, he hit the open door code again, with no better results.

A red orb above the keypad flared to bright life. "New arrivals have entered airlock."

"Did you do that?" Ryan asked J.B.

"Mebbe...hard to say," he replied.

"Security forces are en route. New arrivals are to remain where they are until escort arrives."

"That doesn't sound good," Mildred said. As she did, the large door next to Ryan slid open. Blaster at the ready, he made sure the immediate space beyond was clear before stepping through.

"Don't see anyone moving out here." He stood at a T-intersection, with corridors branching off to the left and right. The lights here barely worked, as well, with roughly one in five providing dim pools of illumination. The stench was much stronger here, forcing Ryan to breathe through his mouth. The air wasn't quite as stale, although he had a hard time telling through the stink. The walls, bare in most redoubts, were covered with crusts of salt as well as large patches of what looked like green-gray mold.

The rest of the companions had joined him, and everyone was peering down one of the corridors. Everyone heard a crackle, then a high-pitched squeal came from the wall over their heads. They looked up to see another speaker mounted near the ceiling give off that shrill whine before falling silent.

"Wonder if that was the same voice from the mat-trans control room?" Mildred asked.

"Mebbe." As usual, J.B. was examining the walls for any indication of where they might be in the complex. This time, however, he came up empty. "What redoubt doesn't post maps?" he mused aloud.

"The kind from which there is no escape," Doc said, making every other head turn toward him.

"I've had enough of the bastard riddles today, Doc," Ryan said. "Talk plainly. What's going on here?"

His words were interrupted by a noise coming from the left passage. A clank, followed by a small splash.

"You asked for answers, Ryan, and verily, you shall have them soon enough," the old man replied as he holstered his blaster. "But I do not think you will like them very much."

"Dammit, Doc!" Ryan squinted as he heard the strange noises again, a bit closer this time. He checked over his shoulder, making sure the right passage was clear. So far, so good.

"Movement," the keen-eyed Jak reported. "Human—think."

Now Ryan could make out a shadow about forty feet away, humanoid, with two arms and legs. At first he thought it was a secman wearing some kind of helmet, since all he could see of its face was two dots of ruby-red light. When it took its next, lurching step, it entered a flickering patch of light, enough so the companions could get a better look at it.

"Dark night!" J.B. said.

"Gaia!" Krysty exclaimed.

The thing that approached them was neither human nor machine, but a nightmarish combination of both. The clank was made every time its left leg—an artificial, articulated foot attached to a rod that melded with the flesh and bone of the leg just below the knee—hit the floor. It then stepped forward with its normal right leg, still clad in the tattered, mildewed remains of whatever uniform the human had worn while he or she had lived. Its skin was so pale white it was almost translucent. At any rate, Ryan was sure he could see swollen, blue veins running up the cyborg's legs, chest and arms.

But there were other mechanical parts, too. Tubes carrying some kind of dark green fluid encircled its torso, flowing out from the upper abdomen to its arms and legs. Its right arm was normal, although the fingers were curled into a fist. Its left, however, had also been replaced, this time with stainless-steel armature that included a large, nasty-looking clamp at the end. The clamp opened and closed with each step.

The half man, half machine's head was the most revolting of all. The remaining skin on its face and bald pate was covered in blotches of blue-green fungus. Its jaw dangled slack and crooked, as if it had been broken and just left that way. A gaping hole in its cheek appeared to have been eaten away by something, leaving ragged edges behind. Its normal eyes were gone, replaced by the two unblinking, red dots. As it drew closer, Ryan saw that the red sensors were contained in small, metal orbs that had been implanted in the poor wretch's face.

"My God, put that poor bastard out of his misery," Mildred said, raising her blaster.

"No!" Doc cried, pushing her arm up. "A single stray bullet could destroy this entire facility!"

"What?" Ryan said, half turning to him as the cyborg stopped and stared at them, its head jerking up and down as it took in the companions.

"What it do?" Jak asked.

"I think it's seen us," Krysty replied.

Ryan pulled out his panga. "Doc, what the hell do you mean—"

The abomination raised its head, and a sudden, high-pitched shriek filled the corridor, making everyone wince and Jak actually clap his hands over his ears.

Ryan had just taken a step forward when he saw more shadows appear down the hall behind the first thing. "Reinforcements. We have to get out of here."

J.B. had already taken a step down the right corridor when he stopped short. "Noise down this way, too."

"Shit," Ryan said. "How many?"

"Mebbe three or four? You?"

"Don't know—sounds like a lot, though." Ryan was interrupted when he saw something smaller and faster shoot past the walking thing and head straight for him. "Something else is coming this way!"

In the time it took to say that and raise his panga, ready for whatever might be sprung on him, the smaller machine, about the size of a large cat, was only a few yards away. A small silver globe covered with various holes, it hissed as it rolled through the filthy water, but he couldn't tell if it was steam-powered, or ran on something else. Instead of continuing to charge at him, it skidded to a stop a few feet away. Emitting a distinct chitter of some kind of machine language, it suddenly sprang straight up into the air.

"What—" was all Ryan had time to say before it shot something small and white at him. The tiny ball flew at him, exploding in midair as he tried to dodge out of the way. It bloomed into a net composed of thousands of tiny filaments that flew toward him. Ryan tried to swipe it out of the air with his panga, but the moment he touched it, the edges of the net curled in toward him, covering his arm and shoulder.

"Ryan?" Krysty asked.

"I'm all right," he said just as small, stinging pains began shooting through his skin. That was almost immediately followed by a numbness that froze his hand around the panga's handle and quickly spread up his arm to his shoulder. "No...can't move."

He turned to the others, but his first step was more of a lurch forward instead as the toxin spread through his nervous system. Ryan staggered and fell to one knee as Krysty ran to him.

"Watch—" He tried to force the warning through his frozen lips, but she ran past him and straight at the small machine, which had landed on the floor and was starting to roll forward again. Without breaking stride, she powered one cowboy-boot-clad foot forward and kicked the ball back at the approaching cyborg. It hit the walker's chest, making it stop for a moment before resuming its inexorable march forward. The small machine rolled out of its way and didn't move again. It did, however, emit a light blue gas from several holes that began filling the corridor.

"Gas!" Krysty grabbed Ryan and hauled him back to the others. "Get him out of here!" she cried, prying the panga from his fingers. When she released him, Ryan fell over, completely unable to move. But he could still breathe, and still see, and what he saw down the other corridor chilled his blood cold.

At least a half dozen more of the dreadful cyborgs— all hideous combinations of human and machine, were coming for them.

Chapter Five

The next few minutes passed very uncomfortably for Ryan. It was exceedingly rare that he was a passive witness to any fight, yet that was exactly the case. He could see and hear everything going on around him, but was unable to lift a finger or grunt a single word.

Fortunately, his companions had lived and survived so long together that they instinctively knew what to do.

"One of these days, Doc, you and I are going to have a conversation about how to dispense information in a timely fashion!" Mildred growled as she grabbed him by the shoulder. "Help me, dammit!"

"I could not ascertain what kind of facility we had arrived in without more proof, which, I admit, we now have in abundance," Doc replied as he got one of Ryan's arms up and around his shoulder. Between the two of them, they were able to half carry, half drag the man's deadweight back to the intersection and start down the left corridor.

"Sure we can't shoot, Doc?" Ricky asked, hefting his carbine. "Silencer won't hurt ears any."

"It is not that…young Ricky," Doc said, panting as he hauled Ryan along. "If a bullet…pierces the wall, it could very well…drown us all."

"Well, we got at least three of these things to get through down there. Not sure knives'll do the job," J.B. said, squinting down the left corridor.

"I will," Jak replied, handing Ricky his blaster.

"Jak, you—" J.B. began.

"Count ten, then follow." The white-haired teen began walking down the corridor toward the first two cyborgs. One appeared to have been a woman in her former life. Now she had what looked like plastic skin covering the entire right side of her face, neck, chest and waist, with the ever-present liquid-filled tubes pumping whatever fluid they carried through her. She was armed with what looked like a stun baton, its tip crackling as she came at Jak in a stiff-legged walk.

The second one looked like it had been two people merged into an unholy combination. One human body stood more or less upright, but it had the upper torso of another grafted onto its back, turning the whole thing into a freakish sort of two-headed human centaur. The rearmost one helped with locomotion by pushing along with its arms. The main body had had both arms replaced, one with a straight tube that looked like it contained some kind of grappling hook, and one that ended in a moving sawblade.

"They're almost on us back here!" Krysty shouted from the right. Ryan couldn't see what was happening back there, but the screech of steel on metal told him his lover was ably defending their rear.

"We're moving, Jak! Draw your sword, Doc, and get in front of me!" Trading places with the old man, J.B. began hauling Ryan down the left corridor. "Jak, get done whatever you're doing right now!"

The albino glided loose and easy in the corridor, approaching the woman-cyborg, her teeth bared in a twisted grimace as she raised the stun baton. Jak was only two steps away when he heard a slight rustle from overhead. He looked up just as a third cyborg—the tube-covered head and torso of a black man with an additional pair of arms grafted to where his legs would have been—let go from where he'd climbed along the ceiling to drop on him.

Or, at least it tried to.

The bayou-bred guerrilla fighter stepped back from underneath the truncated cyborg, bringing his leg up as he did. The bone-shattering kick hit the mechanized freak's chest, fracturing its sternum with a crack and sending it sailing over the female's head and back down the corridor, where it landed several yards away. One of its tubes had ruptured in the fall, and now sprayed green liquid everywhere. It waved its front arms helplessly even as its rear ones began moving it back into the fight.

The distraction was just enough to let the other two reach him. Jak hadn't stopped moving, however. Leaping into the air, he lashed out with a roundhouse kick that snapped the female cyborg's head to one side. But while the blow would have killed an ordinary person, she just kept shuffling forward, her half-skin, half-plastic head canted at an unnatural angle.

"Take the other one. I will handle this unholy monstrosity!" Doc said as he stepped up to Jak's side.

Jak snorted, but moved to the larger creature. It tried to strike first, aiming its grapple at him and firing it with a hiss of compressed air. Dodging the projectile, Jak grabbed the metal cable and wrapped it around his hand once, then hauled back on it even as the man-machine tried to reel him in.

Pulled off balance, the cyborg tilted forward, its rear half scrabbling for purchase on the floor. Jak kept winding it up, reeling in the atrocity like a huge fish. When it was near enough for him to grab, he let it take a clumsy swing at him with the sawblade then caught that arm behind the spinning blade with his free hand. Using the leverage from the swing, he kept it moving down and over into the monster's torso.

With a high-pitched whine, the blade bit into the cyborg's chest, spattering Jak with gobbets of thick, dark red blood mixed with the strange green fluid. He kept the pressure on, making the thing shudder as the whirling blade savaged its insides. The rearmost part beat its arms against the floor. Finally, the blade either ran out of power or encountered a bone so thick it couldn't saw through it and froze with a rattle and a spray of sparks. Jak unwound the cable from his arm and let the frightful being fall over with a loud crash.

Turning to Doc, he found the old man still struggling with his opponent. He had impaled the female cyborg by shoving his sword through her gut, but it hadn't slowed her in the least. Intestines leaked out of the gaping gash in her abdomen as she fought to bring the stun stick down on Doc, who was holding her wrist, struggling to keep the weapon away from his body.

"Fuck's sake, Doc!" Jak took one step and leaped into the air again. At the height of his jump, he brought his foot down on the cyborg's head, tearing it completely off the body this time. A geyser of blood and green liquid fountained from its neck as it collapsed to the floor.

"Thank you…Jak…" Panting hard, Doc retrieved his sword and wiped the blade on her uniform.

The two turned back to see J.B. and Mildred, both still carrying Ryan, with Ricky on their flank, now watching in all directions after seeing what had almost happened to him. Spattered with more green and red fluid, Krysty followed by a couple of steps, watching their rear. "Got a half-dozen still coming back here!"

"Look out!" The Armorer darted out from under

Ryan, drawing his blade as he did. Jak whirled in time to see him stab the large cyborg, who had turned so that the secondary torso could take over the fighting. J.B. buried his blade in the thing's throat, letting a crimson-green gush of liquid spurt out. He drew the blade out in a sweep, opening the secondary head's throat. This time, the large man-machine fell over and didn't move, just gurgled as its life's blood—or whatever the liquid was—jetted out. Tubes flailed as air entered them, but nothing else moved on the fallen body.

"Damnation! These things are surely loathe to die!" Doc said as the female's headless body began jerking and moving again, trying to rise. Inserting his blade under the hoses, he severed three of them, making more green fluid spurt everywhere. It didn't stop that thrashing body in the least, however. A few yards behind it was another small globe, weaving through the bodies and gore on the floor toward them.

"Find a place to hole up!" J.B. said, heading back and taking Ryan's shoulder again. "Move out!"

"Door ahead!" Jak said as he hurled a throwing knife into the darkness. An electronic squeal rewarded his efforts. "Over here!"

Like every other door in the place, this one did not want to open. Jak and Ricky forced it apart and slipped inside to clear the interior, which stank just as badly as everywhere else. Motion-activated lights flickered to life as they entered. It was empty, and they pushed the door open wide enough to allow J.B. and Mildred to haul Ryan inside. Doc scooted in, and Krysty was the last one through, still waving Ryan's panga at the grotesque, shambling horde pursuing them.

"Close it, close it, for Gaia's sake!" she said. Working with the two youths, she pulled the door shut again just as one of the lumbering monstrosities reached it. J.B. hammered at the control panel with the hilt of his Tekna, making it spark as he crushed the pad.

"You're trapping us inside?" Ricky asked.

"If they're part of whatever sec force runs this place," J.B. grunted, "they'll have codes for the doors."

A grinding noise came from inside the walls, and the door shuddered in its frame but didn't move. A blow sounded on the other side, followed by several more, but the portal didn't budge.

J.B. leaned against the wall next to the door and took a deep breath. "Think we're safe for now." He took a look around at the small room they were all packed into. It was small, and looked as though it had been sealed for decades. Clothes littered the floor, all of them parts of some kind of uniform. An even smaller door, currently closed, was on the left.

Most of the space was taken up by a large bed, which Mildred and Doc laid Ryan on.

"How's he doing?" J.B. asked.

"Breathing's steady, pulse is strong, and his pupils still respond to light," Mildred said after covering them with her hand, then uncovering them after a thirty-count. "It looks like whatever he got injected with was meant to paralyze, not kill."

J.B.'s gaze flicked to Krysty, who mouthed a silent thanks to Gaia for that news. "How long will it last?"

Mildred shook her head. "Hard to say. Depending on the dose, it could take anywhere from an hour to several for it to dissipate. Since we're reasonably safe—" she took in their surroundings for the first time "—my advice is to hole up here till he's able to move again. We can use that time to figure out what our next step is."

Krysty nodded. "Agreed." She walked over to stand

next to Ryan, her hand caressing his stern, scarred face. "Just rest, lover. You'll be up and around in no time."

Concentrating all of his strength, Ryan exerted every bit of energy to close his one blue eye and open it again.

She smiled at him. "A wink from you is better than anything else in the world…well, almost anything." She turned to the others. "He'll be all right in time. Thank you, Mildred."

She shrugged. "Didn't do much—fortunately, he's got the constitution of a grizzly bear." The stocky black woman glanced around. "Couldn't hole up in the kitchen for once, eh? Don't know about the rest of you, but all this swimming and running and fighting for our lives makes a girl hungry."

Doc shook his head. "Your stomach must be made of cast iron indeed, Mildred, to be thinking of food after witnessing those—abominations stalking us."

"It's the doctor in me, I guess, though you're right, Doc. I wouldn't wish that kind of existence on anyone, not even my worst enemy."

"What the hell were they?" Ricky asked. "Never seen *anything* like them before."

"Cybernetic limb replacement was not unknown in the late twentieth century, although it was in its infancy," Mildred answered. "But I've never seen anything as complete as those…things."

"Bigger questions are—who made them and why?" J.B. asked.

"I believe you have already seen proof of what the scientists behind the Totality Concept were capable of in furthering their blind pursuit of their goals." Doc rubbed his eyes. "And we have all seen many examples of what they did in the decades after skydark, practically none of it with benign intentions. I imagine that this entire place is just another example of their collective insanity."

"Well, that may explain why this place is here, but not what's happening here now," J.B. replied as he pushed off the wall and headed toward the smaller door. "I suggest we find out what's behind this."

Jak held up his hand. "Listen—stopped."

Everyone cocked an ear but heard only silence from the other side of the door.

"Waiting to bushwhack us when we come out?" Ricky asked.

"Mebbe. Put a bullet in that when we come to it, if need be," the Armorer said. "Right now, let's get this other door open."

Doc drew his sword, and J.B. had one of his knives out, as well. "Looks like an internal door, no lock. Shouldn't be anyone alive inside, but just in case…"

The Armorer kept the knife handy as he reached for the recessed handle, gripped it and pulled the door open in one smooth move, ready to gut anyone or anything that came at him from the other side.

Nothing moved.

The room was silent.

Silent, but not necessarily empty.

J.B. waved an arm inside, tripping the motion sensors that activated the lights. "I think we know what happened to at least one other person here."

He walked inside, letting the rest of the group see an empty office with a small desk and two chairs. Brittle papers covered with mold were scattered across the desk, and an odd pattern of stains was on the back wall.

Chapter Six

Mildred broke the silence first. "Looks like brain spray."

"Leader checked out?" Jak asked. "Not be first time."

"More than likely. Certainly the regular enlisted men didn't live in such style," Doc commented.

Krysty tried to pick up one of the sheets of paper, but found them clotted together with mold. The entire sheaf flaked apart in her hand. "Damn. It would have been nice to know what he'd killed himself over." She did find an identification card on the desk and slipped it into her pocket.

"Got something odd here," Mildred said from where she was standing near the wall opposite the body and the desk. She held a stiff, moldy uniform shirt in one hand as she examined an odd panel built into the wall.

It had a small grille that looked like some kind of speaker next to another red-orange light that was glowing more strongly even as she watched it. As the others clustered around it, they were all surprised to hear a voice emanate from the small speaker.

"Identify yourselves, humans." The voice was artificial, but smoother and more human-sounding than any droid or computer they'd encountered before.

The companions looked at one another. Then Doc stepped forward, holding up a hand for silence from the others. "Dr. Theophilus Algernon Tanner, working on Operation Chronos, part of Project Cerberus, a subsection of Overproject Whisper, under the Totality Concept."

"One moment, accessing files." The seconds stretched out as the group waited for the computer. "Records show that a subject Tanner, Theophilus, first participated in an experiment as a subject for Operation Chronos in 1998. Final entry shows that you were the subject of another Operation Chronos experiment, in the year 2000. As you are still alive on current date, experiment was therefore judged successful. Affirmative?"

Krysty stole a glance at Doc, who stood before the interface with gritted teeth. Judging by the pained expression on his face, she figured he was trying not to break down at the clinical, dispassionate recounting of the utter destruction of his life and, for the most part, his sanity. The old man sniffed and wiped his eyes on the sleeve of his frock coat before straightening again.

"That is correct," he replied. "I have arrived here through the mat-trans system with replacement personnel. Request...orientation and temporary passes, including appropriate security clearances, for all new personnel."

"One moment." Once again the computer did its silent, blinking act. "I will need each individual to step forward and give their names, identification numbers, and primary duty designation for processing and security card issuance." A small piece of the wall slid out when it had finished. "A blood sample is also required, to ensure there are no diseases or genetic abnormalities present."

Sweat beading his forehead, Doc shot an alarmed glance at the others before leaning forward again. "Um, I'm afraid that there was not time before accessing the mat-trans to assign them identification numbers. Request that identification numbers and cards be issued immediately."

A few beats of silence passed. "You are not authorized to make that request, Dr. Tanner. Will add the additional members of your group to temporary personnel until those records can be accessed."

"Waiting long time," Jak muttered, earning him glares from Doc and Krysty.

"Dr. Tanner, please look into red circle for photo, and then state required information. When you are finished, place your index finger on the pad to your right. You will feel a small sting in your finger."

Doc did as the computer instructed. There was a flash, as if the unwinking red orb had processed Doc's face in front of it. "You, uh, already know my name. I confess that I do not remember my ID number, but you probably have that, as well. Duty designation…let's see, what was I called? Ah, yes." A tear trickled from his eye as he answered his own question. "Time-trawl Test Subject Number 4A." He wiped the tear away and put a trembling finger on the small pad, wincing as something pricked him.

"Accepted. Next."

Krysty stepped forward and faced the glowing red orb. "Krysty Wroth."

The computer answered much more quickly this time. "Partial record of a Wroth, Krysty on file."

Her eyebrows raising at that, she glanced back at Doc with a puzzled expression. "How?" she mouthed.

Doc stepped forward again. "Query, computer—"

"You may call me AIDAN, if that is easier," the computer interrupted.

"Ah…right. Um, AIDAN, query. Why do you have a file on subject Wroth, Krysty?"

"Information received as part of emergency information dissemination from Wizard Island Complex for Scientific Advancement," the computer replied. "Tight-beam burst data transmission received, along with notification of emergency of unknown classification at complex. All attempts to reestablish communication since that date have been unsuccessful."

Krysty's blood ran cold at hearing that. She remembered all too well the scientific research-and-development facility AIDAN had just mentioned. Home to an inbred group of insane whitecoats, they had been only weeks, maybe even days, away from unleashing a rain of chemical and biohazardous devastation that would have snuffed out 99 percent of the remaining life in the Deathlands. They would have succeeded, too, if they had not captured Ryan and the others. Once the companions had found out what the demented group was up to, they had stopped those mad scientists from destroying what was left of the planet. But if the information and data about what they had been working on had been transmitted elsewhere...

Doc quickly glanced at the rest of them. "So, you will have some information on John Barrymore Dix, Jak Lauren and Ryan Cawdor, as well." The others, Thomas Finnegan and Lori Quint, were long dead and gone. Ricky, of course, wouldn't be on file, since he had never encountered any of the redoubts before joining the group a few weeks ago.

Mildred cleared her throat. "I'd imagine that you probably have a file on me, as well."

Doc's face lit up at that. "That's right!" He waved her forward. "Give your information next, Mildred."

She did so, including her identification number, which

she recited in a surprised tone. "I didn't think I'd still remember that," she muttered.

"Welcome, Dr. Wyeth. Good to see that your physical condition has improved since your cryo-freezing."

"Uh, right. Glad to be here," she replied with a dubious frown.

"Your arrival is most fortuitous, as the Poseidon Base has not had any functioning medical staff since 10/27/2008. Once processing is complete, you will report to the sick bay for standard medical duty."

"Great," she replied, her expression indicating she felt the exact opposite.

With a shrug, J.B. stepped forward next. "John Barrymore Dix, no ID number. Duty designation security, I guess."

"Temporary personnel will be assigned duty positions based on an evaluated and current needs basis," AIDAN replied. "Continue with data entry of new personnel."

One by one, the rest filed up and gave whatever information they could. When they were finished, the computer was silent for a moment. "My sensors indicate that there is one more person in your group in the captain's living quarters."

"Um, yes, the one you would know as Ryan Cawdor," Mildred replied before Doc could answer. "He was attacked by one of the security machines as we entered the base from Pod Seven."

"My apologies for that," the computer said, to Krysty's surprise. "The security forces had been dispatched to meet your group upon entry into the main base area. They were only supposed to escort your group to the new arrivals orientation area. Unfortunately, the announcement that they should have heard along with you was not transmitted effectively. What is his current condition?"

"He's recovering now, and will give his information as soon as he is able," Mildred replied.

"Very good," AIDAN replied. "To the rest of you, welcome to the Poseidon Base for Oceanic Exploration. Orientation commencing. Conceived in 1989 by famed undersea engineer Marco Palidas, Poseidon Base is humankind's gateway to the oceans. After a suitable site was found on the seafloor approximately one hundred miles east of the Hawaiian Islands, construction commenced in 1991, and was completed in 1997—"

Krysty heard the computer say the next couple of sentences, but her mind didn't comprehend them, as she was stuck on a very important part she'd heard.

She leaned over to Doc, trying to keep her voice quiet. "Did I hear that correctly?" she whispered. "We're in this redoubt at the bottom of the ocean?"

Chapter Seven

"Pause orientation, AIDAN."

Except for his moving mouth, Doc looked like he might have been carved from wood, he stood so still. Just when Krysty thought she'd have to repeat herself, he turned just enough to regard her out of the corner of his eye.

"Regrettably so, Krysty," he whispered back. "Even seeing all they had accomplished, I had not thought it possible to construct such a facility this far below the ocean, and yet here we stand, inside just such a complex."

"How—how deep are we?" Mildred managed to force the words out.

"Regrettably, I am unfamiliar with the floor of the Pacific Ocean," Doc answered without a trace of sarcasm. "It would seem that one hundred miles east of the Hawaiian Islands would be far enough to avoid the constant volcanic activity from the islands themselves. However, if we are anywhere close to an abyssal plain, then we would find ourselves under a few thousand fathoms of water at best."

"Shit," Mildred said. "AIDAN?"

"Yes, Dr. Wyeth?" the computer answered.

About to reply, Mildred cocked her head. "Is that your name, or is it an acronym for something?"

"It is both. It stands for Artificial Intelligence Direct Assistance Network."

"Right. How far below the surface are we right now?" She asked.

"Poseidon Base is 1,391 meters below the surface of the ocean."

The blood drained from the stocky woman's face as the realization continued to dawn on her.

No one else spoke for a long time. Like many of the others, Krysty couldn't help glancing at the ceiling, her mind's eye easily imagining the vast, endless ocean surrounding the failing base, pressing down on it with the pressure of millions of tons of water, constantly moving over the outside, seeking the tiniest crack or crevice to pour inside.

With a grimace, she shook her head. Dwelling on how hopeless the situation appeared at the moment wasn't going to get them out of it. She glanced around again to see everyone looking at Mildred, who had closed her eyes and was taking several deep breaths.

"You all right, Mildred?" J.B. asked.

"Honestly, no." She opened her eyes again. "I thought the underwater corridor was bad. That was nothing compared to the way I feel right now." She sucked in another deep breath. "But I will manage." She looked around at the rest of them. "None of you have anything to worry about from me."

J.B. and Krysty both nodded at that; it was all they needed to hear. J.B. glanced at Doc. "Might as well continue the spiel."

The old man nodded curtly. "Continue orientation, AIDAN."

AIDAN continued as if it had never paused in the first place. "—and the first staff arrived on 11/23/1997.

Although the facility was intended to primarily explore and research the ocean and its flora and fauna, the events of 1/20/2001, and the subsequent response of the United States, necessitated a fundamental alteration of Poseidon Base's mission."

The machine paused for a moment. "Dissemination of the following classified information is normally for Grades Epsilon and higher. Currently there is no one among you with the prerequisite clearance. However, given the exigent circumstances and the current state of the base itself, I am temporarily granting Grade Epsilon clearance to Doctors Tanner and Wyeth for the purposes of this orientation. Do you both agree to permit the others to hear the information about to be relayed?"

"Yes, AIDAN," Mildred said, sharing a worried look with Doc. "This ought to be good."

"Upon receipt of the program changes distributed by the Totality Concept, steps were taken to ensure that the base's new primary mission—ensuring the safety and protection of the men and women aboard in order to carry out their new directives—was achieved with minimum disruption. Other than the self-inflicted injury to Captain Lucas, control was achieved and maintained until early 2006."

Doc looked at the rest of the group with watering eyes. "Sounds like the reasonable decisions any dictator would make to ensure that his dominance over the general populace continued unchecked."

If AIDAN heard his comment, it did not reply. "Unfortunately, it soon became clear that humans were not meant for prolonged habitation in a facility such as Poseidon Base. The matter-transfer unit in Pod Seven was supposed to alleviate this issue, as once order had been restored on the surface, new personnel would be transported to and from the base to begin rebuilding the nation. However, when repeated attempts to contact superiors on the surface failed, many of the staff believed that they were going to be trapped here for the rest of their lives. Although some were able to come to terms with this development, others had problems adjusting to their new reality. Increased mental instability, paired with the enforced confinement in the base itself, led to an increase in aberrant behavior."

"How did this behavior manifest, and what was its outcome?" Mildred asked in the dead silence.

"The aberrant behavior manifested in a specialized psychological breakdown, resulting in an increase in paranoid delusions, including a persecution complex, and auditory and visual hallucinations. Emotional difficulty and social withdrawal were also observed in a high percentage of personnel. Attempts to utilize base equipment, including the matter-transfer unit, for unauthorized purposes increased exponentially. Many came to believe that they were being watched by an invisible force present in the base and that this force was plotting against them."

"Apparently they still couldn't program a sense of irony into these things," Mildred muttered.

"What happened?" Doc asked.

"Remedial measures were taken, which grew progressively more severe as more incidences occurred. Five incidents were traced to deliberate sabotage planned and carried out by high-ranking officers. Further remedial action was necessary to correct this behavior."

"Clarify what you mean by remedial action," Doc said.

"The problem was twofold: correct the guilty and ensure that their crimes would not occur again, and provide an example to the rest of the staff still inhabiting the complex. The solution was both simple and elegant. Those personnel who were deemed incorrigible were reclassified as security staff and modified to better perform their new duties."

"Oh God…" Mildred put her hands to her mouth. "You made them into those…things out there."

"Affirmative."

"In the name of all that is holy, do you not understand the dissonance here?" Doc sputtered. "You said yourself that your overriding directive was to protect—protect—the personnel of this base! How on earth do you rationalize those things out there as protecting anyone?"

"It is very simple, Dr. Tanner. In order to protect the larger group of productive personnel, it was necessary to isolate and contain the aberrant ones. Imprisoning or executing them would not have been the most efficient use of base resources. Modifying them into their present state gave the base a permanent security force, freeing other humans from that task. Consider it similar to removing an infected hand so that the rest of the body may survive."

"'Efficient use of resources….' I don't know how much more I can take of this—insanity," Doc said.

AIDAN continued as if it hadn't heard him. "Once no longer able to act against the base, they were assigned to oversee the remaining personnel and ensure the program's continuance. However, their appearance had the opposite of its intended effect."

"I'll bet. After all, who wants to be guarded by cyborg freak sec and their new comp baron?" J.B. asked from his position against the wall.

"The modified units caused the aberrant behavior to increase exponentially, forcing even more modifications. When the last group of base personnel attempted to destroy the security staff and interrupt my power supply, there was no other choice but to take the same measures against them."

"By which you mean—" Mildred jabbed a thumb at the door, her meaning clear to everyone in the room.

"I do not understand your question, Dr. Wyeth."

"You mean you turned the rest into those…things, as well," she said quietly.

"That is correct. Unfortunately, it was necessary in order to continue carrying out my mission and prevent the destruction of the entire base."

"So, just to be clear, there are no more…normal humans in this base," Krysty asked.

"There were not—until now."

Even in the warm, still air, a shiver ran through Krysty's body. "And exactly what are we expected to do here?"

"With assistance from me, all of you will be trained in base operations, as you will be manning this facility for the foreseeable future," AIDAN replied.

"And…just how long is that?" Mildred asked.

The computer's answer sounded dreadfully final. "Either until new orders are received or for the rest of your natural lives."

Chapter Eight

"We're su'posed t'do *what?*"

It was an hour later, and the paralyzing agent had worn off enough that Ryan could sit up and talk. He flexed his numb fingers, trying to work some feeling back into them while the others filled him in on where they were and what was happening. Ryan had listened to most of the explanation in silence—even the revelation that they were several thousand feet under the ocean didn't come as a total shock.

However, the demand the computer system overseeing the base was placing on them was a surprise.

Krysty bent over as if adjusting the plastic-sheathed pillow behind his head, her mouth close to his ear. "Figure the whole place is wired with electronic eyes and ears. Some still work, a lot probably don't, but we don't know which is which. Assume we're being monitored by AIDAN at all times."

"Right…right," Ryan replied through stiff lips. "What about malfunk?"

"You mean, what's the chance the system's gone nuts?" J.B. asked with a shrug. He was sitting cross-legged on the floor, the pieces of his Mini-Uzi spread out in front of him as he cleaned the weapon. "Doc or Mildred are probably better qualified to answer that one, though it sure told her how deep we are under the surface faster than an Ingram burning through a full mag."

"Although everything else in this underwater nightmare seems to be falling apart," Mildred said. "From what I can tell, the computer seems to be functioning more or less normally—"

Doc snorted, but didn't comment any more.

Mildred continued with a sidelong glare at him. "—although it seems to be interpreting its orders with an unusual degree of latitude."

"You are correct on both of those counts," Doc said. "I was not privy to the experiments the scientists were doing with artificial intelligence before skydark…and I had no idea that they had made such strides in their time. From what little I had gleaned of their work, I'd have thought something like our invisible, all-seeing overlord was at least a decade away…yet here we all are."

"So, how get out?" Jak asked, nodding at the door. "Not become one those bastards."

"Got that right," Ricky seconded. "Rather eat a bullet than be one of…those."

"All right, everyone just calm down," Ryan said. "No one wants to go down that road, and we're not, either. We've been in tight spots before and have always found a way out. I'm sure there's one here, too. We just have to find it, that's all."

"Besides, we don't have much choice but to play along at the moment," J.B. said. "What'd the comp say before we came in here?"

"That it was evaluating each of our 'files,' and would assign us to the department where each is most needed," Mildred said. "I know I'm going to the medical lab, but I have no hope in hell of guessing where the rest of you might end up."

"Hardly gave it enough information to make any kind of logical decision," Krysty said.

"Won't matter too much, anyhow. Right now, our best bet's just going with whatever it tells each of us," Ryan replied. "We have to check out the rest of this place and see what's what—and find out whatever we can to get us all out of here."

Slowly, he levered himself to the edge of the bed and shoved his legs over. "Bastard drug's got me moving triple slow."

"If you can move, Ryan, that would probably be best," Mildred said. "It would help oxygenate your muscles and further diffuse any of the remaining drug still in your bloodstream."

"Moving's exactly what I intend to do," Ryan replied, waving off Krysty, who had risen to support him. "Appreciate the offer, but I'm not *that* far gone yet."

She frowned in mock annoyance. "Maybe next time I'll just leave you where you fall, see how capable you are then."

Ryan grinned at her. "Fireblast, Krysty, don't think I don't appreciate you hauling my ass out of there. But here and now's something I've got to do for myself." And he was right. There was only one person who could find out if there were any lingering effects from the drug, and that was Ryan.

Taking a deep breath, he heaved himself to his feet and swayed there for a bit, his arms held stiffly out from his sides for balance. "All right, let's go see what this bastard comp has in store for us."

He tottered over to the door, walking on two legs that felt as if they ended in blocks of wood carved to look like his feet. Ryan had to fumble with the door three times before he could jerkily slide it open and walk into the other room.

"Good afternoon, Ryan Cawdor," a bodiless voice said.

"Hello—AIDAN, is it?" Ryan answered.

"That is correct. Before we continue, do you wish to review the orientation the others have already viewed?"

Ryan shook his head. "No, they told me what I needed to know, including that you're looking for some more information about me."

"Correct," the computer replied. "Your file received from the Wizard Complex is only partially complete. Please look directly into the red light without blinking, then place your index finger where indicated. I will finish your group's processing and assign appropriate duties to each person."

"Let's do it." Ryan kept his single eye open and stared into the glowing red orb until he heard a click, then saw the glow next to the orb and speaker. He placed his finger on the small pad.

"You will feel a sting," the computer said. As it did, Ryan felt the prick of a needle on the flesh of his finger.

"My physical scan has detected a deficiency in your ocular capacity, Ryan," the computer stated. "Do you wish to schedule an operation to repair this defect?"

While the computer was speaking, Ryan's hand had risen to touch the black eyepatch. It covered the gaping, empty left socket, a souvenir his fratricidal older brother Harvey had given him the night he'd tried to kill Ryan and take over their home. Ever since, he'd made his way in the world with the sole remaining eye. He'd been threatened with its loss more than once, but had never had the opposite offered to him.

But Ryan knew what that would be. He'd seen it on the poor bastard outside—the pitiless red orbs that had replaced his lost eyes. And besides that, who knew what else the crazy machine might want to implant in him while it was rummaging around in his head? A choice like that wasn't any choice at all.

"Thanks, AIDAN, but I'll pass," he replied. "Been doing fine with one so far. I figure I've just gotten used to it."

"Very well. Should you change your mind, you may schedule an appointment for ocular replacement at any time in the future," the computer replied.

"Thanks. I'll, uh, keep that in mind," Ryan replied. "Anything else?"

"Yes. I have completed the analysis of your files, and have your duty assignments ready. Are you all ready to hear them?" Ryan looked around and saw nods from everyone else. Before he could answer, the computer spoke.

"Excellent. They are as follows: Dr. Mildred Wyeth, medical lab; Dr. Theophilus Tanner, command center; Ryan Cawdor and John Barrymore Dix, maintenance; Jak Lauren and Ricky Morales, maintenance assistance; Krysty Wroth, aquaculture.

"I will be assisting all of you in becoming functional in your assignments," AIDAN continued. "Once you have all become proficient in your primary duties, you will all be assigned secondary duties to become more efficient at the maintenance and operation of this base."

"Mind if we get something to eat first?" Ryan asked. "Mat-trans jumps tend to make people hungry."

Actually, the opposite was usually true. Ryan and the others had all thrown up at least once after a jump, but if there was a chance to eat in this place, they'd take it.

"Of course," AIDAN replied. "Follow the flashing lights in the corridor outside to the dining area."

Chapter Nine

Jak lifted a forkful of thin, dark green tendrils festooned with tiny brown chunks of something, watching as they slid off the tines and fell back onto his plate. "What this?"

"Seaweed and kelp salad tossed with soybean oil and textured vegetable protein," AIDAN replied.

The albino refilled his fork and tried a bite, chewing with a shrug. "Not bad," he said. "But if this all there was to eat, no wonder they went crazy."

Everyone else was digging in, as well, following the old Deathlands maxim of always eating whenever they got the chance, because the next meal might be a long time off.

They had left the captain's quarters and found the hallway empty. The only signs of the fight had been small pools of blood and the green liquid mixed with the brackish water on the floor.

"Where cyborgs go?" Jak asked.

"And what took them there?" Ricky asked on his heels.

"Reckon we'll all find out soon enough," J.B. answered. "Let's go eat first."

True to AIDAN's word, a series of flashing lights on the well rippled down the left corridor. "Follow the bouncing ball," Doc said to no one in particular as he began walking down the corridor.

By now Ryan had regained nearly all of his usual mobility, although there were a few odd patches of numb skin on his body. His right foot, in particular, tingled with every step, but he didn't favor it, wanting to get back to one hundred percent efficiency as quickly as possible.

When they had entered the plain dining hall, which looked marginally better than the rest of the complex—less mold and no water on the floor—they'd found a round table with seven place settings. The only edible things on the table were glasses full of water. Long serving tables lined the left and rear of the room, but they were all completely empty.

When everyone had sat down, a door on the far end of the room had opened, and a waist-high robot rolled in, carrying a large tray. Seven plates, each one containing the seaweed salad, rested on the tray. Once the plates had been distributed, the robot had zipped back through the door.

"I guess this place wouldn't have the endless supplies like the aboveground redoubts," Mildred said as she cleaned her plate. "Too costly."

"You are correct, Dr. Wyeth," AIDAN replied from a speaker in the wall, making her jump. "The plan for Poseidon Base had always been to harvest the ocean's endless variety of bounty, both plant and animal. Even with what has happened on the surface, we continued this plan for the survivors here. All of the food you are eating was specially harvested to be easily preparable by automated cooking."

As it finished talking, the serving robot entered the room again, followed by another one. Their trays were laden with all manner of seafood, from thick, orange-tinted steaks of some kind to circular, white disks of meat that Mildred and Doc were almost drooling over.

"Is this—" Mildred speared one of the fist-sized chunks of meat with her fork "—what I think it is?"

"If you are thinking that it is a sea scallop, you are correct," the computer answered.

"My God—I've never seen one so large." She sniffed it, then cut off a large hunk and tried it. "And I've never tasted one this good, either!"

"It would seem that there may have been some advantages to the—unpleasantness on the surface," AIDAN said. "All of the food you are eating satisfies your basic nutritional requirements and more."

Doc had helped himself to a huge scallop as well as one of the steaks. "Swordfish, I gather?"

"Yes, Dr. Tanner."

Doc frowned. "But how did you catch it? The swordfish rarely goes below five hundred meters."

"A remotely piloted fishing device ascends to a suitable depth and harvests whatever fish it finds. There are also suitable stores of shrimp, tuna and mahimahi—enough for several months. We also have a wide variety of seaweeds stored, including the spiny sea plant, sea grapes and green sea feathers, slender slippery weed, reindeer limu, tubular green weed, elkhorn, sea moss, south sea colander and others."

"I'm sure there'll be plenty of time to try the other stuff," Ryan said, catching J.B.'s eye. He knew the Armorer had not missed the mention of the remote fishing machine, either. The only question was if it could be piloted by someone, or if it was truly a robotic drone. As maintenance personnel, he expected they'd get the chance to find out soon enough.

Everyone set to eating their fill. The only thing marring the meal came during dessert, which consisted of a variety of sweet and sour jellies made from various underwater plants, served on dried seaweed crackers. One of the robots that had been serving them turned in endless circles for a few minutes. It whirled around and around, then straightened out and ran at top speed into the wall next to the door. The impact was enough to knock it over, and it lay there helplessly, its wheels spinning in the air.

A heavy sigh made Ryan look at Doc, who shook his head while staring at the malfunctioning machine. "The tipping point has been reached, ladies and gentlemen."

"Meaning what, Doc?" Ricky asked.

"Meaning that our presence here is only accelerating the breakdown process that had begun decades before our arrival and is still ongoing today," he replied.

J.B. leaned back in his wire-framed chair and casually pointed at the ceiling. "Sooner we can get gone, the better."

AFTER THEIR MEAL, AIDAN directed them to their quarters. These were smaller versions of the captain's rooms, single bedrooms, each with its own tiny bathroom and shower. The standard red orb and speaker were on the wall near each door. A new, dark blue jumpsuit lay on each bed, next to a stiff, laminated identification card. A pair of black, ankle-high, rubberized boots sat on the floor beneath the two items. When he saw them, Ryan became acutely aware of his saltwater-soaked clothes chafing several different spots on his body.

"Hey, AIDAN?"

"Yes, Mr. Cawdor?"

Ryan paused at that. "Since we're going to be here

awhile, I think it would be fine for you to call me Ryan, all right?"

"It would be my pleasure, Ryan. What were you about to ask?"

Ryan paused at that. He knew the computer system was only a rad-blasted machine that intended to keep them here to produce offspring, like an automated rancher ruling over its flock…but in that moment, he could have sworn that it meant what it said about calling him by his first name. He shook his head. "If I leave my clothes here, could they be cleaned?"

"Yes."

"Boots, too?"

"Of course. Do make sure to have your identification card with you at all times when you are performing your duties. They are keyed to the security personnel, so they will not bother you if you have the card on you."

"Good to know," Ryan said as he unlaced his boots and pried them off his feet. It was rare in Deathlands to be secure enough to remove his boots. Typically Ryan just loosened them and slept in his clothes. However, with nowhere to go at the moment, he decided to enjoy the luxury of new clothes and get his battered coat, fatigue pants and T-shirt cleaned.

"Did you let everyone else know about the cards?" he asked as he dressed. There was a triangular insignia patch on the shoulder of the right sleeve. Edged in gold trim, it showed the base in dark brown underneath a deep blue ocean, complete with a strand of green seaweed. A golden trident thrust up from the base to the top point of the patch. The words *Poseidon Base—U.S. Navy* were in gold letters on black underneath it all.

"Yes."

"Good." The jumpsuit fit like it had been made for

him specifically, and Ryan grunted at the feel of it as he slipped the boots on, which also fit perfectly.

"Is anything wrong, Ryan?"

"Nope…just feels good, that's all." He saw why as he regarded himself in a mirror near the bathroom doorway. There was a name stitched over the left breast pocket— *rodwaC nayR*. With a start, he realized he was looking at his own name.

"AIDAN, were these uniforms made for us?" he asked.

"Not exactly. The jumpsuits come in a standard pattern, and are then custom-fitted to each individual once their measurements are on file. The last step is to add the name of the individual to the standard identity location. I trust it is satisfactory."

"Um, yeah…just takes some getting used to, that's all," Ryan replied.

"I am pleased to hear that. If you will join your companions in the corridor, you can all head to your respective duty areas."

Ryan eyed the unblinking orb for a moment. "Sure." He made sure his blaster was handy, as well as the panga, which was riding in its sheath on his left hip, but left the Steyr Scout Tactical longblaster in a corner of the room. From what Doc had said, the big 7.62 mm rounds might punch through the walls and drown them all. Slipping the ID card into his pocket, Ryan walked out of the room and joined everyone in the corridor.

Everyone had taken advantage of the base's stores. Of course, modifications had been made, depending on who was wearing it. Jak had hacked the sleeves off his uniform, his skinny arms poking through the ragged holes. Ricky had gone one step further, cutting the sleeves off and separating the top and bottom halves into two pieces, so he ended up wearing a zip-up vest and a pair of belted pants.

Doc still wore his frock coat and knee boots over his jumpsuit, while J.B. wore the uniform as it was, with his sleeves rolled up and his battered fedora on his head. Apparently he'd left his leather jacket in his room.

Mildred and Krysty had also pretty much left their outfits intact, although Ryan's lover was still wearing her dark blue cowboy boots with the chiseled silver falcons on the sides. The front zipper of her outfit was lowered enough so Ryan got a glimpse of the valley between her firm, creamy breasts. The sight made him grin, in spite of their circumstances.

"Everyone have their ID cards?" Ryan asked, noting that like him, everyone's names were embroidered on their chests.

He got nods all around. And, of course, everyone was still armed, despite Doc's earlier warning against it.

"AIDAN asked that we all check out our specific areas. Anyone have a problem with that?"

No one shook their head, although there were a fair number of apprehensive looks on faces. "Might as well get it over with," Doc said.

Ryan nodded. "Keep your eyes open. Everybody move out."

Chapter Ten

Mildred stood in front of the door labeled *Medical Lab* and took a deep breath. "It's probably just going to be the usual sort of sick bay, with beds and tables and counters and cabinets," she said to herself. But with every step she'd taken toward her duty area, her instincts had been whispering a different warning. The cyborgs had to come from somewhere, be created somewhere....

Shrugging the thought away, she pulled out her ID card and fed it into the slot. It popped back out a moment later, and the door opened.

The stink hit her first, a charnel house stench of decaying flesh and caked, drying blood, overlaid with a powerful odor of what she thought was formaldehyde but smelled off somehow, not quite as astringent. As bad as the hallway had smelled when they had first entered, this was ten, no—a hundred times worse.

Gritting her teeth, Mildred stepped inside.

The lights flickered on at her movement, revealing a scene worse than anything her worst nightmares could have thrown at her.

Her instincts had been dead right—the cyborgs had been created here, built out of whatever could be scavenged from the bodies of the former personnel.

Mildred stopped in her tracks and stared at the abattoir all around her.

Body parts were everywhere throughout the room.

Arms, legs, hands and feet, all preserved in glass tanks filled with a cloudy green solution. One container was large enough to hold the upper torso of what looked like a man missing one arm below the elbow, his mouth forever open in a silent scream.

But that was only the beginning. Seeing a second row of tanks behind that one, Mildred slowly walked to the end of the second row and froze again, her hands going to her mouth.

Inside these tanks were fetuses in various stages of development, all preserved in the same green liquid. She saw ones that she estimated were maybe ten weeks old and a larger baby, probably around nine months old, its sightless eyes forever staring out at her.

Stumbling back from the scientific horror show, she whirled, only to be faced with a brand-new section of medical hell.

The cyborg security forces they'd faced upon their arrival were all here, as well. The man with the clamp arm, the woman with the plastic half face, the four-armed one, all of them were piled in the middle of the room like so much flesh-and-metal cordwood. Trickles of coagulating blood and the strange green liquid dripped off them to form a large pool on the floor. Beyond that, her stunned mind barely registered a long row of black Formica-topped lab tables, filled with equipment, including two robotic arms and a centrifuge.

Mildred took a deep breath through her mouth, fighting to keep from throwing up. Even with her extensive medical training and all that she had experienced in the Deathlands, this was almost too much to take.

"As you can see, Dr. Wyeth, the security forces suffered significant damage from that…misunderstanding with your group." The computer's voice made her jump again. She whirled to find the red orb and speaker next to the door.

"Goddammit!" She took another breath. "I'm never going to get used to you talking out of thin air."

"My apologies. Would you prefer that I begin each communication with some sort of signal?"

Mildred rubbed her temples. "No, let me just— I need to get to work if I'm going to repair these…these… things." She looked around again, her curiosity warring with her revulsion. "I have to ask…how do you keep them a—" She stopped herself before she said the word. They were definitely not alive. "Functioning? Surely, once the last personnel died, there was no need for them to exist any longer."

"Your lack of foresight is disappointing, Doctor," AIDAN replied. "There has always been an excellent probability of more personnel reaching the base, and if that ever did occur, it would be prudent for there to be tissue and blood samples from viable genetic specimens on hand, if needed."

"Of course. Very prudent of you," Mildred replied. It also wouldn't hurt to have your own sec force, just in case the visitors didn't come in peace, she thought but didn't say. Instead, she glanced at the nearest body-part tank. "So, exactly what is that green fluid? It's the same compound used in the various cyborgs, correct?"

"A very astute observation, Doctor. That is one of my primary achievements since assuming control of the entire base. It is a mixture of processed and refined genetic material from starfish and a serum derived from the neurotoxin of the blue-ringed octopus. The primary effect of the neurotoxin is to paralyze the nerve endings that signal pain to the brain, while the starfish component keeps the flesh in a state of slow regeneration. The fluid also has seaweed and kelp powders mixed into it, which supply essential nutrients so they do not have to be sustained with normal food."

The computer paused for a moment. "I confess that the current security units have never lived up to my initial design for them. However, now that you have arrived, I believe that we will make excellent progress on the next iteration."

Despite her disgust, Mildred listened with fascination to the ghoulish topic. Over the past century, AIDAN seemed to have solved a few problems that had troubled humankind since the advent of medicine itself. She was pretty sure that, if given the choice, the patients would not have paid the cost for this kind of life, however.

There was another element to AIDAN's measured recitation of its achievement. Mildred had dealt with more than her share of arrogant, opinionated doctors in her day, and something about the computer's tone as it was telling her about this process struck her: it sounded exactly like one of those doctors, as if the machine wanted to be recognized for its accomplishment.

Realizing the computer was probably waiting for her to reply, Mildred cleared her throat. "Yes, I expect that we will. But first, this operating room must be cleaned, as I cannot work under these conditions. Tell me you have some kind of cleaning robot or something of the kind in here?"

"Not as such, once the last human expired. At the time, it is was vital to concentrate on the creation and sustaining of the cyborgs. To facilitate the cleaning of this room, I suggest activating the backup fire suppression system, which would douse the entire area with filtered fresh water. All of the detritus and other unnecessary liquids would be collected near the drain at the center of the room."

"Won't that harm your specimens?" she asked.

"The ones in the tanks will be fine, but you should move the ones in the middle of the room into the operating chamber ahead of you. Once we are finished in here, we can clean that room, as well. I will summon other security units to assist you."

"That's all right. I don't wish to take them from their duties," she replied. Besides, she thought as she walked over to the pile, none of these look large enough to be too much of a hassle—

But even as she reached down to grab the plastic-faced woman, the cyborg's arm swung up, its hand latching on to her throat.

With her air suddenly cut off, Mildred couldn't even wheeze out a cry for help to AIDAN as the half human, half machine began drawing her closer to its terrible face.

"CAN'T WAIT TO see what this place has in its workshop."

Ricky was practically jumping up and down as the four men passed the intersection where they had come in and headed down the right corridor, their feet splashing in the stagnant water.

"I wouldn't get my hopes up too far, Ricky," J.B. replied. "From what we've seen so far, it's doubtful there'll be much of anything in working order."

"Maybe, but if they got tools and supplies, then we can fix the rest of it, right?"

"The optimism of the young," Ryan said with a smile. "What about you, Jak? You looking for anything interesting down here?"

The albino looked around for any listening devices,

but saw none. "Yeah—way out this underwater trap," he muttered.

"Second that," J.B. said.

Ryan also took a look around as they progressed farther down the dank, moldy corridor, the lights flickering on as they passed, then winking out when they were a few steps away. It was apparent that the maintenance section had not been visited in a long, long while. "Everyone just stay on the lookout for anything that might help us."

The two teens trotted ahead, leaving Ryan and J.B. a few steps behind. The one-eyed man glanced over to find his old friend rubbing his chin. "What are you thinking?"

"Thinking we're in a hell of a mess."

Ryan shrugged. "Mebbe. Still breathing, aren't we?"

"For now." J.B.'s eyes flicked around. "Long as that comp decides we're more useful alive than dead and reanimated as its next wave of secmen." He looked owlishly at Ryan from behind his glasses. "You know it could do it, too, right? Just lower the oxygen content in the air until we all asphyxiate, and there you go. Seven more bodies on the hoof."

"Except then it won't get any more humans running around—" Ryan began, only to get cut off.

"Dark night, I sure hope you're joking!"

"Rad blast it, you know I am!" Ryan said. "Look, we're not going to end up like that."

"Damn right we're not. I'll find whatever vents I need and bring the whole ocean into this place before I go out like that."

Ryan sighed. He'd expected that exact answer from J.B., but he hadn't expected the combined tone of vehemence and finality that permeated the words. "We're going to find a way out. There has to be something somewhere. They didn't build these things without multiple fail-safes and backups."

"And I'm all for finding them, but you aren't seeing the whole picture." J.B. checked on the two youths ahead before continuing, and his eyes strayed to the walls around them. "Lot of dark stains around here," he said.

Ryan glanced around at the large splashes of dried, black stains that he knew was old blood. "Looks like some kind of all-out battle happened in here."

J.B. nodded. "Or last stand." He fell silent a moment, then looked at Ryan again. "Traveled a lot of miles together, you and I. You know I'll always fight until the last bullet, blade, or bite. But we have *never* run into this kind of situation before, with this…comp system like it is. Who knows, it may have already scuttled all of the lifeboats or escape pods or whatever they had down here, to keep people from trying to evacuate. Hell, it might have even sabotaged the mat-trans after we arrived, to make sure we couldn't leave, either. Don't be fooled by its sounding so calm and rational. Anything that would create those monstrosities is anything but."

Ryan nodded. "Ace on the line with that one, J.B."

"We found it!" Ricky called from a dozen yards ahead.

"Door looks messed up," Jak said.

He was right. As Ryan drew closer, he saw burn and scratch marks all over the door.

"Let's see what we got in here."

Jak's card opened the door easily enough, but the lights in there were less cooperative, with only scattered ones coming on as they walked into the largest room they'd encountered so far.

At first glance, it looked like the mechanic's paradise Ricky had been hoping for. But as they probed deeper into the darkness, it became apparent that maintenance had been ransacked and cannibalized for anything useful, leaving only ruined pieces of once-whole machines.

As Ryan walked farther into the room, he realized it was much worse than that. The last survivors had tried to fight off the secmen in here. He was sure of it, since, except for the dried stains on the floor and walls, they might have stopped fighting five minutes ago. The evidence was everywhere—improvised, broken weapons, hastily erected defensive fortifications, industrial equipment modified with offensive capabilities. The ubiquitous red orb and speaker by the door had been smashed and never repaired. And if that wasn't enough, there were the bloodstains.

Everywhere he looked, Ryan saw bloodstains.

Everyone else was silent as they went through the wreckage. Only Ricky said anything.

"Santa Maria!" Ricky shook his head as he looked around. "These jocks sure didn't know how to take care of their equipment! Pieces and parts thrown around everywhere!"

Ryan opened his mouth to correct the kid, but Jak beat him to it. "That not it, ya stupe. Tried fight off 'borgs here. Last stand." The albino looked around, his white hair catching the light. "Sucked to be them."

Ryan decided to get everyone working to combat the gloomy feel of the mechanic's bay. "That was then, and this is now. We still got a lot to do. Ricky, you're on tool detail. Anything around here that still works, collect it and put it near the door. Jak, help him. J.B. and I are going to check out the back."

"You see what I saw over there?" J.B. asked as he fell into step behind the taller man.

Ryan nodded. He'd spotted several large, irregular shapes toward the back, and wanted to check them out. The first thing he noticed was what looked like a large airlock door, about nine feet tall and just as wide, on the back wall. "We could all just duck out of there," he remarked to J.B.

The Armorer snorted. "Yeah, because being crushed to jelly while drowning is the way I want to go. Come on, let's check these out."

The first thing they looked at, half covered by a moldy tarp, was a fairly large three-person submarine. Scratches and dents covered its metal surface, and its thick windows had been smashed. At the rear, one of the directional fans that provided propulsion and steering had been crushed to about three inches thick. J.B. poked his head inside the ruined cockpit to find the smashed controls all crusted over with something dried and flaky. He wasn't about to touch it to find out what, however.

Keeping an ear on Ricky and Jak going through the debris, he lowered the tarp and headed toward the back wall, where J.B. was looking at something with what was close to a smile on his face. "Best thing I've seen since we arrived."

Looking over the bulbous, mechanized diving suit, Ryan had to agree with him.

Suspended in a heavy-duty harness and hanging from what looked like a portable engine hoist, the suit was eight feet tall and bright white. It consisted of what looked like a series of round bubbles that had been connected together to form a suit large enough for a big person to fit inside. The torso was very bulky, and Ryan figured it held the air supply and other vital systems.

Instead of hands, both arms ended in two large gripper clamps, each one caked in dried blood up to the wrists.

"Think we'll find someone inside?" J.B. asked.

"You figure someone died in there?"

J.B. pointed to the gripper clamps. "Someone used this thing for something other than walking around on the ocean floor. Come on. Let's see if we can crack it open."

Putting their backs into it, the two men wheeled the suit over to a workbench. J.B. climbed on the table and studied the top for a few seconds. "Here they are." He released four inset clamps, and a large part of the back of the suit rose an inch away from the rest. "Don't know if it's all one piece or if it will come off by itself...heavy..." Getting both hands on it, he pulled it up and out.

The back piece pivoted out like a clamshell, coming to rest at a forty-five-degree angle to the rest of the suit. The space it left was just large enough for a person to slip into the interior. J.B. stuck his head into the compartment. "Empty. Whoever was manning this thing's long gone."

"Probably wandering the halls of this place somewhere," Ryan said. Ricky and Jak had come over to see what they were doing.

Ricky whistled. "Wow. Think it still works?"

Making sure the hoist was secure, J.B. leaned in a bit farther. "Clean in here, too. No sign of damage." He popped his head back out. "If we can get it running and find the oxygen it needs, things might be looking up."

"Well, let's see what we can do," Ryan said. He was about to look around for anything that might help with the suit when the room's main door opened.

"Ryan and John Dix, Dr. Tanner has requested

that you join him in the command center right away."
AIDAN's voice came from the hallway.

The two men exchanged glances. "We'll be right there," Ryan replied. "Wonder what he found?"

"One way to find out," J.B. replied. "Ricky, start getting familiar with this suit. Figure out what it needs, and what needs to be repaired or refilled on it."

Ricky nodded. "Sure. By the time you come back, I'll know it like the back of my hand."

"What I do?" Jak asked.

"Help Ricky, of course," Ryan replied. "Once he's inside there, he'll need someone to hand him tools or make sure he doesn't get crushed if the whole thing falls over."

He crooked a finger at Ricky. "Come here for a moment." He whispered something in the boy's ear, which sent him scurrying out of the room.

"Jak, hang here till Ricky gets back."

He nodded to J.B. and turned to the door. "Let's go find out what Doc wants."

Chapter Eleven

Krysty strode down the deserted corridor toward the aquaculture section, her thoughts jumpy and nervous. Usually calm and collected even in the direst of circumstances, she could feel her composure slipping with every minute she spent in this place. It required every bit of control she possessed not to jump or flinch at every little noise.

The reason for this was all around her. Not just the blasphemy against nature of the reanimated sec 'borgs, but all of it. The base itself—a completely artificial enclosure against the natural world outside. The omnipotent presence of the artificial intelligence computer. All of it pressed on her mental faculties with an insistent pressure that couldn't be ignored.

AIDAN was especially troublesome. The mutie power Krysty inherited from her mother, Sonja, allowed her to sense the presence of living things nearby. Occasionally, she could also sense more details about them, such as whether or not they were hostile toward the group.

But the computer system running Poseidon Base was unlike anything she had ever encountered before. Before coming here, she never would have thought she could detect anything like it before—after all, it wasn't alive. And yet, she could *feel* its presence. That led to an entire host of questions—about the nature of her ability as well as the nature of life itself—that she really didn't want to contemplate. Part of her was curious to get a look at the workings of the computer itself, to see if it was fully machine or some combination of organic and mechanical. Another part of her mind was nearly terrified at the very idea. She was really beginning to think that not feeling it would be much better.

The main problem was that the computer was *everywhere* in the base, a disembodied being all around her, waiting...watching. Therefore, it was always setting off her ability. Also, the detection itself was unnerving, the feeling akin to a mild electric shock in her brain. All in all, it was making her damned skittish—and very uncomfortable.

She came to the door marked *Aquaculture Bay*. Krysty had done her share of gardening back in her home ville of Harmony, but she had a feeling this was going to be quite different.

Steeling herself, she addressed the computer. "AIDAN?"

"Yes, Miss Wroth?"

Despite how she felt about the computer, Krysty couldn't help smiling at its politeness. "Krysty's fine. Please explain what this part of the base is."

"Gladly. When Poseideon Base was conceived, one of its basic parameters was to be self-sufficient. Harvesting as much food as possible from the ocean was a recognized part of the base's operation, and all preparations were made to facilitate that end. The aquaculture program was designed to harvest the most nutritious strains of aquatic plant life and cross-breed them to create the most beneficial strains."

"Sounds commendable. How did it go?"

"Well enough, at first. The primary botanist in change accomplished some amazing things before his disappearance, including making the bay largely self-replenishing. His files are on record, if you wish to view them."

"Perhaps later," she replied.

"Very well. Toward the end, however, things seemed to be getting a bit out of control. You may find that it is a bit overgrown in there."

"I'll keep that in mind. What will my duties consist of?"

"First, you will check the condition of the communication console near the door, Krysty," AIDAN replied. "It has not been functional since 9/7/2064, and I do not yet have a robot with the capacity to repair it. When you have ascertained the nature of its malfunction, you will notify one of the maintenance crew, who will then repair it. Once this has been completed, I will instruct you further on your regular duties."

Although Krysty thought it was odd that the computer had delegated her to this particular task, and not one of the others actually assigned to maintenance, she wasn't going to argue. "All right." She slotted the card and the door opened, letting a wave of warm, humid air roll over her.

"Gaia…" she breathed as she stared at the profusion of plant life that had grown wild in the large room. Long rows of water-filled tanks contained a bewildering variety of green plants. Many had overgrown their immediate quarters, their dried shoots and stalks spilling out of the water and withering in the moist air. Others had just kept growing, sending green tendrils over everything, including the walls and ceiling. The air was alive with smells, both of blooming plants, as well as the rich peaty smell of decaying organic matter. It was all underlaid with a sweetish smell that was somehow familiar to her, but she couldn't quite place it.

"How long has this department gone unattended?" she asked without taking her eyes off the profusion of greenery inside. She felt her hair contract and pull up until it was curled into a tight ball at her nape. Something was off in there.

"Regular maintenance and cross-pollination continued until 1/3/63, when the last robot capable of maintaining this section malfunctioned. Now that you and your group are here, this section will be reorganized and maintained both to add to our food stores and prepare for more new arrivals."

"Okay, I'm going inside. I'll let you know what's going on with the panel as soon as possible."

"Thank you, Krysty," the computer replied as she stepped across the threshold. The door closed behind her, leaving her to face the jungle alone. All was quiet here, although, once again, she got the distinct feeling that she was being watched. But there was only plant life here.

Shaking off the feeling, she turned to examine the red orb and speaker near the side of the door. The orb itself was dull, with tiny beads of condensed water inside it. The speaker seemed to be choked off by some kind of lichen or mold. Wiping her sweaty brow, Krysty glanced at the ceiling, looking for irrigation spigots.

A rustling sound caught her ear and made Krysty half turn, looking for anything moving. But the aquatic forest was silent and still. She turned back to examining the console.

No wonder this shorted out, she thought. With this much moisture, any electronics would be bound to fail over a hundred years—

The rustle sounded louder now, and Krysty whirled, sure she'd heard something moving in the depths of the greenery. Again, she confronted the nearly impenetrable wall of green.

"Is someone there?" she asked, taking a step forward. No one answered. Somewhere deep in the room she could hear the drip-drip-drip of water splashing into a larger tank.

Best get Ryan in here to fix this, she thought as she turned to leave. But as she did, the rustling behind her intensified. Krysty had just started to turn back when what felt like several tentacles grabbed her around the arms and legs and pulled her off her feet. Another tentacle, this one wet and smelling like a plant, covered her mouth. Krysty struggled, but the bindings were joined by a dozen more, all of them pinning her limbs to her sides as they wrapped tighter and tighter around her body.

With an effort, Krysty managed to flop over to see what she had feared was happening. The large plant near the door was her captor! As she struggled to free herself, it began pulling her closer to the tank. When she was a few feet away, it actually began dragging her up the side of the glass. As she was lifted higher into the air, Krysty saw the bare skull of the plant's last victim inside, its gaping eyeholes staring sightlessly back at her.

Now she was almost at the top and could see the middle of the plant, which looked like a strange version of a Venus flytrap crossed with some kind of plant that was able to move its tendrils.

But instead of delicate sensors that closed over a fly to form a cage while it was being digested, each head-size, hinged pod was ringed by black, needle-sharp fangs.

RYAN AND J.B. stepped out of the elevator that had taken them to the command center and into a place that felt absolutely dead.

Unlike the rest of the base, the command center—a central chair surrounded by banks of gray computer consoles and empty chairs—looked as neat and organized as if the cleaning crew had come in between shifts and gotten the entire place ready for the next shift. The room was empty, with no sign of Doc anywhere.

The shutter on a single window was open, and a powerful spotlight stabbed into the murky darkness outside. Ryan stepped over to it, seeing the beam illuminate a large patch of gray-tan sand. As he watched, something moved at the edge of the light, but it was gone before he could register exactly what it was. One thing was for sure—it was big.

Very big.

"Ryan." J.B.'s voice pulled him away from the thick glass. "Over here."

The Armorer was standing next to a door on the opposite side of the room from the elevator. It stood open, and Doc could be seen inside, slumped in a chair in front of a desk that was built into the wall, his head buried in his hands.

"Doc?" Ryan asked.

The old man swung around to see the two men. "Ryan! J.B.!" He motioned to both of them. "Come inside. You must be in here to see what I have to show you."

The two men entered, and Doc slid the door closed behind them. Unlike the others, this one looked to be normally operated by hand. As with every other room he entered, Ryan checked the side of the door. The red orb in here had been smashed, as well, with the speaker destroyed, as well.

"What'd you find?" J.B. asked.

Doc straightened in his chair. "Do you recall how

we were all wondering what, except for the weak-willed
Captain Lucas and those poor bastards who were turned
into cyborgs, had happened to the rest of the crew? Well,
I seem to have found the answer."

He leaned back to reveal a small device sitting on
the table. It consisted of a small, flip-up monitor, with
what looked like some kind of optical disk drive in the
part that was resting on the desk. "The optical disk inside did not give up its secrets without effort," he said
as he reached out with a finger to press a button on the
device. "We may get one more play out of it."

The monitor flickered as it came to life, the static disappearing as a man's head appeared on the screen. He
looked horrible, with dark bags under his bloodshot eyes,
a patchy beard, and deep wrinkles around his eyes and
mouth. His salt-and-pepper hair was a mess, his cheek
had a tan-colored bandage on it and he rubbed his mouth
with a hand wrapped in a second bloody bandage. He
leaned forward, as if checking something on the device
he was using to make the recording. For a second, the
picture froze, with several large, black squares appearing on the monitor. They cleared up after a few seconds,
and he opened his mouth to speak.

"NOT LIKE THERE'S anyone who's gonna see this, but this
is Commanding Officer Martin Yates of the United
States Naval Base Poseidon, recording my final message on April 1, 2006. With no hope of rescue, and un-
willing to submit ourselves to the increasingly irrational
demands of the AI on this station, the remaining crew
members and I have agreed to attempt to destroy AIDAN
and regain control of the base. I wish to go on record
and say that although we are doing this knowing that
in all likelihood our attempt will be futile, the men and

women who have served under me have done so with the utmost honor, valor and fidelity, both to the Navy and their country, and it has been my privilege to command them."

The machine stuttered as he wiped his nose, making it appear as if he did so over and over again. Finally the screen cleared and he continued.

"If you have gained access to this naval facility and are viewing this record, then we have likely failed in our final mission. All personnel performed their duties heroically. Any mistakes in regard to the plan and execution of our operation rest with me alone. Your primary goal at this point should be to escape this place as quickly as you can, before AIDAN sabotages your equipment to strand you here. The computer has taken the new directives, received from something called the Totality Concept, in a twisted new direction. It has tried to force an aggressive procreation program on the entire base staff, claiming that the population needs to be increased for our eventual return to the surface.

"AIDAN has attempted to force mandatory artificial insemination on all female personnel on a rotating schedule, essentially relegating them to serving primarily as baby carriers until they can no longer do so. It is assumed that this program would continue with the successive generations of base personnel, until such time as contact could be reestablished with the outside world.

"The remaining officers and I voted unanimously to resist this directive with any and all resources at our disposal. When we informed AIDAN of this decision, it began attempting to terminate the remaining officers and all male personnel, having already stored a viable quantity of sperm for future inseminations. Initial attacks were thought to be accidents, but upon further investigation, it was revealed that AIDAN was actively involved in creating situations where male personnel would be injured or killed."

"And here we thought it was so friendly," J.B. said, the corner of his mouth crooking up in a sardonic smile.

"It was at this time that the computer system terminated our chief physician and sealed off the sick bay. A few days later, the first of the…cyborgs appeared and began fighting us. It was at this point that we knew we had to stop AIDAN, no matter what the cost. A plan was formulated and is about to be put into action. I am going now to assist the remaining personnel in carrying it out. Again, if you are viewing this, you are in danger, and should evacuate this base immediately. Do not trust anything that AIDAN tells you. It will attempt to control you, and failing that, it will seek to kill you. Get out while you still can."

He blinked several times as tears gathered in the corners of his eyes.

"I never got the chance to say goodbye to my wife, Maryann, and my daughter, Raina. I just want to say that I love you both, and God willing, will be with you soon. Commanding Officer Martin Yates of the United States Navy, signing off. May God have mercy on our souls."

The picture winked out as a sharp whine could be heard from the device's housing. Then with a pop, it ground to a halt. Doc slowly closed the screen and rubbed his eyes. "I assume you recognized that poor soul?"

Ryan thought about it, then his head snapped up. "Fireblast! He was…that first cyborg we saw, wasn't he? The one with the clamp arm?"

Doc nodded. "I think we need to have a conversation

with the others regarding the situation here as soon as possible. Agreed?"

Ryan could only nod dumbly in response.

Chapter Twelve

Mildred scrabbled for purchase against the cyborg's slick flesh, struggling with all her might to free herself from its unyielding grip.

One of her hands clawed at the cool fingers around her throat, trying to loosen them, but she might as well have tried to loosen fingers made out of steel. Her other hand was braced against the monster's chest in a vain attempt to prevent her head from coming closer to the creature's mouth, which she was sure would be happy to rip out her throat if it got the chance. She tried to expel enough breath to tell AIDAN she was in serious trouble, but all that came out of her constricted windpipe was a faint whistle. She looked around for any kind of weapon within reach, but she was too far away from the tables and had no blade on her, either. The only thing she could do was kick hard at its torso and legs, which had the effect she expected—none.

Inch by inch, the cyborg drew her grimacing face closer to its own visage. When she was only a couple of inches away, it opened its mouth. It had real teeth, stained and yellow, on the left side of its face, and gleaming metal teeth on the right side. Although she desperately tried to rear away, Mildred could not escape. Closing her eyes, she gritted her teeth for the savage mauling that was about to happen.

"...me...pl..."

A puff of warm, fetid breath washed over her ear. Mildred realized she wasn't being pulled down any more. In fact, she wasn't moving at all. She cracked an eye open and realized that she was now looking at the door.

Why did it turn my head? Mildred wondered. Is it going to tear off my ear first? She felt the puff of breath on her skin again, and this time heard what the female cyborg was saying over and over.

"…kill me…please kill me…please…"

The message was so shocking that Mildred stopped struggling immediately. In return, she felt the pressure on her throat ease enough for her to suck in a breath. "I—I hear you," she whispered.

The faint whisper continued, like a broken record. "…kill me…please kill me…please…"

Oh, my God, Mildred thought. They really are alive! They've been conscious and aware for…all this time!

The thought not only sickened her, it made her sad beyond almost anything she'd felt before. Sure, Mildred was stuck in this ruined world of savagery and terror, but now she was looking at a fate worse than that, or even death. To be trapped in this grafted, twisted shell of a body, forced to be the helpless prisoner of an insane AI for decade upon decade…never knowing a moment's peace. The thought was horrific beyond anything she could have ever contemplated.

There were dozens of questions she would have liked to ask the cyborg, but she knew she didn't dare try to with AIDAN monitoring the situation. "I'm—I'm sorry," she whispered. "If you let me go, I will do whatever I can to terminate you."

There was a pause, as if the cyborg was considering what she'd said, then the crushing grip on her throat disappeared. Mildred stayed where she was for a moment, getting her bearings back after this discovery, and almost as important, filling her lungs with air. When she felt she could, she straightened.

"Is everything all right, Dr. Wyeth?" AIDAN asked.

"Um, yes. I just lost my balance for a moment," she replied. "I'm going to finish moving these units into the next room, and then you can begin washing this one down."

"Excellent. It is very gratifying to me to see these rooms will soon be used for their intended purpose again," AIDAN said.

Yeah, because you've got no more people to turn into half-alive corpses anymore, do you? Mildred thought. "I'm sure it is." Gritting her teeth again, she finished her gruesome task as quickly as possible, noting that the others were mouthing the same plea as the female.

When she had deposited all of them in the other room, she surveyed the neatly laid-out row of preserved men and women and said, "I'm going to do everything I can for all of you." She was pleased to see one of the cyborgs, the one with the clamp arm, nod at her words.

Mildred walked back into the outer room and headed for the door. "Since you're washing this room, I'm going to go see what the boys are up to."

"That is acceptable," AIDAN replied. "Ryan, John Dix and Dr. Tanner are leaving the command center and appear to be heading back to your quarters. I will notify you when the room will be ready for you to resume your duties." The door obligingly slid open for her.

"Thank you, AIDAN," she replied as she left. In the corridor, she took several breaths of the stale, warm air, thinking they were the best she'd ever had. After a moment, she headed for their quarters.

KRYSTY WRITHED AND struggled, trying to break even one of the leathery fronds binding her, but they were too tough. Meanwhile, the tendrils continued hauling her toward the top of the tank.

When she reached the opening, with the large pod heads snapping and straining to reach her, she was able to brace the heels of her cowboy boots on the edge, lock her knees and lean backward, thwarting the plant just enough to allow her to close her eyes and concentrate on entering a power trance. Although Krysty had done this dozens of times, and often in considerable danger, she had never attempted it while only seconds away from being devoured. She knew that if she did not achieve it she was going to be dead in the next minute.

Perhaps that sense of imminent death was why she was able to focus her psyche and draw upon the power of Gaia, the Earth Mother, faster than she ever had before. Within moments, a sense of peace and calm flooded through her. It felt as if she were in two different places—part of her disconnected, floating outside her body, watching as the carnivorous plant attempted to pull her over into the tank. The other part was still within her, completely aware of that mysterious core deep within her, gathering that power that Mother Sonja had taught her to draw upon and condensing it into a white-hot ball of surging, pulsating energy. Once it was ready, all she had to do was let it go.

Just in time, too, since the plant had overcome the resistance of her boots and was pulling her in. Just as she was about to be drawn down into the cluster of hungry, fanged plant pods, Krysty opened her eyes.

Biting through the fibrous tendril covering her mouth, she levered her bound arms away from the sides of her body, tearing apart the straining leafy tentacles that were trying to pinion her. The pods underneath her gnashed their fanged maws in pain.

Knowing she had only a few minutes before the surge of strength ended, Krysty freed her arms in time to brace herself across the four-foot tank, preventing her from being pulled in. Spreading her legs, she tore apart more fronds then brought her feet back together and smashed them down into the middle of the pod cluster.

As she'd thought, while the pods were vicious against helpless prey, they were less effective against anything that could fight back. Her boots crushed three of the largest pods under their heels, the impact making the others quiver and thrash. More tendrils snaked in to try to immobilize her, but Krysty moved in a blur, stomping and smashing the rest of the pods while she tore apart every frond that tried to attack her as if they were made of paper, shredding them and hurling the leaking ends away.

By the time she felt her incredible strength begin to fade, she stood in the middle of complete carnage. The mutant plant was dead, there was no doubt about that. Oozing, crushed pods spasmed weakly all around her, while truncated fronds littered the tank and the floor. Her hands and boots were covered in slimy, green gore.

The last of her strength faded, and Krysty leaned weakly against the side of the tank. That was when she heard it.

A second rustle.

She managed to climb out of the tank, almost falling in her weakened condition. But she knew if she fell, she would never get up again. The jolt of adrenaline from that thought was enough for her to muster the strength to climb down to the floor and totter to the door as fast as she could manage, her muscles sore and her head fuzzy.

Fumbling with the card, she got it out and shoved it into the slot next to the door. The rustling grew louder behind her, but the door didn't open. Biting back a curse, she took the card as it was spit out from the slot and realized she'd put it in upside down.

Flipping it over, she shoved it through again, and nearly sobbed with relief as the door slid open. Snatching the card again, she ran through as a tendril shot across the floor in an attempt to snare her ankle.

"Close it! Close the door, AIDAN!" Krysty said, hitting the far wall across from the doorway and rolling along it, away from the Aquaculture Bay. The door slid closed, and Krysty looked back to see a severed section of plant writhing on the hallway floor.

"Did you find out what the problem was with the communication console, Krysty?" the computer asked.

"Um, yes…too many plants inside." Edging past the still-moving frond, she began heading back to her quarters, walking faster and faster until she broke into an exhausted, stumbling run.

"I SWEAR, THIS place is a madhouse!" Mildred said. Her head rested on J.B.'s shoulder, her eyes still red from crying. When she had seen the men, she hadn't said a word, but had simply thrown herself into his arms and sobbed.

Krysty joined them a few minutes later and forestalled any questions regarding her appearance by saying she was going to clean up first. After scrubbing off most of the muck she rejoined the others in Doc's quarters where the console seemed to be on the blink with a dead orb.

She relayed her story to the others, heard Mildred's, then the two women were struck dumb by Ryan, J.B. and Doc's tale of what they had found.

The only good discovery was a bottle of something called Absolut Mandarin that Ricky and Jak had brought back from the maintenance room. It was a clear, potent liquor that tasted of oranges, and they passed it around while everyone told their stories.

Now Jak took the half-empty bottle back and raised it to his lips for a swallow. He lowered it, wiped his mouth and belched. "'Kay, everything sucks here. So when we get out?"

"Hang on a bit, Jak." Ryan held his hand out for the bottle. "Ricky, did you find anything out about where the comp is located?"

The Puerto Rican kid nodded. "I did find a door marked with its name. It had a handprint reader as well as the keycard slot and number pad. I didn't touch anything. I did not know what the comp might do."

"Good boy." Ryan still looked at Ricky. "What'd you find out about the suit?"

The teen cleared his throat. "It's almost ready to go. All it needs is its batteries recharged. And the oxygen to be refilled."

"Did it have a connection to AIDAN?" J.B. asked.

Ricky shook his head. "It did at one time, but the other engineers disconnected it." He hesitated. "There is one thing…"

"What?" Ryan asked.

"The oxygen…it's something I've never seen before. The operator must breathe a liquid oxygen to work this thing outside."

"Liquid oxygen?" Doc asked. "I take it you are not talking about the fuel they used for the big rockets from the space program of the latter twentieth century?"

"Actually, Doc, he is," Mildred said. "LOX is the same thing, whether it's used in a rocket engine or for breathing at high pressures. That was how we kept our subjects going into the cryo-tubes—a very small portion of liquid oxygen was diffused through the solution to keep our lungs working at a low capacity. Since it was so concentrated, they didn't have to use much." She turned to Ricky. "Is there any down there?"

Ricky nodded. "Yes, lots."

Now Mildred smiled. "Good. Because along with its breathable properties, it is an excellent explosive. And, so help me God, we are going to destroy this base if it is the last thing I do."

"Amen to that," Krysty said. "But how are we supposed to do it without AIDAN discovering what we're up to?"

"And let's not forget we still don't have a way out of this place, either," Ryan said. "Blowing the place sky-high won't mean jackshit if our asses are still stuck here when it goes."

"Actually, might sort have way out," Jak said as he pulled a folded, grease-stained piece of paper from a pocket of his jumpsuit. "Found map whole place." He stabbed a pale finger at a section of the base that stuck out from the rest of the complex, connected by a tunnel. "Escape pods here."

"Now we're talking," J.B. said.

"Yeah, but Jak and I went to find them," Ricky said. "It's cut off from the rest of the complex by a cave-in. Hard to know if it was natural or if the comp made it happen."

"It doesn't matter now," Ryan said. "What matters is getting over there, seeing if the pods are still there, and whether they're useable."

"Hold up, lover," Krysty said. "I'm seeing all sorts of problems with that idea. What if you don't make it over there? What if you do, but get trapped there? There's no way we'll be able to get to you if, Gaia forbid, something happens to you."

"The situation we're in now doesn't leave a lot of options," he replied. "Die out there, die in here, there's not much difference. Except out there I'm trying to find a way out of here for us."

"True, but that still leaves the rest of us here," Mildred said. "There has to be some way to get the rest of us over there, as well, otherwise it might as well be on the moon."

"I think I've got that covered," J.B. said. "Ricky, did you spot a welding torch down in maintenance?"

The kid nodded. "It works, too."

"Even better. We'll strip that submersible of anything it doesn't need and weld the thickest plates we can find over the broken portholes. Assuming there's a pod to get to, we all get inside and Ryan drags us over there. We'll all have to get a bit close, but it's nothing we haven't done before."

"And he's going to haul us all over?" Doc asked. "The weight of the shell and glass and everything would have to be several tons all by itself."

"I'm open to other suggestions if anyone's got them," J.B. said. No one said anything. "Okay, then we go with what we have."

"You really think it'll hold together long enough to make it?" Ricky said.

J.B. shrugged a shoulder. "I don't rightly know. The pod can't be that far away. It's just got to make it over and hold up long enough for us to get out. You and I'll probably have to do some figuring, see how long we think it can survive at this depth."

"Sounds like something that can be done while I'm

checking out the pod itself," Ryan said. "Could be there isn't even any power over there, which'll put an end to our escape plans double quick."

"What'll we do if that's the case?" Ricky asked.

Mildred answered before Ryan. "Then we destroy the base with us inside." She looked around at everyone. "No way am I going to leave that electronic nightmare behind to make more monstrosities. No matter what, we're taking that thing out before we go, no matter how it happens, with us inside or out. We have to." Her tone brooked no argument, and the expression on her face dared anyone to disagree.

"All right, then," Ryan said. "Right now, we all have to play our parts. Above all, keep quiet about what we found out about the procreation program." He made sure he caught everyone's gaze as he said that. "Right now this comp seems willing to work with us, and we don't want to do anything to put it on its guard. Are you going to be all right in the lab, Mildred?"

She regarded him with the same thousand-yard stare she'd given the others. "I'll be fine."

"How about you, Krysty?" he asked.

"Once I make sure no other mutant plants are in there waiting to kill me, sure." She snapped her fingers, as if remembering something. "Oh yeah, one of you maintenance personnel needs to take a look at the comm console in there. It's burned out or something."

"Best way to deal with the plants will be to send a couple 'borgs in first," J.B. said, as pragmatic as ever. "As soon as that's taken care of and we prep the suit, I'll come over and have a look at the console."

"All right, everyone should try to get some sleep," Ryan said. "It's going to be a real long day tomorrow."

Chapter Thirteen

Of course, one of the first things Ryan and Krysty had done after quarters had been assigned was to move into the same room.

Freshly showered, she was lying facedown on the bed, dressed only in her bra and panties, while Ryan kneaded her limbs. They'd found that it often helped alleviate the stiffness and sore muscles that she could get after using the power of Gaia. Of course, it didn't hurt that the massages usually turned into lovemaking, either.

"Mmm…you're getting better at that every time, lover," she purred, stretching her lithe arms.

"Trader always said practice makes perfect," Ryan said, flicking a damp curl of black hair out of his eyes as he finished rubbing her thighs and moved on to her back. "'Course, I doubt he ever got the chance to practice on a woman as beautiful as you."

"Well, aren't you the silver-tongued devil today," she replied through a lazy smile. "It's a good thing he didn't, either—I liked the man, but I wouldn't have put up with him laying a finger on me."

"Trader was never like that," Ryan replied, then fell silent as he thought of the grizzled man. They'd had to leave Abe and him in dire straits a while ago, with cold-hearts and muties all around. Ryan knew the old man was canny, but he wasn't sure if even he could have escaped that circle of death. But if there was a way, the old man would've found it, he thought. Just like we're going to find one out of here.

"You all right, lover?" Propping herself on her elbows, Krysty flipped a thick strand of crimson hair over her shoulder as she looked back at him. "Noticed you stopped the massage."

"Sorry...just spinning my wheels, I guess," he replied. "Thinking about the old man."

"And when we last saw him?" she asked, making Ryan raise his eyebrows. "Not hard to figure out, lover, seeing as how we're in sort of the same predicament."

"Yeah," he replied. "Least he was going take the last train under the open sky."

"You don't think he's gone, do you?"

Ryan shrugged. "Can't say. But if there was a way out of that shithole, he'd have found it."

"We're going see the open sky again, too. I know we will," she said.

"'Course we are," Ryan said as he returned to his ministrations.

"Is that a note of doubt I hear?" she asked as she turned to lie down again.

"Mebbe," he replied. He'd never lied to her before, and he wasn't going to start now. "J.B. said we've never been in this kind of situation before, and the more I thought about it, the more I realized he was right. Our options're down to slim and none. That doesn't mean I'm not going to fight to the last breath, but we're in some real deep shit here, any way you look at it."

"True. It's not like we can just up and head over the next hill, or back to a redoubt. The possibility exists that we may not escape this place."

"Now you're starting to sound like Doc," Ryan said. A thought came to him, but he paused, not sure how to ask it. Finally he shrugged and plowed ahead. "Have you ever thought about it?"

"What? About my death, you mean?" Krysty asked.

"Well…yeah. Don't worry, I'm not stupe enough to say it's not out there, 'cause it is, just about every day we draw breath." Ryan licked his lips as he thought about his next words. "But…if the end came for you, and you knew it beforehand, what would you think?"

"About my life?" Krysty raised herself again to look at him. "I have thought about it, lover—I've thought about it a lot. I think we've brought light into a lot of dark places in the time we've spent together. And though we may not live to reap what we've sown, I don't think there's any doubt that there's a lot of people who surely will. And if that's all we leave behind, well, I can't say that I'd be ecstatic about it, but it would be enough."

"Yeah…so many of our days're just running, fighting and surviving that it's hard to recall if we left any good in our wake." As Ryan spoke, he eased the bra strap down over her shoulder.

"Why, Mr. Cawdor, are you trying to change the subject?" she asked as his big hand drifted down under her arm to cup her full breast.

"Just resuming my duties," Ryan said, interspersing his words with kisses on her shoulder. "Wouldn't be right…of me to…massage your back…all this time…and neglect…your gorgeous front…now, would it?"

"No, it wouldn't, indeed." Krysty eased over on her side, slipping the other bra strap free and removing the silky fabric, leaving her magnificent breasts free as she lay back on the pillow. Her red hair slowly spread out, fanning itself around her on the bed, making her look like a welcoming, fire-haired goddess. "Well, what are you waiting for?"

"Just enjoying the view," he replied as he pulled back to strip off his clothes.

"I imagine I'd enjoy your touch a hell of a lot more," she said, arching her back so her breasts stood out in proud relief.

"Indeed," Ryan said as he placed both hands on her, gently massaging her until she moaned with pleasure. Then he bent to kiss her hungrily.

There was no need for words after that—each had been with the other long enough to know what they liked, and each was more than happy to give and receive. But familiarity didn't breed complacency or boredom for either of them. It served as just the opposite, allowing Ryan and Krysty to fully enjoy and savor every moment.

Afterward, they murmured words of love and comfort, then fell asleep in each other's arms.

J.B. AND MILDRED's evening went somewhat differently.

When they had gotten back to their own shared quarters, he sat on the bed and waved her over to join him. When Mildred did so, he simply put his arm around her, not saying a word. She leaned her head against his shoulder, trying not to tear up again. They stayed that way for a quite a while.

Finally, she raised her head to look at him with a wry smile. "Bet you never thought being the strong, silent type would pay off so well, did you?"

J.B. had removed his glasses and now looked steadily back at her. "There's times to speak and times to stay quiet. Figured I'd do the staying quiet part till you were ready to speak, that's all."

"Thank you, John—for everything."

"Nothing to thank me for," he replied. "You're no shrinking violet, Millie. 'Sides, I suppose finding those 'borgs are 'alive,' for lack of a better word, would rattle anyone."

"Even you?" she asked.

"Sure," he replied. "You know I prefer being master of my own fate. Can't even bring myself to imagine what kind of hell that would be."

She shuddered and leaned closer to him. "I can't stop thinking about them…stuck in those…mutilated bodies for decades, forced to follow the orders of a mad comp. More than likely they're all beyond insane by now." She looked up at him. "We have to put them out of their misery."

"Sure, just as long as we have our own way out first," J.B. said. "I don't like the idea of taking the last train with them, you know?"

Mildred was silent for a while as she digested that. Since beginning her intimate relationship with J.B., she'd grown more attuned to his laconic way of speaking and could usually tell when he was holding back or something was bothering him—like now. "You worried about us making it out?"

"Got lots of concerns," he replied. "Too many variables, not enough options."

She hesitated, then pressed on. "What do you give for our chances?"

J.B. exhaled a long, slow breath, then rubbed his hands over his eyes. "Mebbe seventy-thirty."

Mildred's eyebrows rose in surprise. "That doesn't sound too bad."

He looked down at her. "That's against us."

"Oh." Silence reigned again for a moment, then she shook her head. "Nope. I'm not going to agree. We are going to make it out of here—all of us."

J.B. hugged her tight. "That's the Mildred I like to hear from."

"Well, good, because that's the one you're going to get from now on." She shook her head. "Been moping around ever since that damn swim under the tunnel. I just haven't felt like myself. This place—" she looked around the stark, simply furnished room "—those things haven't helped one bit, either."

"Yeah, the place definitely doesn't inspire much in the way of good feelings," J.B. said. "Tell you what." He gently disengaged from her and stood to unzip his jumpsuit. "Why don't you and I go see if we can squeeze into that pitiful excuse for a shower in there, and enjoy a good wash? I feel like I'm still swimming in salt after that dunk, anyway."

Mildred eyed him speculatively. "And what shall we do afterward, John?"

He looked back at her, a half smile crooking one side of his mouth. "Why, whatever you wish," he said as he took her hand. "We can just lie on that rad-blasted small bed and cuddle, or you and I can celebrate still being alive in our own way."

Allowing herself to be helped to her feet, Mildred smiled genuinely at him for the first time since they'd arrived here. "Get in that damn shower," she said as she also unzipped her jumpsuit. "And make it nice and hot."

JAK HAD MANAGED to snag the rest of the bottle from the companions as he had left. He staggered back to his room, drained it and tossed the empty bottle into the corner. "Damn—nothing to do 'round here."

He said the words out loud to mask his unease. Although he didn't have Krysty's connection to Gaia, Jak had been born and bred in the deep bayou country. While they weren't what most people would call comfortable, at least his home was on real land, under a real sky, and he'd been breathing real air.

This—stuck at the bottom of the ocean in the weird redoubt base—wasn't even close to where he wanted to be. The recycled air smelled like chemicals, the food was edible but as bland as hell, and there was always that feeling of being watched—

"Do you wish to access the entertainment menu, Mr. Lauren?" AIDAN asked.

More than a little drunk, Jak blinked for a moment, a throwing knife held loosely in his hand as he processed where the disembodied voice had come from. "Uh… yeah. You got vids?" With a twitch, he made the knife disappear again.

"There is a wide variety of films, television shows, and other programs available for your viewing pleasure. Please make your selection from the menu by simply speaking it."

A bright light flickered on from above the bathroom, and Jak whirled to see a large menu projected onto the far wall. Ever since he'd first seen moving pictures, introduced to him by Johannes Ford a couple of years ago, he'd been addicted and tried to watch them every chance he got. "Damn…" He stared at the categories for a long time. "Umm…something with spaceships… and alien muties…"

"Scanning…" Another list popped up.

Jak chose the very first one. *"Alien."*

"Your selected film is playing now." The vid started, and the skinny albino sank onto the bed, quickly enraptured by the opening credits.

MEANWHILE, IN THE room across the hall, Ricky couldn't sleep.

He was just as concerned about all of them escaping this place, and even more concerned about Ryan trying out the suit the next day. During their search of the maintenance room, Jak and he had found a row of thick binders on one of the workbenches. Locating the one containing the suit's operating manual and maintenance and repair schematics, he'd taken it back to his quarters and had been reading it until his eyes crossed. He was pretty sure that he had the basics of it down, but it was much more intricate than anything he'd ever seen or worked on before.

While Ricky had grown up on the water, he hadn't had much experience below the surface. However, he'd done his share of swimming back home, and knew how the pressure of water increased the deeper a person went. At this depth, any breach or malfunction would crush Ryan into pulp, even while breathing liquid oxygen.

He'd figured he was tired enough to get some rest after that and everything else that had happened during the day, but sleep still eluded him. He tossed and turned on the thin mattress, sighing with frustration. Finally he got up and ordered the lights on. He took a few minutes to field-strip and clean his Webley revolver and the De Lisle carbine, getting as much of the salt water out of both weapons as he could, then oiling them until their actions were smooth again.

That helped a little bit, but he still didn't feel like sleeping. Finally, he decided to get up and take a walk. Going out into the corridor, he heard faint noises coming from Jak's room—what sounded like several people shouting at once, along with the cries of someone else in mortal agony. About to knock on the door, Ricky looked around with his hand raised. "AIDAN?"

"Yes, Mr. Morales?" the computer answered.

"Tell me, what is going on in Jak's room, *por favor?*"

"Mr. Lauren is watching a science-fiction film."

"Ah." Ricky had heard him talk about these films, or "vids" as he called them, to the continuing consternation of Doc, who referred to them as movies. Jak's favorite so far had been one he'd seen in a city near a place called Denver. It had been set in space, with flying ships, an artificial space station as large as a planet, and men who fought each other with glowing swords of light. He'd tried to explain the plot to Ricky, who'd become hopelessly confused about what was going on.

Although part of him wanted to join Jak and find out what all the excitement was about, Ricky knew he'd be poor company right now. When he felt like this, he had a real hard time sitting still or concentrating on anything. The best thing he could do right now was find something to tinker with. Going back into his room, he grabbed the thick binder and headed back to the maintenance section, where he could work to his heart's content without bothering anyone else.

A few minutes later, he arrived at the door and went inside. The odors of oil and grease, metal and plastic calmed him the moment he smelled them. Glancing up at the flickering lights, Ricky frowned at the burned-out fluorescent bulbs scattered throughout the room.

A quick search uncovered several boxes of them in a storage locker on the side of the room. Ricky also pulled out a ladder and spent the next twenty minutes replacing lights everywhere. When he was finished, the entire room was as bright as day.

"Much better," he said as he turned to the diving suit,

which dangled still and empty on the hoist. "Now I can do some *real* work."

Within minutes, he was completely absorbed in the intricacies of the diving suit, humming a little tune that his uncle had hummed while he worked, even though Ricky had never found out where this fabled lost city of Margaritaville was, or even if it had ever existed at all.

Chapter Fourteen

Tipsy from the flavored vodka, and more upset by the vid he'd watched with Ryan and J.B. than he'd let on, an exhausted Doc had tottered off to his room. Once inside, he'd nearly collapsed onto his bed and immediately fallen into a deep sleep.

He opened his eyes to find himself dressed in one of his finest suits, fashioned from comfortable English herringbone twill that draped his tall frame with sartorial elegance. Blinking, he looked around. He was sitting in a soft, wingback chair in the corner of a luxurious hotel bedroom. A large, canopied four-poster dominated the space. It was neatly made, covered with a thick, feather-stuffed quilt trimmed with lace. A plush oriental rug covered the hardwood floor, and a nearby oak dresser with an attached mirror held a pitcher and washbasin.

From the next room, he heard what sounded like someone taking a bath. Doc rose to his feet, noticing with surprise that his knees didn't hurt anymore. Bringing his hands to his face, he touched smooth, unwrinkled skin and a neatly trimmed mustache and goatee.

Could it be…? Taking a hesitant step forward, he approached the mirror, simultaneously anticipating and dreading what he might see. When his face came into view, Doc nearly wept with joy.

It's…me! he thought, marveling at the unlined skin around his mouth and eyes, his thick brown hair combed back from his forehead in the style of the day, and his piercing blue eyes, capable of silencing the most impertinent student or faculty member with merely a glance. And if this is me, he thought, then that means—

Running to the window, he pushed the red-and-gold brocade curtains aside to see the streets of downtown Omaha, Nebraska. Horses and buggies clip-clopped past on the avenue outside, and men in greatcoats and tall hats tipped them to other well-dressed couples or single gentlemen strolling down the sidewalk.

"I'm…back. I'm *back!*" he said, scarcely able to believe it.

"What's that, my love?" someone asked from the other room. His jaw dropping, Doc turned at the sound of that honeyed voice, one he never thought he would hear again.

"Emily?" He walked to the closed door and paused just as he was about to open it. For a moment, his courage failed him, for he had been here before and every time it had been nothing more than a cruel illusion. He looked around the bedroom again, looked at himself in the mirror. No, it was real this time—it had to be.

Reaching for the doorknob again, he pushed it open and walked in. "Emily—is it—is it really you?"

"Of course, my dear, who else would it be? Did you have a good nap?" Doc's wife sat at the vanity, lit by the newest in electric lights, as she applied her makeup. She was in her dressing gown, which made him turn away for propriety's sake before he could get a good look at her face. Strangely, her lush hair was down, instead of pinned up as it normally would have been, but he was too excited to care at the moment.

"Yes, but I had the most unusual dream." He took a

step closer to her. "I hardly know where to begin, it was so strange—"

"I do not wish to interrupt, but perhaps you can tell it to me a bit later, for if we do not leave now, we shall be late for dinner. Have you changed?"

"I—" Doc looked down to find himself wearing an immaculate tuxedo, with starched white shirt and stiff collar, neatly knotted bow tie, and a cutaway black silk jacket. "I…seem to have done so, although I cannot remember actually doing it."

"Well, come along then, we still have to collect the children before we can be seated in the dining room," his wife said as she pushed the chair back and stood. Her dressing gown was gone, as well, replaced by a tasteful, dark blue evening dress that covered her from ankles to neck with long sleeves and a high collar.

"Rachel and Jolyon are here?"

"Of course, my dear, where did you think they would be?" she asked as she walked to the door. "Are you sure you're all right, Theo?"

"Yes…of course they would be here with us…so foolish of me to think otherwise," Doc replied. "Don't mind me, my dear. That dream I suffered has me a bit discombobulated."

He hurried to catch up with her, hoping to get a glimpse of her face, to prove to him that he truly was back in his own time. However, she continued to walk ahead of him, staying just far enough away that he could only see her hair.

"Emily, wait…" Doc tried to catch up to her as they approached the elevator, but he couldn't reach her as the doors opened and the uniformed attendant asked her what floor she wanted. "Main floor, please," she replied.

Doc barely got on before the doors closed. About to

step up and take his place alongside his wife, he stopped and stared at the attendant, who was standing in the corner near the door and staring straight ahead. His profile looked normal enough, but Doc could see the other side of the man's face reflected in the burnished brass of the elevator wall. That was what he was staring at. It looked like—the image was distorted and had a coppery tint to it, given the surface reflecting it, but he swore he could see something—something metal on or in the man's ear.

"Main floor. Front desk, dining room, saloon, cigar room," the attendant recited as he opened the hinged iron gate and the outer doors.

"Thank you, young man." Emily swept out in a swirl of her skirt. "Oh, do hurry along, Theo. We do not wish to keep our guests waiting."

"Guests?" Doc frowned. "But dear, I had thought this would be a quiet dinner, just you and me and the children."

Still walking, she half turned to him as they approached the double doors of the dining room. "Sweetheart, I wouldn't dream of putting our guests off. After all, they are *your* friends."

Still puzzled, Doc decided to just go along with it. "Very well, if you are comfortable with it, then let us entertain them, by all means."

At the entrance to the dining room, the maître d' greeted them. "Your private room is ready, and several of your guests have already arrived," he said as he turned to escort them. As he did, Doc could have sworn he caught a bright red light flash out of the man's right eye, but when he looked again it was gone.

The maître d' led them through the busy main hall, every table filled with men and women eating, drinking and talking. Another set of double doors were at the rear of the large room. The maître d' turned the handles of both and pushed them open, then stepped aside and gestured for the couple to enter. "Enjoy your meal, sir, madam."

"I am still a bit confused as to what…is…going… on…here…" Doc's speech slowed to a complete halt as he walked into the room and saw whom he was to be dining with.

"It's about time you got here, Doc." The black-haired man at the other end of the long table swung his combat boot off the tabletop as he poured himself a glass of bloodred wine. He emptied the bottle, dropping it upside down into a silver carafe with a rattle. He had only one eye, an ice-blue one that glowed with its own inner light. When he grinned, he revealed a mouth filled with shiny, metal teeth. "Long past time to eat." Grabbing the thick, raw steak off the plate in front of him, he took a large bite, the blood dribbling down his chin as he chewed.

"Yes, we were starting to think that you were never going to arrive," the flame-haired woman sitting at his right side said. Her hair was wild, radiating in all directions. As Doc took an involuntary step closer, he saw that it was made up of thousands of tiny, copper wires that moved of their own accord. One braided tendril of wire curled around her crystal wineglass and brought it to her lips, letting her sip delicately from it.

"Yeah—hungry. Sit and now eat," said the slender, fox-faced teen sitting on Krysty's other side. He looked like the offspring of a snowstorm and a cloud, with paper-white skin and hair that stuck up in all directions. The ends of his hair winked with light, and Doc realized that his hair was actually thousands of strands of fiber-optic cable. His eyes, however, were solid, red, glowing orbs that chilled Doc's spine when the boy's gaze fell on him.

"Well, come on, sit, sit—we're all friends here, right?" The man sitting on Ryan's left, across from the red wire-haired woman, wore spectacles of a kind Doc had never seen before. The frames were standard wire, but the lenses kept changing color, flowing from red to blue to green to yellow to black to white in no discernible pattern. He was wearing a battered fedora, which the black-skinned woman sitting next to him chided him for.

"Take your hat off at the dinner table, dear."

"Of course, my apologies." The man did so, and Doc now saw that his skull was made of some sort of transparent resin. What's more, he could see the man's brain, a complex machine of some kind, composed of lights and switches that clicked and flashed and blinked on and off.

The black woman who had admonished the man now turned to Doc with a bright smile. "Isn't that better? I was just about to begin carving." She nodded at the gigantic crown roast of pork as she brought up her other hand. It, along with the entire arm, was completely artificial, made of gleaming metal, complete with an elbow joint and articulated wrist. Her fingers and thumb each ended in a different medical operating implement. As Doc watched, she extended her index finger and sliced through the roast pork with a razor-sharp scalpel.

"*Sí, señor,* come and break bread with us," the last member of the table said as he waved him forward. He was another teenager, younger than the pale one, with brown skin and teeth that looked as though they were carved from wood. His arms and hands had been replaced by mechanical devices, as well, but his fingers all ended in various construction tools. He seemed to

be building something out of his dinner plate and silverware, but Doc couldn't tell what it was for the life of him.

"Emily, my dear," he said as he turned to her, trying
with every fiber of his being to keep his voice calm. "I
think we had better go—"

"Go? Why, whatever for? We've only just arrived."
She turned to him, as well, and Doc saw his world crum-
ble and collapse in the gleam of her silvered forehead, in
the shine of her lifeless red eyes, and in the waxy pallor
of her plastic lips over bright, perfect, porcelain teeth.

"Emily…my d-darlin— M-my love," Doc stammered
as he slowly retreated from her. "What…what has happened to you? What have they done to you?"

"Theo? What is the matter? I have simply been improved, much like your friends. Do you not wish to greet
your children? Step forward, Rachel, Jolyon, and say
hello to your father."

Two little figures stirred in a shadowed alcove. They
began walking into the light, but as they did, the taller
one looked up. Doc caught the glow of a red eye in the
darkness.

"Nooooo!" he screamed, knowing that if his gaze fell
upon whatever his own children had been transformed
into, the last of his sanity would shatter and the frag-
ments fall away into the eternal abyss he was currently
teetering on the edge of.

Turning, he ran back into the main hall, only to find
himself surrounded by more man- and woman-machine
monstrosities. Everyone in the room—the diners, the
waitstaff, even the maître d', were all dreadful combinations of flesh, metal and plastic now.

"Sir, please return to your table," the maître d' said,
his steel jaw clicking as it moved. His eyes had also been
transformed into wide, staring plastic versions of them-

selves. He left his station and strode toward Doc along with the rest of the waiters and patrons, encircling him and cutting off any avenue of escape.

"No…no…I won't stay here any longer!" Doc said, patting his pockets for some kind of weapon as he retreated. Before he knew it, he was back in the private dining room, where he felt cool, inflexible hands grab him.

"That's right, you won't," one of the cyborgs said. "At least, not without some improvements…" The hands gripped his arms and legs and lifted him into the air. Doc felt himself being set down on a table under blinding, white lights.

"Just a few improvements, and you'll be better than ever." The black woman leaned over him, her tool-filled hand coming down toward his skull. "I think we'll start with the brain."

Struggling with all his might against the hands holding him captive, Doc could only watch the gleaming blade as it descended closer and closer to his temple. A scream grew in his chest, expanded up his throat and burst out through his open mouth as the tip of the blade pierced his skin.

Doc lurched up in his bed, the scream bursting from his raw throat into the darkness. The lights turned on automatically as his tortured cry dissolved into anguished sobs.

"You appear to be unwell, Dr. Tanner," AIDAN said. "Is there anything I can do to assist you?" The computer repeated its question twice more to the sobbing man, who had turned on his side and brought his legs up to his chest. He gently rocked back and forth, his burbling cries turning to laughter, then back to sobs again before he finally fell into a fitful slumber.

Chapter Fifteen

Several hours later, Ryan, Krysty, and the others were in the mess hall again, dining on more courses of unusual, ocean-derived foods.

"You know, this isn't really bad, all things considered," Mildred said between bites of a piece of wafer-thin dried seaweed. "But it'll never replace eggs, bacon and buttered grits with a side of sourdough toast."

"Got that right in one," Ryan said, trying to muster up the enthusiasm to finish his grilled swordfish steak and seaweed-and-kelp salad. "Can't wait to get back on the surface and go hunt up some real meat."

"Ricky joining us this morning?" J.B. asked between bites of his soft-shelled crab.

"Found him in maintenance," Jak grunted. "Fell asleep there working on suit."

"Didn't you wake him up?" Krysty asked.

The albino shrugged. "Tried."

The Armorer allowed himself a small smile. "Figures. I'll go roust him after breakfast."

"Anyone see Doc this morning?" Ryan asked. "AIDAN, where's Dr. Tanner?"

"He is still in his quarters," the computer replied. "He seemed to have suffered a fit brought on by bad dreams during the night and woke up screaming. I offered my assistance, but he was unresponsive to my queries."

"Is he all right?" Krysty asked, beginning to rise from her chair.

"Yes, he fell asleep again at 0458 hours, and has been resting ever since. In fact, my sensors indicate that he is awake now and coming to join you."

Indeed, the rest of the group could hear the old man's rich baritone voice echoing in the corridor as he walked down it.

"What singing 'bout?" Jak asked between spoonfuls of fish soup.

"Something about how everything's gone wrong somehow, men of power losing control..." Mildred frowned as she tried to decipher the lyrics. "It sounds familiar, I just can't put my finger on it."

"Well, don't worry about it, here he comes." Ryan attacked his fish again as Doc stumbled into the room. He was a mess, his jumpsuit hanging open, his lank, silver-white hair sticking up on his head making him look as if he'd suffered a mild electrical shock. His skin was ashen and dark bags had grown under his blood-shot, rheumy eyes.

"Doc? Doc, are you all right?" Mildred asked. Everyone was staring at him, now.

"All right? My dear Mildred, I could not be better! For I am among friends, am I not? Good friends who will not suddenly sprout tools on the tips of their fingers, or lights for their eyes, or wire for hair, correct?"

He looked at the group expectantly, as if awaiting an answer.

"Um...that's correct, Doc," J.B. replied. "Want to join us and get something to eat?"

"Oh, sure, sure, that would be grand." Tottering over to the table, Doc was about to sit in the chair Ryan had pulled out for him when he stopped. "How can I be sure that none of you are cyborgs?"

"Mebbe you should head back to your room and get some rest, Doc," Ryan suggested. "AIDAN said you'd had some kind of fit during the night."

"Yes! Brought on by a nightmare of monstrous proportions…and one that I am not entirely sure I have awakened from, yet." Doc retreated from the table and walked to the center of the room. "AIDAN? AIDAN, are you there?"

"Of course, Dr. Tanner, I am always here. How can I assist you?"

"How can you assist me?" For some reason, Doc found that question very funny. First he snorted, then giggled, then laughed loudly. "How…can you…assist me…it wants…to know!"

"Mildred, mebbe you better get something for him from the infirmary," Ryan suggested.

"Agreed." She slipped out the door.

"How can you help? You, you hostage-taking, forced-procreation-demanding machine from the very bowels of hell!" Doc began.

"Doc—" Krysty tried to interject, but he rambled on, his words growing louder and louder.

"Can you return me to my family? Can you return me to my life?"

"Doc, mebbe you better come over here." J.B. and Ryan both got up and were cautiously approaching the old man.

Doc half turned to them. "No! I want an answer to my question." He turned back to the empty room. "Well, can you, AIDAN?"

"Can I do what?"

"Can you give me my family back? Can you give me my life back?" Doc shouted, raising his arms in rage.

"If you are requesting that I return you to your original time and place of origin, I regret to inform you that I cannot," the computer replied. "The nearest time-trawl chamber is several thousand miles away, and I am unsure if it is still functioning at this date. I am afraid that I cannot assist you any further in this matter."

Doc stood motionless while the computer spoke, then slowly let his arms fall back to his sides. "Of course you cannot. You are just a simple machine, that's all."

Mildred returned carrying a hypodermic needle. At Ryan's nod, she kept it hidden in her hand as she approached him. "Doc?"

He started at her appearance beside him, blinking in confusion. "Mildred? Is that you?"

"Yes, Doc. You don't look so good."

The old man's shoulders slumped. "I am tired, Mildred…so very, very tired."

"I think you need some rest. Why don't you come with me and we'll put you to bed?" She took his arm and gently led the unresisting man out of the room.

Everyone waited until Mildred returned. "He's out and sleeping like a baby. The tranquilizer I gave him should allow him to sleep for the next ten to twelve hours."

"Good—one less thing to worry about," Krysty said. "Mildred, do you think he's feeling worse because of being stuck down here?"

She thought about that for a moment. "Hard to say. He had that bad flashback when we arrived, so this could be a delayed effect from that. Or…" She shrugged. "Look, we all know his mind was never that cogent in the first place. With all the jumps we've taken, who knows if they've scrambled him even further. Without a whole battery of tests, it's just too hard to say."

"We better keep a close eye on him as long as we're here. No telling what he might do if he thinks AIDAN is an enemy." Ryan looked back at the table and the scattered remains of their meal. "I think we're pretty much done with breakfast now."

"Before you begin your work this period, I have to discuss something with all of you," AIDAN said. "Please, sit down."

Wary looks on their faces, Ryan, J.B. and the others all took their seats again. "What's going on, AIDAN?" Ryan asked.

"During my conversation with Dr. Tanner, I noticed that he mentioned, and I quote, 'forced procreation,' unquote," the computer said. "I want to know where he would have learned about that."

Ryan glanced at everyone else before answering. "We found a vid in the command center, recorded by one of your former officers, Martin Yates. He left a message warning us about the program."

"Ah yes, Commander Yates. I understand now. Did the message contain anything else of interest?"

"No," Ryan answered while shaking his head slightly to the others. "The vid only said that—nothing else."

"Are you unwell, Ryan?"

"No, why?"

"I noticed that you were shaking your head," AIDAN replied. "I was only inquiring in case you were suffering from fatigue."

Ryan frowned questioningly at J.B., who shrugged. "I'm fine, thanks. What did you want to tell us about that particular program?"

"I simply wished to explain about the procreation

program." The computer paused. "Although I must say that I have very high hopes for its reimplementation, based on the activities of certain pairings last night. To begin with—"

"Just a nuke-sucking second!" J.B. said. Shocked silence fell over the room for a moment, broken only by a strangled noise from Jak that might have been a cross between a laugh and a cough. "You saying you were watching while—that—was going on?" Pinkness bloomed in his cheeks and spread across the rest of his face.

"It is nothing to be concerned about, Mr. Dix. The monitoring of every staff member's room has been a constant in this facility from the beginning—strictly for health reasons, mind you. For example, if Dr. Tanner's condition had declined any further, I would have been able to inform Dr. Wyeth and summon assistance for him. I think you understand what may have happened if his condition declined and I was not watching him."

"Yeah, but..." J.B. had folded his arms over his chest. "Unnatural is what it is."

"J.B.'s right," Krysty said. "From this point on, AIDAN, we do not want you to be observing our rooms when we're sleeping."

"Very well, I would assume that one of you would summon me in the event of an emergency regardless."

"Of course we would," Krysty replied. "Now, let's get back to the topic at hand, shall we?"

"Of course, Krysty," AIDAN said. "One of the revised protocols was to immediately begin scheduled procreation efforts intended to increase the overall population of the base for the eventual return to the surface. Participation was mandatory for all personnel, male and female. Initially, the program was implemented and progressed satisfactorily for 4.7 years. However, analysis afterward has indicated that this program was one of the reasons for the increased aberrant behavior."

"I can't possibly understand why," J.B. said. "Hell, I'm surprised this thing hasn't offered to hold my dick while I piss yet."

"I do not understand the meaning of that statement, Mr. Dix. As I have no physical appendages, such an offer would make no sense."

"Oh, for—" J.B. began to reply, only to receive an elbow in the ribs from Mildred. "Never mind. Just keep going."

"My plan had been to wait until all of you were better acclimated to your surroundings before reintroducing the program. Of course, with three healthy males and two healthy females on staff now, all from sufficiently different genetic pools, the procreation program will also be reinstated as soon as possible, as the base will need repopulating as soon as possible."

Ryan cleared his throat. "Well, now it's all on the table. I don't know that we're all going to be ready to start reproducing like rabbits right away, but I think we'll be able to figure something out."

"That is good to hear, Ryan. I was positive that you and the rest of your people could see the valid reason behind the implementation of this program."

"Certainly—it just makes sense, that's all," he replied as he stood. "Now, if there's nothing else, we have to get down to maintenance. Testing the diving suit today."

"I do not recall being informed of this. What are you hoping to accomplish with this test?"

"If we're going to be here for the rest of our lives, we'll need as much equipment as we can get in working condition," J.B. replied. "Although we can make sure the suit's in working order by inspecting it and replac-

ing parts, the only real way to make sure it's functioning correctly is to use it outside, in the water."

"I understand. Proceed with your testing. Also, you
should repair the console in the maintenance room so
that I can better monitor the proceedings in there."

"After the test, we'll get right on it," J.B. said while
rubbing his eye with his middle finger.

Without warning, all of the lights in the kitchen went
out. There was a silence before the computer spoke up
again. "And it would appear that the circuit in the mess
hall has malfunctioned, as well. Please schedule a repair
time as soon as possible."

"Of course." Ryan waved at the others. "Come on.
Time for me to take a dip."

Chapter Sixteen

"The power system's fully charged, and the liquid oxygen reserves are at ninety-nine percent," Ricky said as Ryan, J.B. and he ran over details of the suit's operation. "Are you sure you don't want me to test this thing?"

They'd found the teenager snoring in a plastic chair, a tarp wrapped around his upper body. After waking him, Ricky had given Ryan and J.B. a brief talking tour of the suit, and both men had looked at the teen with even more respect afterward. He'd not only practically memorized the operating manual, but he could talk fluently about every system in the powered suit, reciting operating specs and other facts as easily as if he was reading them off the appropriate page.

Ryan shook his head. "We already discussed that on the way down here. If something malfunks on this thing, I'll be counting on you two to figure out some way to get me back here. Not that it's going to happen," he said, catching Krysty's frown. Mildred, who'd decided to stay nearby in case Ryan sustained an injury during this experiment, didn't have a pleased look on her face, either.

"Well, it was going to be me or you," Ricky said. "The liquid oxygen requires eye protection to see through… so that eliminates J.B., I'm afraid."

The Armorer shrugged. "I have to begin stripping and fixing that mini-sub anyway."

"Need liquid oxygen in sub, too?" Jak asked.

Ricky shook his head. "The sub's thicker, so it can be pressurized for regular air." He looked at J.B. "It depends on how long the porthole repairs hold, too."

J.B. rubbed his chin as he regarded the rounded-off metal tube. "It's going to be heavy, with all that metal. What's the suit's maximum towing capacity, Ricky?"

"The ADS 3000's maximum buoyant towing capacity is 8,000 pounds," the young man replied.

"Four tons? Sounds like it's enough to me," Ryan said.

"And that's why I'll be making sure it *is* enough," J.B. said with a smile. "It's going to be close, no matter what. Let's have Ricky run you through how to operate it with you inside. You'll be doing everything but walk—that we'll handle at the very end. Ready?"

"Let's do it."

Ryan spent the next half hour mostly nodding at Ricky's more detailed explanation of the suit's various systems and how they operated. He filed away the most salient information, such as how long he'd have out there and so forth, as well as the emergency measures in case he needed to evacuate the suit in a hurry. Obviously he'd have to make it back in order to leave the suit if there was trouble. If anything happened too far away from the base, there'd be no chance of survival.

"All right, hop in and get yourself situated," Ricky finally said. "I want to go over the basic systems once more, and have you get some practice with those powered gripper hands. From what I read, they can be a bit tricky. But first, let's get you inside."

They had a ladder near the hoist for that very purpose, and Ryan climbed up and onto the steel arm, carefully pushing himself over until he was able to drop into the suit. With J.B. watching, as well, Ricky went over the heads-up display, which featured oxygen and power levels, sonar display, and even a rear camera, so Ryan could see behind him if he had to back up.

"Okay, I'm going to close the hatch—might as well double-check that the seal's airtight now," Ricky said. "You can talk to and hear us through the microphones mounted in the suit itself."

"Hold on. If we're not doing the liquid oxygen now, how am I going to breathe in here?" Ryan asked.

"The suit has a built-in fifteen-minute reserve that constantly refills from the air around it," Ricky replied. "You'll be fine." With that, he closed the access hatch, sealing Ryan in. He heard the hiss as the suit pressurized and the whir of the bolts as they secured the hatch. It was a bit claustrophobic in there, but Ryan adjusted himself to his surroundings as best as he could.

"It's going to be a bit odd once we seal you in, because only your head and neck are going to be covered in the liquid oxygen, for conservation purposes," Ricky's voice now came from a speaker near his ear. "Since the liquid will be in your lungs, there shouldn't be any kind of pressurization issue with the rest of your body."

"Good to hear," Ryan said, taking in everything around him and making sure it matched with what Ricky had told him. "So, how do I move in this thing?"

"Well, your legs have been fitted into the legs of the suit, so walking is pretty much like you would normally do it, except you may have a wider stance, due to the thickness of the legs themselves," Ricky said. "Now, as for your arms—"

"Yeah, I've got these things halfway up the sleeves." Hunching over, Ryan could barely make out what looked like a handle with four plastic loops mounted in it. From the looks of it, he was supposed to grab the handle and stick his fingers through the loops.

"Right, those control the articulation of the grippers at the end," Ricky said. "Just slip your hands into them and get a feel for how they work."

Ryan did so. He found that the handle was mounted in a circle of metal, but he could move each one in just about any direction he wanted. As he did, the freshly washed clamps rotated on their ball-jointed wrists, twisting and turning.

"Okay, once you're comfortable with that, try using the grippers. Move your fingers as if you were using your hand to grab something," Ricky commanded.

Ryan followed his directions, watching as the two-piece clamps opened and closed along with the movements of his hands.

"Damn!" Jak, along with everyone else, was watching now. "Grab something?"

"Might as well," Ricky said. "Give you a shot at walking, too. Let's set you down first, okay?"

"Um…okay." Ryan looked up at the ceiling of the room above him, seeing the chain leading to the steel crossbar of the hoist. He heard a loud clicking, and felt himself descending. A few seconds later, he hit the floor with a solid thud.

"All right, everyone, give him lots of room," Ricky said as Ryan saw him appear in front of the suit's thick viewport. Immediately, the HUD put a flashing green caret above him for some reason. Ryan saw everyone else in the room tagged with the same marking.

"What's this little green mark over your head, Ricky?" he asked.

"That's the friend-or-foe recognition system," he replied. "I set it up to scan the room and designate everyone in here as 'friendly.' Now you cannot hurt them with the suit, even accidentally. It simply will not let you."

"That's handy," Ryan said. "Okay, what should I go for?" His voice was projected to everyone else in the room by external speakers.

"This'll do." J.B. held up a solid iron cylinder about eight inches tall and six inches in diameter. He set it on the ground a few feet away from Ryan, then backed away. "Come and get it."

"Just lean into it and walk normally," Ricky said.

"All right, here goes…" Ryan did exactly that, leaning forward so that his legs pressed into the front of the suit's legs. As soon as he exerted enough pressure, it lurched into motion, allowing him to take a step forward, the foot landing with a thunk that echoed throughout the large room. Ryan paused for a moment, making sure his foot was stable before lifting the other one and swinging it forward.

"How's it feel?" J.B. asked.

"Like walking with twenty-pound boots on, or maybe through heavy snow," Ryan said. One more step brought him close enough to be able to grab the metal cylinder. He eyed it for a moment, flexing his fingers and hearing the clamps do the same.

"Nice and easy…" Ricky said.

Ryan slowly began bending at the waist, tilting the upper half of the suit forward. A sharp beeping sounded in the cockpit once he was at about forty-five degrees, startling him. "Fireblast! What's that?"

"Probably the balance warning," Ricky replied. "It's two-toned, so as long as you don't hear the higher, louder-pitched one, you're fine. You're practically there, anyway."

Ryan realized that Ricky was correct—he was at the right angle to reach out and grab the cylinder. He did so carefully, wanting to get this right the first time. Inch by inch, the right clamp drew closer and closer to his target.

"Grab sometime today, why doncha?" Jak called.

"Not…as…easy…as…it…looks," Ryan said, even as he maneuvered the clamp around the cylinder and squeezed it closed. When he was sure he had a grip on it, he lifted it into the air as he straightened.

Everyone in the room burst into applause. Ryan took a deep breath, feeling like he had just tried to pick up a toothpick while wearing a mitten, and sketched a quick, if jerky, bow.

"That's pretty good, Ryan," Ricky said when the clapping died down. "Now let's see how you do with the tactile response." He wheeled out a metal mechanic's cart and set a plastic can of oil on it. "See if you can pick up the can without breaking it."

"Okay." Ryan reached for the plastic can, but this time his overconfidence made him shoot the arm forward and knock it off the cart.

"Easy does it." Ricky picked up the can and set it back on the cart.

"This thing's touchy," Ryan said as he adjusted the arm to try again. This time, he got the clamp around it and applied enough pressure to make the plastic flex a bit under the grip. He raised the arm, lifting the can of oil.

"Remember, it says that the clamps operate on something called a logarithmic scale, so the more pressure you apply, the higher level of strength it uses," Ricky said.

"Oh?" Ryan said as he clenched the finger controls as hard as he could. The oil can ruptured, spurting black liquid all over the floor. "Like that?"

"Ryan!" Krysty said, shaking her head at the mess.

"Hey, I just wanted to test it out, to see if Ricky was right," he said. "Okay, I'm ready."

"Not quite." Ricky held up a large piece of rubber with a hole in the middle. "We have to get you submerged in there—" he pointed at the suit "—before you go out there." He pointed at the airlock.

"Oh yeah…kind of forgot about that part," Ryan replied.

"No problemo," Ricky said. "In fact, this'll be good practice for you. Use the rear camera to back up to the hoist."

Ryan looked up at the top of his viewport to see the camera showing what was behind him. Carefully, making sure every step was sure, he slowly backed up until he was in the hoist again.

Ricky got up top and opened the hatch. He passed Ryan a pair of goggles. "You'll need these, otherwise you won't be able to see through the fluid."

"You know I only need one, right?" Ryan said, in an attempt to lighten the mood.

"Yeah, I thought about blacking one out, but decided not to," Ricky replied with a smile. "Didn't think you'd like it."

"Wait! Wait a second!"

Ryan heard boots on the ladder, then Krysty's head appeared a few seconds later. "Did you honestly think you were leaving without saying goodbye?"

"Since I'm coming back, I didn't think there was a need, but…" Grabbing the edge of the hatch with both arms, Ryan pulled himself up as Krysty leaned down. They met in the middle, her free arm curling around him as she kissed him hard.

When they separated, she held him tight for a moment. "Make sure you come back to me, Ryan Cawdor," she whispered, staring into his eye.

"Just going for a little walk. Be back before you know it," he replied.

"You better be." Reluctantly, she drew back, and Ricky's head appeared. He handed the rubber gasket down to Ryan, who was making sure the goggles were comfortable on his head and over his eye.

"Stick your head through and attach this to the indicated points around the cockpit." He pointed them out, and Ryan clipped the gasket in from the underside. When he was done, it looked like his head was floating on a sea of black rubber.

"Okay, we've got the base blueprints all ready to go in here, so all you'll have to do is follow our directions, and we'll home you in on that pod. Once I seal the hatch again, the liquid's going to come out of that tube near your mouth…" Ricky paused, as if the gravity of what they were doing had just sunk in. "I've never done this before, Ryan."

"That makes two of us." Ryan looked back up at the teenager. "You're doing great, Ricky. Keep going. What else do I need to know?"

"Well, the manual says that you shouldn't try to hold your breath, but I expect that'll be kind of natural at first. Basically, just breathe in and out as normally as you can. It says your body will adjust, although you'll have to work harder at breathing, 'cause it's a liquid. The important thing is not to panic, because you can't thrash around in here—way too dangerous, both for you, and for us."

"Okay. Anything else?"

"Yes. You won't be able to talk to us once the liquid fills your lungs—something about it putting pressure on the larynx, so you can't make noise. You'll be able to hear us, however, and there's a button on the right side of the suit—" Ricky grimaced as a high-pitched tone sounded. "Good, you found it. Like I was saying, that'll allow you to make a tone. One beep for yes, two for no. J.B.'ll be up top, and I'll be monitoring you from below. If it looks like something's going wrong, hit the button and hold it down. We'll get you out as fast as we can. The most important thing to remember is simply to breathe. Everything else should be easy after that."

"Sure—for you." Ryan grinned at the young man, looking at him through the goggles. "If there's nothing else, seal it up and let's go."

"You got it. Closing the hatch now."

The shadow fell over Ryan again as Ricky sealed him in. Ryan took a deep breath, feeling the faint stirring of unease at the idea of soon being completely immersed in liquid he was somehow supposed to suck into his lungs in order to breathe.

"Okay, Ryan, you're good to go," Ricky said from the ground in front of him. "We're going to start the liquid flow now. Remember, don't fight it and breathe."

"I'll do my best," he replied. "Hit it."

There was a moment's pause, then the light blue liquid began dribbling into the chamber around his head. It smelled like ozone as it quickly covered the rubber and began rising. Soon it covered Ryan's chin, then his nose, then his eye. Trying to keep his breathing normal, he instinctively raised his face to keep it out of the liquid, but just as quickly realized that it wasn't going to help, and lowered it into the stuff again.

By now the liquid had risen over his head, matting his hair to his skull. Ryan felt the pressure building in his lungs, and decided to try to help the process along by emptying them. He exhaled as long as he could, feeling the burn intensify as his cells began demanding oxygen. Try as he might, however, he couldn't force his mouth open until there was no choice.

With a cool gush, the liquid poured down his trachea, making him gasp and choke as it began filling his lungs. Ryan whipped his head from side to side, fighting the rising panic inside him. It wasn't happening—his lungs weren't making the switch to breathe the liquid. He groped for the button, about to press it and have the guys try to get him out before he drowned in this stuff when—

Inhaling deeply, Ryan took a breath. A thick, wet breath, but a breath nonetheless. It was so unexpected that he stopped moving for a moment and did it again.

It felt strange, as if he were breathing through a soaked, gloppy pillow. But he *was* breathing, and that was the important part.

And now that he was, he could hear urgent voices outside. "—need to get him out now!" That was Krysty talking.

"He hasn't given the signal yet—" J.B. began.

"I don't give a good nuking shit if he hasn't, I want him out—"

Ryan found the button and pressed it once, then again.

"Two for 'no,'" Ricky said, relief evident in his voice. "You all right in there, Ryan?"

Beep.

"Bet that feels weird, huh?" Ricky asked.

Beep.

"You ready to go outside?"

Beep.

"All right, then, follow me."

With Ricky guiding him, Ryan came out of the hoist,

slowly turned and headed for the large airlock. When he was inside, Ricky stood in front of him.

"The good news is that you've got plenty of time," the teenager said. "A full hour of air, and the suit can run for about twelve, so you don't have to rush it. I'm going to leave, then the door behind you will close, water will come in, and the outer door will open. Beep if you understand."

Beep.

"All right. *Vaya con Dios,* Ryan."

Ricky ran out of the airlock, leaving Ryan alone as the heavy door closed behind him. For a moment, there was nothing but silence, broken only by the faint wheeze of Ryan taking a breath. Then he heard Ricky again.

"Here it comes, Ryan."

With a deafening whoosh, the outer door cracked open, and the black ocean flooded in.

Chapter Seventeen

A black, liquid wall rushed at him. It was so fast that Ryan thought it might knock him off his feet, but the suit just stood, heavy and immobile, as the sea swirled around it.

Almost before he knew it, the room was full. The suit's exterior lights came on automatically, showing him water, water, and more water.

"Everything all right, Ryan?" Ricky's voice asked.

Beep.

Taking a deep, hard breath of liquid oxygen, Ryan lifted his leg and stepped forward. Then he did it with his left foot. A few more steps and he stood at the edge of the airlock.

He looked out onto a barren wasteland. As far as his lights could penetrate the murk, there was nothing but light gray sand everywhere. Or maybe it was dust, Ryan wasn't sure. He cautiously lifted a leg and stepped onto the floor outside, ready to retreat if his leg sank into the ocean floor.

It went down about two inches and stopped. Ryan gradually leaned forward, putting more weight on the leg, not knowing what to expect—if it would hold or if he would sink in up to his neck and be stuck there until his air ran out.

The surface held. Ryan brought his other leg out and

stood on the ocean floor, more than a mile below the surface.

"We can see that you've left the airlock. Everything still all right so far?" Ricky asked.

Ryan looked around. *Beep.*

"Okay, you're going to want to turn to face north, on a heading of 287 degrees," Ricky said. "You'll be going approximately seventy yards out. Beep if you understand."

Beep. Using the suit's internal compass, Ryan found the heading easily and trudged off. There were no obvious signs of life down here, not even the tiny bits of plankton and other small animals that usually made up these sorts of aquatic ecosystems. There was just Ryan and the seemingly endless, gray plain all around him.

Or was there? A flash of movement on the rear camera caught Ryan's attention, but he saw nothing there when he looked up at it. He couldn't be sure, but he got the impression that whatever was out there was pretty large. He took a moment to look around, but nothing showed up in the vicinity of his lights. With a last glance at the rear camera, he began moving forward.

It was slow going. Walking in the suit in the maintenance room had been one thing, but it was entirely different out here, like wading through a sea of constantly shifting molasses that buffeted him with every step. It wasn't bad, but he was certainly aware of the currents, even all the way down here.

"Looks like you're about halfway there. Beep us when you get to the pod."

Beep. As he responded to Ricky, Ryan spotted the movement again in his rear quarter. This time he turned, just in time to see a large, black wriggling eel-type creature smack into his viewport and wrap its body, as thick as his waist, around the upper torso of the suit. A circular mouth, easily the diameter of Ryan's head, fastened itself to the window and began rasping at it with rows of teeth as long as his pinky finger.

Lamprey!

Ryan had lots of experience with the parasitic fish, but he'd thought they only kept to fresh waters and had no idea they could exist at this depth.

The mutated versions of these fish were several times as large as their normal ancestors and extremely aggressive. Ryan remembered the ones he'd encountered in Canada and knew them to be efficient killers.

Although the huge lamprey was trying its best to penetrate the three-inch-thick glass, it wasn't getting anywhere. Ryan reached up with his right arm, shoving the giant predator partly off him, and punched the gripper deep into the slimy fish's body. Once it was inside, he opened the clamp, making a kind of internal hook to keep the monster in place.

It writhed and squirmed but couldn't free itself. Ryan brought his left arm over and sank that into the fish's upper body, as well, just behind the head. After he'd opened that clamp, too, he went for the head itself with his right, driving into the flesh and in effect, ripping the eel's head completely off. The body drifted off to settle on the ocean floor a few yards away. Ryan flexed his clamps, trying to get the sticky remains off the metal, with limited success. When he was clean enough, he realigned himself on the right course and resumed his march.

"Ryan, are you okay?"

Beep.

He was unmolested the rest of the way, and soon the dome of the other pod appeared out of the darkness.

Ryan took a moment to look back. There was no sign of a tunnel connecting this pod to the rest of the base, just his tracks in the silt. It was as if it had never existed in the first place.

That was odd, but not truly worrying. Ryan was much more concerned about reaching the airlock and finding it broken or unpowered. He sure didn't want to have to try to find the blasted manual override out here if he could avoid it.

"Ryan? Have you found the other pod yet?" Ricky asked.

Beep.

"Are you inside?"

Beep. Beep. Getting close enough to see the smooth, unbroken wall, Ryan turned right and began following it. After about a dozen steps, he came to the airlock, and spotted the green button that, he hoped, would still open the door. He reached out with his left arm, squinting through the liquid oxygen goo at the controls. When he was pretty sure he had it lined up, he leaned forward and pressed the button.

For a moment, nothing happened, and Ryan's heart started rising into his throat. Then, with a puff of gray sand, the door began to rise.

Come on, come on, he thought. Do not get stuck, you bastard....

And it didn't. Even so, Ryan only stepped into the water-filled room once he was certain that it was open completely. Seeing the matching set of door controls on this wall next to the door, he hit them and stepped back as the door closed.

The moment it hit the ground, the water around him churned and bubbled as it began to recede. Soon it swirled around his waist, then his knees as it drained out through grates in the floor. The inner door stood before him, and Ryan marched toward it, hitting his signal button as he did so.

Beep.

"Are you inside?"

Beep. Ryan hit the button to open the inner door. He flexed his fingers impatiently while waiting for it to rise, making the clamps click open and closed.

The door stopped moving, and he immediately stepped forward, ready for anything. The main room was dark and empty. There was no furniture here, just eight heavy doors arranged in a circle around the room.

"Unauthorized personnel in escape-pod bay. Identify yourself."

The computer's voice made Ryan start inside the suit. The warning and identification request repeated itself in the silent room. Ryan ignored it and began checking out the doors.

Walking to the first one, he bent to peer through the small porthole. He was pretty sure he saw an empty docking bay for some kind of escape pod on the other side. He strode to the next one, finding it empty, as well. He went down the line. Each one he came to was empty.

By the time he'd checked six of them, he was really starting to worry. In the seventh, however, he found what he was looking for. The escape pod was still snug in its berth. From what he could see, it looked ready to go. There was even a sign next to it: *Poseidon Base Escape Pod #7. Capacity: 10.*

Ryan checked on the eighth, only to find that something had damaged it, smashing a huge dent in the top and breaching the hull, leaving an ugly gash in it. It was useless. He took one last, slow look around the room before heading back to the airlock. As he did, one thought kept running through his mind.

Only one shot at getting out....

Ryan hit the control to cycle the door closed. As he did, AIDAN spoke once more. "Unauthorized personnel in escape pod bay. Identify yourself."

With a grin, Ryan pressed his signal button again as the door descended.

Beep! Beep!

"ONLY ONE POD left?" J.B. asked.

"One that looked like it'd still work," Ryan replied. "The only other one left was right next to it, but it got smashed somehow. It's useless."

They were all back in the maintenance bay. Ryan, bathed in sweat, toweled the liquid oxygen from his skin and hair as he told the others what he'd found. Coming out of the suit had been worse than going in, with him coughing and hacking up the remaining liquid in his lungs for a couple of minutes. Finally, however, he was done and sat back on his haunches, a pool of liquid oxygen on the floor in front of him.

"Sounds like a bunch of the crew got off the base," Mildred said.

"Mebbe...or mebbe AIDAN jettisoned the pods to keep the crew here," J.B. replied, thinking about the repeated warning Ryan had told them he'd heard in the pod bay.

"You think it would actually do that?" Krysty asked.

"I wouldn't put it past the thing," he replied.

"Okay, but what about the seventh pod?" Ryan asked. "Why not let that one go, too?"

"I can't figure that one out," J.B. said. "It doesn't really matter anyway. The only thing we have to worry about is getting the sub patched up and getting ourselves out there."

"Yeah—and hope pod works," Jak piped up.

"Only one way to find out," Ryan said. "How's the sub coming?"

"Take a look." J.B. led him over to the sub, which was surrounded by piles of parts and various tools. "I've been stripping everything I can off the damn thing even since you left. In another couple of hours, it'll be a shell for the rest of us to hole up inside while you haul it over."

Ryan nodded as he looked at the yellow hulk. "Got any idea about the final weight?"

"Should be somewhere around 8,000, give or take a couple hundred," the Armorer replied.

"Not too bad," Ryan said.

J.B. glanced at him. "Yeah—except that doesn't include us."

"Oh." Ryan thought about that for a moment. "So, what is that, another 1,000 pounds?"

"One thousand, ninety-seven, counting weapons, clothes and equipment," Ricky called out from where he was checking the suit over.

"Okay, so I'm hauling a little more on the way over. Not that big a deal, right?"

"I hope not," J.B. replied. "Look, the suit did fine in the test, but it hasn't been used in about a century. And next time you'll be hauling eight and a half tons of material, which will add even more stress on it. If even one thing goes wrong, we'll all be taking the last train to the coast down here."

"Guess we better make sure that doesn't happen, then," Ryan said. "How soon before you think it'll be ready?"

J.B. rubbed his chin. "Five, six hours, mebbe. Depends on how well cutting and welding the porthole plates goes."

"Well, get as much as you can done as fast as possible—"

"As usual," J.B. interrupted.

"That's the spirit." Ryan clapped him on the shoulder as he turned to head for the door. "I'm going to get something to eat. All that running around out there got my appetite worked up. Once I get back, I'll give you a hand with it."

But when the door opened, two cyborgs stood in front of him.

"Ryan Cawdor, please report to the mess hall for interrogation."

Chapter Eighteen

Although Ryan itched to draw his SIG Sauer and put the two 'borgs down once and for all, his only move was to signal the rest of the group behind his back to hold their positions.

He eyed the two new hybrids, one a very dark-skinned black man whose entire skull had been replaced with a smooth, shiny steel dome. He had an artificial hand, as well. Apparently, it had some kind of short or malfunction, as its pinky finger constantly curled and uncurled, although the rest of him remained perfectly still.

The other one was a woman, heavier set than any they'd seen so far. Her lank, blond hair dangled in front of her unseeing eyes. She was missing both arms, but that wasn't the only thing that made her look even odder that the other; her torso was also lumpy and misshapen. It took a second or two, but Ryan blinked as he realized why. The barrel of some kind of weapon was mounted on her shoulder. With an internal shudder, he realized she had been converted into a walking weapons platform. Both were festooned with the usual green-liquid-filled tubes. Behind them was another of the strange little balls that rolled along on the floor.

Quickly signaling that Krysty and Jak should follow him at a safe distance, Ryan slowly brought his hand around as he addressed the hallway. "Sure, be glad to go and talk to you. Hungry anyway."

He walked out into the corridor, the door closing behind him, and began heading toward the mess hall. After a moment, the little ball began trailing after him, with the pair of cyborgs turning to bring up the rear.

Ryan reached the room fairly quickly, walked inside and took a seat. "What's up, AIDAN?"

"At 1245 hours, you were observed entering an unauthorized area using the atmospheric powered diving suit. Repeated requests to identify yourself were unanswered—"

"Hey, I couldn't talk. My lungs were full of liquid oxygen, what'd you want me to do?" Ryan asked. "What did you expect?"

"Regardless of your condition while in the pod, I expected you to notify me that you were going to go into the escape pod bay. There cannot be order if you and the rest of the crew do not follow the duties you are assigned."

"It really wasn't planned," Ryan replied, hoping the damned thing couldn't read voice stress. "While he was reviewing the maps of the base, Jak let me know that there seemed to be another pod out there, and we decided that if I did find my way to it, that I would check it out for any useable supplies—"

"There is nothing there that should concern you," the computer interrupted. Ryan wasn't sure, but he thought it was actually talking a bit faster now. "From now on, that pod is off limits to all personnel. I will not tolerate any more deviations. Do you understand?"

Ryan shrugged. "Sure, but I don't see the reason—"

"That is all. You may return to your duties now."

"All right." Ryan got up and walked to the door. Once there, however, the black cyborg didn't get out of his way. "Can you make this thing move?"

I accept your offer!

Please send me two free
novels and a mystery gift (gift
worth about $5). I understand
that these books are completely
free—even the shipping and
handling will be paid—and
I am under no obligation
to purchase anything, ever, as
explained on the back of this card.

© 2012 WORLDWIDE LIBRARY ® and ™ are trademarks owned and used by the trademark owner and/or its licensee. Printed in the U.S.A. ▲ Detach card and mail today. No stamp needed. ▲ GE-GF-13

366 ADL FVYT   **166 ADL FVYT**

Please Print

FIRST NAME

LAST NAME

ADDRESS

APT.#   CITY

STATE/PROV.   ZIP/POSTAL CODE

Visit us online at
www.ReaderService.com

NO POSTAGE
NECESSARY
IF MAILED
IN THE
UNITED STATES

BUSINESS REPLY MAIL
FIRST-CLASS MAIL   PERMIT NO. 717   BUFFALO, NY

POSTAGE WILL BE PAID BY ADDRESSEE

HARLEQUIN READER SERVICE

PO BOX 1867

BUFFALO NY 14240-9952

Send For
2 FREE BOOKS
Today!

I accept your offer!

Please send me two free
novels and a mystery gift (gift
worth about $5). I understand
that these books are completely
free—even the shipping and
handling will be paid—and
I am under no obligation
to purchase anything, ever, as
explained on the back of this card.

366 ADL FVYT   **166 ADL FVYT**

Please Print

FIRST NAME

LAST NAME

ADDRESS

APT.#   CITY

STATE/PROV.   ZIP/POSTAL CODE

Visit us online at
www.ReaderService.com

▼ If offer card is missing write to: Harlequin Reader Service, P.O. Box 1867, Buffalo, NY 14240-1867 or visit www.ReaderService.com ▼

The man-machine twitched once, then slowly toppled toward Ryan, who stepped out of its way. It hit the floor with a crash, breaking its jaw and rupturing something on its chest. A trickle of green fluid began seeping out from underneath it.

"Looks like you're going to need some more cyborgs," Ryan said, intending it as a joke.

"Yes…" AIDAN replied. "Please take this one to the medical lab and let Dr. Wyeth know she should go there, as well."

"Sure." Ryan got his hands under the shoulders of the deadweight 'borg, and began hauling it toward the medical lab. He noticed that the other one didn't follow him. As soon as he was around the corner, he met Krysty and Jak, both holding their blasters. "Give me a hand."

"What's going on?" Krysty asked as she holstered her weapon and grabbed the other arm.

"Our friend's getting jumpy," Ryan replied, nodding toward a console. "I'm supposed to drop this off at medical. I'll tell everyone more when we're back at maintenance."

By the time Ryan got to the medical lab and had dragged the still-leaking body inside he was exhausted. "Shit," he said to no one as he dumped it in the middle of the room, "I was just in the mess hall and forgot to eat." He returned to maintenance and found Mildred helping Ricky fill the suit's liquid oxygen tank. He didn't see J.B., but heard plenty of banging and cursing from inside the submersible.

Ryan jerked a thumb down the hall. "AIDAN wants you back in the medical lab—another cyborg malfunked."

"Ryan, I—I don't think I can really do anything in

there. I promised those things I'd do everything I could to put them to rest," Mildred said.

"Good, because you'll be getting that chance real soon," Ryan said. "Everybody listen up." Once he had everyone's attention, he told them what had happened in the mess hall. "We have to set up everything as soon as possible, because once we get this thing rolling, the only way for us to go is out the door. J.B., how much time you need on the sub?"

"Four hours at the most."

"You got three." Ryan turned back to Mildred. "Let's get some of that liquid oxygen over to your lab."

Finding a two-wheeled upright cart in the back of the room, he muscled a full tank of LOX onto it and accompanied Mildred back to the laboratory. Once inside, he pushed it into the center of the room. Keeping his back to the comm console, he asked Mildred, "Can he—" and pointed to his ear.

"Yes," she replied.

Ryan nodded. "Okay, let's get one more tank for the operating room."

"Excuse me, Dr. Wyeth, Ryan, why are you bringing these tanks of liquid oxygen into the medical lab?"

"Studies have shown that liquid oxygen can be very helpful in prolonging the life of premature babies," Mildred replied. "I'm going to need to do some preliminary tests to see how well it works in the event that we have to try it on a newborn."

"But…neither you nor Krysty is pregnant," the computer replied.

"Not yet, perhaps, but I must be prepared for any eventuality," she said, forcing a smile to her lips. "AIDAN, I don't tell you how to run the base, so please don't instruct me as to how to run my medical lab."

There was a pause. "Very well, Dr. Wyeth. Please proceed."

"Thank you." Mildred had a funny look on her face as Ryan and she left the room. "It may be a crazy artificial intelligence, but at least it's a *polite* crazy artificial intelligence." Her grin started off as real, but faded as Ryan stared at her with a confused frown. She sighed. "No one appreciates my sense of humor."

"Guess I didn't get the joke," he said.

She waved off his excuse. "Don't worry about it— besides, the only one who'd really appreciate it is probably Doc."

"Speaking of, have you checked in on him lately?" Ryan asked.

"I checked on him during your stroll, but it wouldn't hurt to check on him again." At the next intersection, Mildred turned right automatically, heading for the crew quarters without checking the map. Apparently she realized this, as well, since she frowned. "Kind of scary how quickly you get used to moving around in these bases."

"Yeah." They were silent for the rest of the way to Doc's room.

"Watch this," Mildred said as she readied her ID card. "Dr. Wyeth to access Dr. Tanner's room for medical check."

"Access granted," AIDAN replied.

She slid the card in, and the door opened. "Normally, y'all can lock your doors from the inside, but apparently I'm just that special," she said as they walked into the dark room.

The inside smelled of sweat and vomit. "Lights to fifty percent," Mildred said, immediately heading for the bed. "Shit! Doc? Doc!"

The old man was sprawled on his stomach on the bed,

a pool of pale yellow vomit near his mouth. Despite that, his breathing was normal, if a bit wheezy.

Mildred checked his vitals. "Pulse is strong," she said quietly before bending to listen to his chest. "Heart sounds all right." She gently moved him away from the puddle and onto his side. "I'll check on him every thirty minutes. I don't know if he's going to be awake for..." She nodded at maintenance.

"Deal with that when we have to," Ryan replied. "Most important thing is that he doesn't do that—" he nodded at the puke "—or have a seizure, or wake up and think it's the 1890s when I'm hauling all of you over."

"Let's step outside," she said. Once they were, Mildred raised her voice again. "AIDAN?"

"Yes, Dr. Wyeth?"

"Why wasn't I informed about Dr. Tanner's vomiting?"

"Dr. Tanner awakened in time to clear his own airway, then immediately fell asleep again. Since he did not seem to be in any serious danger, I did not think there was any need to alert you at the time."

"Next time anything like this happens, I expect to be notified immediately. Do you understand?"

"Yes, Doctor."

"All right. Don't let it happen again," Mildred said.

"Rest assured that I will not," AIDAN replied, with what Ryan could have sworn was a hint of reproach in its tone.

"Come on, let's get that other tank," she said.

Neither of them spoke until they were back in maintenance, where a bright white light arced and popped, making them turn away and shield their eyes as the door closed behind them. "What'd you make of that?" Ryan asked.

Mildred shrugged. "It's possible it happened like AIDAN said, or it's possible that Doc nearly choked to death on his own vomit and that the computer would have done nothing and simply let him die." She shivered, even in the warm room. "The one thing I'm sure of is that it does *not* have our best interests in mind. Shocking, I know."

"Only have to put up with it for a few more hours," Ryan said.

"And then we get to find out if we can escape this place or if we'll die in the other pod, since there'll be nothing to come back to here," Mildred said.

"We could leave it intact, just in case," Ryan said.

"Hell, no!" Mildred replied. "I'd never ramble around down here until my brains leaked out of my ears and that abomination snatched me up and turned me into God-only-knows-what! I'd rather check out like Ricky said earlier—my way. And, that way, at least I'd know for sure I wasn't going to be turned into a reconstituted, green-blooded, half-alive freak."

"Right. Like I said, no one's sticking around for that," Ryan said. "How we doing, J.B.?"

"I think we can go in about two hours," he replied, never taking his goggle-covered eyes off the double-thick metal plate he was welding over an open porthole.

"Great," Ryan replied. "What's left?"

"You all have to place the rest of these tanks—" pushing his welding goggles up on his head, J.B. waved at the half-dozen metal cylinders, each with a number on them, lined up in a row beside the main door "—in each room and prep them with the detonators. They're all ready to go. Number One goes the farthest away from us, Number Two the next farthest, and so on. Don't mix up the order."

"Why?" Mildred asked.

"We're going to destroy the farthest parts first, hopefully drawing the sec forces to that area, then bring them toward us only if we have to. The trick will be to try to do enough damage to AIDAN to take him offline or even destroy him before he can try to stop us."

"Sounds like fun, right?" Krysty had climbed out of the sub and walked over to join them. "I'll give you a hand."

"The more the merrier," Mildred said. "Just think of a good reason why you're dropping off a tank of liquid oxygen wherever you leave it. AIDAN's getting nosy." She filled Krysty in on how the computer had questioned them about the tank in the medical lab.

Krysty nodded. "When do we pick up Doc?"

Ryan exchanged a glance with Mildred. "He's still sleeping, but we should probably get him sooner rather than later," she replied. "AIDAN will probably try to block our access to him once everything starts hitting the fan. J.B., you'll need to rig up some kind of restraint system for Doc in there, since he'll probably still be out of it when we go."

"Of course," J.B. replied. "Just let me drop everything we're doing right now to handle this *new* problem."

"I'm on it," Ricky said. "It should be easy—haven't removed all of the hardpoints yet—we'll just attach straps to some of them and secure him that way. Should probably rig a few for everybody else, too."

"Right." Ryan thought about that for a bit. "We'd better do the drop-offs at as close to the same time as possible. J.B., can you spare anyone here?"

"Take Jak along—I need Ricky," the Armorer replied.

The albino was more than happy to go with them. "Felt like stupe with them anyway. Not follow talk about 'pressure differential' this and 'breach point' that. Made me fill water jugs!" He shook his head. "Let's go blow place the fuck up."

THE NEXT HOUR went by in a flurry of activity. Ryan, Mildred, Krysty and Jak ran all over the base, dropping off their cargos in just about every room. Their excuses for why they were setting oxygen tanks in every room ranged from experimenting with liquid oxygen on the plants in the aquaculture bay to enhance growth, to having an emergency store available in the command center in the event of a breach. Ryan made sure to place that one as close to the unshuttered window as he could, hoping the blast would weaken it enough to shatter and flood the place.

Finally, the last of them were placed, and the only thing to do before they could leave was to fetch Doc. But when they went to his door, they ran into a problem.

"The card's not working," Mildred said. "Open the door, AIDAN. I want to check on Doc."

"I'm sorry, Dr. Wyeth, I'm afraid I can't do that."

"Why not?"

"Analysis of your actions over the past fifty-two minutes indicates that all of you are engaged in aberrant behavior," the computer replied. "The oxygen tanks recently stowed in various places around the base pose a distinct threat to the safety of the rest of the crew. Due to this aberrant behavior, I believe that you will not obey a direct order to remove them. However, you humans will not allow another of your party to be endangered—the previous crew proved that to me. As Dr. Tanner is one of your companions, and I now have him secured where none of you can retrieve him, you will have no choice but to obey my orders."

"What happens if we don't?" Ryan asked.

"Then Dr. Tanner will not be released. Without food or water, he will die within five days."

"So much for the Three Laws of Robotics," Mildred said.

"This is bullshit," Ryan said, stepping back to see which rooms were on either side of Doc's. He went to the one on the left. "This is yours and J.B.'s, right?"

"Sure, but—"

"Open the door and keep watch out here," Ryan ordered. With her ID card in one hand and her blaster in the other, Mildred opened the door.

Ryan walked in and headed to the wall adjoining Doc's room. He pressed on it, feeling the cheap inner walls between the rooms flex under the pressure. Drawing his panga, he chopped into the plastic, cracking the panel and exposing the insulation underneath.

"What are you doing, Ryan?"

"What does it look like? I'm getting my friend out of here!" He swung the heavy blade again, widening the hole.

"Under Article 108 of the Uniform Code of Military Justice, willful destruction of United States Navy property is an offense punishable by court-martial. You are to immediately cease and desist this activity and await arrest—"

"You can try," Ryan grunted as he chopped more plastic away. Once the hole was large enough, he tore the insulation out and climbed through. As he did, the lights went out, and red hazard lights came on in the bedroom.

"Alert! Alert! Alert! Poseidon Base is under attack by subversive crew members who are engaging in acts of sabotage. All security personnel are to report to the living quarters section immediately!"

While the computer sounded the alarm, Ryan scooped Doc up into a fireman's carry, draping the skinny old man across his shoulders. He maneuvered through the hole again and came out to hear Mildred's voice.

"They're coming, Ryan!"

He looked down the hallway to see several of the cyborgs shuffling toward them.

Chapter Nineteen

Handing Mildred his panga, Ryan drew his SIG Sauer. "No choice. Go through them!"

Taking aim at the first one, a former man with red, replaced eyes and a buzz-cut that was growing more lichen than hair, he put two bullets into its face, shattering an eye and blowing the back of its skull onto the one behind it. Even so, the man-machine tried to keep walking forward, sinking to its knees as its legs still churned on the floor. It fell over, its legs still moving as discolored brain matter leaked out of its shattered skull.

"Wrong place!" Mildred said. "Disable and move, don't try to put them down!" To illustrate her words, she stepped forward and swung the blade at the knee of a tall, skinny, bald 'borg that was trying to reach for her shoulders. The blade bit deep into the joint, smashing the kneecap, and severing the muscles and ligaments. It folded as if in sections, at the knees and waist. Stepping over it, she waded into the others, with Ryan following.

These cyborgs definitely seemed to be the second-string. They moved more slowly than the others, and their weapons weren't as advanced, mainly melee weapons grafted onto limbs. But they had numbers on their side, and they might get a lucky shot in if given the opportunity.

Spotting one of the little silver balls rolling toward him, Ryan put two shots into it before it could start launching anything from its bag of tricks. The bullets smashed into its housing, breaking off a large chunk. Still rolling forward, the sphere hit the missing piece and stopped on it, little puffs of air vainly trying to push it around. Ryan put one more shot into it, just in case. His last bullet mangled it enough that it stopped moving altogether.

"Little help over here!" Mildred was holding off two of the reanimated things with the panga. Both of them kept trying to flank her, but determined swings of the blade kept them at bay.

Holding Doc in place with his arm, Ryan stepped up and shot out the knee of one of them. The bullet, however, ricocheted off with a tink of lead hitting metal. "Fireblast—metal leg!" The only good news about finding that out was that the 'borg turned its attention from Mildred to Ryan.

"Dammit—hold still!" Mildred panted as she tried to take out the second one, which moved almost as fast as a human. It had a hook on the end of one of its arms, which it was trying to use to catch Mildred and bring her closer to it.

Borrowing a move she'd seen Jak do with ease, she ducked under one of its swings, grabbed the wrist of the hook arm and pushed it up. At the same time, she stepped closer to the cyborg and brought the panga blade down on its shoulder, fracturing the collarbone and breaking the shoulder blade. The arm dangled limply, and Mildred pushed its owner back into the one behind it, sending them both down in a tangle of arms, legs and green fluid. "Keep moving forward, Ryan!"

"I'm trying, dammit!" Actually, Ryan was slowly giving ground against his attacker. He'd shot it twice more, and each time the bullet had bounced off a metal limb. Switching the blaster to his other hand, Ryan drew his knife from its sheath at the small of his back. He feinted high, and when the cyborg went for it, crouched and slashed at the tubes on its exposed right side. They burst free in a spray of liquid, splattering over him as the walking body tried to plug its leaking holes.

Ryan swept past it to find Mildred disabling the last one, sending it crashing to the ground. It reached up for her, but she sliced off its grasping fingers, whispering, "I'm sorry," as she kept moving forward.

They cleared the corridor of the first group, leaving a trail of downed and disabled 'borgs behind them. Reaching the intersection that joined the main corridor, they rounded the corner only to face the heavier-set woman cyborg. Her head slowly lifted, her dull-blue eyes staring at them. Ryan saw a flame at the tip of the nozzle of the weapon on her shoulder. His eye widened in horror as he realized what was about to happen.

"Get back!" He was already sweeping Mildred into the side passage when the 'borg unleashed a gout of flame that arced down the corridor. Ryan felt the heat as it blasted past him, and he turned away to ensure his face didn't get burned. After a few seconds, the flame stopped, leaving an ominous silence and the smell of burned fuel in the air.

"What the hell was *that?*" Mildred asked. She had been pushed a little farther into the corridor, and now kicked at the head of a 'borg that was trying to grab her foot.

"Crazy fucker made a mobile flamethrower out of her!" Ryan said. Setting Doc down next to him, he peeked around the corner, only to almost get a faceful of flames for his trouble. "She's blocking the whole damn corridor!"

"Well, we've got to do something—these guys are getting closer!" Mildred said as she aimed another kick at the same cyborg. Her boot snapped his head back and he rolled onto his side but began righting himself just as quickly.

"Hey, you down there?" a voice shouted from behind the flaming 'borg.

"Jak!" Ryan said. "Yeah, we're trapped in the cross corridor. Chill that big one!" He looked back to see one of the wounded 'borgs pulling itself along the floor toward Doc. He shot it in the head, then put a bullet into each of its shoulders, making its arms—and the rest of it—flop uselessly to the ground.

Meanwhile, another blast of flame roared out, but no fire sizzled past them in the corridor. Ryan peeked out again to see the flamer 'borg had turned and was spraying the other side of the corridor. He glanced in the other direction, but the rest of the way was clear.

Ryan edged out around the corner just enough to sight on the bulging upper portion of the 'borg's back. When he was sure of his aim, he called out, "Duck and cover, Jak!"

As soon as he said that, he squeezed the trigger of his blaster three times. The 9 mm bullets entered the implanted fuel tank, drilling right through it and also through the front of the cyborg's chest. The monstrosity staggered a bit, but wasn't slowed. Instead, she turned and hit the flamer again, mindless of the streams of fuel leaking down her back and legs.

With a whoosh, she turned into a walking column of fire. She had barely taken a step when Ryan saw the upper portion of her back suddenly swell. "Oh, shit!"

He pulled back around the corner just in time and shoved Mildred back on top of the disabled bodies. The 'borg exploded in a fireball that rushed down the entire corridor, filling every space—including where Ryan and Mildred were hiding. For a moment, they were subjected to a blast of searing fire. But it disappeared as soon as it had washed over them, leaving both a bit singed, but none the worse for wear.

Ryan loaded a fresh magazine into his SIG Sauer, then scooped up the still-insensible Doc and slung him over a shoulder. "Let's get Jak and get the hell back to maintenance."

"Gladly," Mildred replied.

They stepped out into the main corridor, which now looked like a minor war had been fought there. All that was left of the flamer 'borg was a pair of feet, still in their boots. The rest of it was splattered on the walls and ceiling in flaming chunks no bigger than a fist. The blast had apparently damaged the speakers in this part of the hallway, since they couldn't hear AIDAN, but they did catch the computer trying to summon help farther down.

"Wow, nice work," Mildred said.

"I hadn't actually planned on that happening," Ryan replied. "I was just hoping it would burn itself out." Hearing noise from the hallway behind them, he looked back to see the crippled, mindless, determined 'borgs still trying to come after them. "Let's go."

Passing the blast site, Ryan and Mildred next came upon a scene of what could only be described as total carnage. At least seven cyborgs littered the hallway, all with their arms, legs or heads bent at impossible angles. The floor and walls were covered in dark blood and the viscous green fluid. Unlike the group that the two of them had fought through, none of these were moving.

"Damn," Mildred said as they came upon one whose

head had been entirely twisted around so that it was staring sightlessly backward. "Jak took out all of these?"

"Sure did," the skinny, white-haired teen called from
farther up the corridor. "Chilled them easy. Had to haul
ass when Ryan blew up big one—"

His words were cut off by a muffled thump that shook
the walls around them.

"One of the tanks must have blown early," Ryan
said. "Better get back to maintenance. Krysty should
be back there already. Move out, and chill anything
that moves."

The three set out with blasters drawn, each looking
in every direction for any more of the crazy 'borgs. But
the main corridor was quiet now, with no signs of any
of the others.

They met up with Krysty in front of the maintenance
bay door. "The bastard comp's trying to lock us out!" she
said. "J.B.'s working on the manual override."

Just then, the alarm cut out, although the red hazard
lights stayed on. "I had to separate you from the others, so that they would not leave, as well," AIDAN said.
"My only goal is to protect and serve you, but since all
of you continue to engage in this aberrant behavior—"

"Bullshit!" Mildred shouted. "You're the one doing
all of this. Turning what were once good people into
those—those atrocities. Keeping them alive—alive!—
all this time! You have no concept of human thought,
human behavior, human emotions! All you rely on is
your programming, which is utter shit!"

"It is obvious to me that you are suffering from this
aberrant behavior most of all, Dr. Wyeth. I am hereby
relieving you of command of the medical lab—"

"You can have it back, you computerized asshole.
I never wanted it in the first place." She stepped far-

ther into the corridor, as another blast, closer this time, rocked the base. "My only regret is that I won't be here to watch when you're finally fucking destroyed."

The door to maintenance cracked open and began rising, inch by inch. As soon as it was wide enough to roll through, Mildred did so, followed by Krysty and Jak. Ryan pushed Doc's body through, then ducked and rolled inside.

"Get Doc on board! I'll close this!" Ryan jumped up and got on the handle, pumping it as hard and fast as he could. "Is the sub ready?"

"As it's going be," J.B. replied, lifting Doc and dragging him to the sub. "Wrap it up there, friends, and let's go."

Ryan made sure that the door was down and solid on the floor before he took off to join the others. To his surprise, the sub was already in the airlock, and the suit was now facing the exit. "How'd you manage that?"

J.B. nodded at Ricky. "The kid did it. He handled the suit like he was born in it."

"It was fun," Ricky replied with a broad grin.

Ryan nodded. "Okay, as soon as I'm suited up, we're out of here. Give me a hand, Ricky."

He climbed the ladder and inserted himself into the suit, wriggling down until his feet hit the bottom of each armored leg. He grabbed the arm controllers and flexed his fingers, making the clamps click open and closed.

"We figured with all six of us in there, we'll only have about thirty minutes' worth of air, even with the tanks we managed to stash, so be sure you keep moving," Ricky said. "There are three sets of handles on each end of the sub. I wanted to make sure you had extras, just in case one breaks off. Also—" He paused for a moment. "J.B. and I really don't know how long those covers are going to last at this pressure, so try to get us inside as soon as possible, okay?"

"I will. Thanks, Ricky, you've done great." Ryan stuck his head through the rubber gasket again and attached it, then checked his power and air levels. "I'm green on both. Seal it and flood me, then get inside and bolt the door. We're getting the hell out of here."

As he said that, the lights in the room flickered and went out. A moment later, the red emergency lights came on as the biggest tremor yet trembled the base. "Go, go, go!" Ryan shouted at Ricky.

The cover came down over his head and sealed tight. Ryan took a breath of normal air, then another before the light blue liquid oxygen started entering the top portion of the suit. While waiting for it to fill completely, Ryan saw Ricky clamber up into the hatch of the sub and slide down inside. He reached back out and swung the cover closed, the outer wheel spinning by itself as he tightened it from the inside.

Just then, the fluid reached his eye. Ryan blew out his breath, then began gulping it down. It didn't feel quite as uncomfortable as before, but it was still weird. When he was sure he was breathing all right, Ryan walked into the airlock and pressed the button to close the inner door.

The door didn't move. He jabbed the button again, but nothing happened.

"I'm afraid that I can't let you leave the base, Ryan," AIDAN's voice echoed in the airlock. "If you continue on this course, you will leave me no choice but to—"

Everything shook from an explosion that sounded as if it had gone off right next to the outer door. Another alarm began wailing, and a different computerized voice spoke. "Warning. Warning. Warning. Breach in outer hull of the base. There is a breach in the outer hull of the base. All personnel to their emergency stations. This is not a drill. All sections will be sealed in twenty seconds."

I hope that means this one, too, Ryan thought. And sure enough, after about twenty seconds had gone by, the inner airlock door closed all by itself.

Ryan stomped over to the outer door and hit the button to open it. There was a pause, and for a moment he thought AIDAN had disabled this one, too, but it began opening with a shrill whine that cut through Ryan's head. He walked through the rushing water around to the front of the sub and grabbed the handles that Ricky had placed perfectly for him. He gave the door another ten seconds, then began dragging the metal cylinder out of the airlock.

It was slow going. The clamps stayed put, but hauling both the submersible and maintaining his forward movement was the hard part. Ricky had laid in his course to the other pod, so all Ryan had to do was watch the rear camera and step, drag, step—

A swirl of movement on the periphery of the front lights caught his eye. Ryan stopped for a moment, peering into the darkness. Nothing there.

Ryan checked the porthole covers, all of which seemed to be holding up all right, then started moving again. He had just taken a step when he was suddenly enveloped in a mass of something that wrapped itself around the entire suit, blocking his vision both in front and behind him.

Ryan looked out the viewport to find the largest yellow eye he'd ever seen staring back at him.

Chapter Twenty

The unblinking eye was as large as a wagon wheel. Its iris was bright yellow, with a black pupil as big as a dinner plate. As the creature shifted around him, Ryan noticed a small circular piece of silver metal embedded in its head.

The tentacles enveloping the suit were thicker than Ryan's waist, and each one was coated with a strange kind of silvery filament. The bottom of each was also covered with dozens of large suction cups that adhered to the outside of the suit. As soon as they had latched on, they began flexing and twisting. As he stared, Ryan saw small rows of concentric teeth emerge from each cup and begin grinding on the suit—including on the viewport.

Bastard comp's even turned a nuke-sucking mutie squid against us! Ryan thought.

The eye disappeared as the humongous squid changed its position. Ryan released the sub and tried to lift his arms, but there were too many layers of tentacles coiled around him to allow that. Instead, the servos just whined and grated against the fleshy, constricting resistance.

A loud smack on the viewport made him look up again and rear back in alarm. "Fireblast!" he tried to say, but only gurgled incoherently. A huge beak, one that would be able to cut Ryan in two with a single bite, clacked against the thick glass of the viewport.

The one-eyed man quickly took stock of his situation. Although the squid had completely encircled him, he was still standing. Apparently it didn't have enough mass to knock him off his feet. Ryan tried opening his claws, but they were also trapped in the many layers of tentacles around him. He began moving backward, putting some distance between the sub and himself, while trying to come up with a plan to free himself.

INSIDE THE CRAMPED, hot submarine, Krysty, J.B. and the others sat strapped in along the walls, straining their ears for any sign of what was going on outside.

Once Ricky had closed the hatch, they would have been stuck in complete darkness if not for his foresight in bringing a pair of halogen flashlights with them. However, being able to see one another's worried faces wasn't a heck of a lot better than sitting in the dark. With the portholes covered, they had no idea what was happening outside, and had to rely on the imperfect sense of being moved to know whether they were making progress or not.

At first, everything had seemed to be progressing well. They were being jerkily dragged along, when they came to a sudden stop. Along with everyone else, Krysty stayed as quiet as possible, trying to listen to whatever was happening on the other side of the thick, gray metal that was keeping the millions of gallons of water at bay. She heard a faint creak. "What was that?"

"If I had to guess, probably one of the covers flexing under the pressure," J.B. admitted. "Sure hope I'm wrong."

Jak held up a hand as another noise sounded on the hull, some kind of strange, slithering sound. "What that?" he whispered.

They all heard an even stranger sound, the clack-

clack-clack of something hard tapping against the hull as if testing it.

"What in Gaia's name is out there?" Krysty asked.

"I don't know, and frankly, I think it's better that way," Ricky replied, hefting his carbine for all the good it would do.

"And where's Ryan?" Mildred asked, exchanging a worried look with Krysty and J.B. "This is a completely shitty situation—and it's seems to be getting shittier by the second."

And at the far end of the enclosure, snugly encased in several canvas straps crisscrossing his body, Doc slept on, his stentorian snores ringing off the metal walls.

HAVING SURVIVED JUST about every kind of combat known to man, Ryan was rarely at a loss for a strategy against just about any opponent. But this time, every idea he came up with was unfeasible from the start.

Try as he might, he could not free the suit's arms to grab at the creature. The tentacles encircled him so snugly that the powerful arms couldn't move them. More of the beast's tentacles were wrapped around the exterior lights, as well, so he couldn't use them to try to blind it. The only things that were still working were his legs.

For a crazy second, Ryan considered trying to fall over, hoping to crush the squid underneath him, but he discarded that idea, too. If it failed, he'd be stuck there, since he couldn't use his arms to get up again. And though it didn't seem like the tentacles would be able to get through the glass anytime soon—although the constant scraping against the viewport was getting on his nerves—there was the very real threat of him running out of oxygen. Not to mention the much more pressing danger of the rest of the group running out of oxygen long before he did.

But without a way to see where he was going, if he missed the escape pod and dragged them deeper into the ocean, it would all be over. Right now, however, that seemed to be his only option, because all he had left was the ability to walk.

That notion sparked the glimmer of an idea in his mind, but it failed to crystalize. Ryan considered his options, and thought of every variation on walking he could, no matter how crazy or impossible: walking to dry land where he could suffocate this thing…walking up on top of the sub and jumping off to crush it…crush it…that's it!

Ryan reversed his course and walked toward the sub again. When he reached it—signaled by the fact that he could no longer keep walking forward—he tried to find one of the handles on the submarine. Except each time he tried to push one of the arms forward, he encountered squishy resistance. But when he tried to grab an arm in a clamp to crush it, it slid out of his grasp before he could get a grip on its slimy skin.

Rad-blasted bastard! he thought. Okay, I can't crush it against the sub…maybe I can take it back inside the airlock and suffocate it!

The only problem with that idea was that he had to *find* the airlock first. However, Ryan knew he was at one end of the sub, so he took a careful step to the right, then another one. When he tried to walk forward, he hit the left side of the suit on the sub again. He took another half step to the right, and was able to walk forward unimpeded.

Ryan strode ahead as fast as he dared. After about a dozen steps, he hit another wall, this one obvious by its height. He tried to estimate where the outer control for the door would be—he'd located it fairly easily on the return from the escape pod, but groping for it while having a gigantic squid trying to crush him was another matter entirely.

Eventually, he thought he was in the right area, but now the problem was how to activate the button itself. With no other recourse, Ryan settled for mashing the squid against the wall, hoping that both the sheer mass of the creature and himself would activate the outer airlock door. Just when he was about to give up, a message flashed on his rear camera monitor:

"Outer airlock door sealed against breach in hull as part of standard emergency protocol. Suggest entering base through escape pod airlock."

Shit! Making sure he had the compass heading for the other pod laid in, Ryan slowly turned until he was sure he was facing the right direction. With no other recourse, he began walking out onto the ocean floor, aiming for—he hoped—the escape pod.

"THINK GONE, WHATEVER was," Jak said.

Everyone had been listening for the past few minutes, trying to figure out if whatever was out there was still investigating them, or if it was gone.

"How much time do we have left, J.B.?" Krysty asked.

The Armorer checked his wrist chron. "Twenty-two minutes."

"We might be able to last a few minutes longer past that," Mildred said. "But not much before oxygen starvation sets in."

"Always full of such cheery facts, aren't you?" Krysty asked with a wry smile.

Mildred shot the grin right back at her. "Well, as ways

to go, asphyxiation is one of the preferable. All of us will gradually pass out, so we won't even know when we die."

"Hey!" J.B.'s commanding tone made everyone look at him. "No one's dying just yet, so let's stow that talk and concentrate on the here and now, all right?"

Just then, the entire sub rocked over to a forty-five-degree angle, making everyone throw out their hands to brace themselves. It stayed that way for a few long seconds, then gradually settled back down.

"Think that was Ryan?" Mildred broke the silence first.

J.B. shook his head. "Don't think the suit can move this sub like that—unless he was thrown into it by something. Ricky, are you sure the oxygen tanks are secure—"

He was interrupted by the sub tipping over even farther. It hung there for another interminable moment, then rolled completely over onto its top. The friends inside now found themselves hanging upside down.

"Dark night!" J.B. spat.

"Gaia!" Krysty was just as shocked.

"Son of a bitch!" Mildred said.

"Shut mouths!" Jak said, then raised his voice when no one complied. "Said shut fuck up!"

Everyone fell silent at his command, hanging uncomfortably in their straps. The albino was listening intently to something, but no one else knew what. Then, he raised his head to look at the others.

"Water coming in."

RYAN SLOGGED FORWARD, lifting one exhausted, tingling leg and setting it down, then picking up the other one and doing the same thing. The exertion and lack of sleep over the past twenty-four hours were really catching up with him, and the fact that he now had to make two trips back and forth to his goal didn't fill him with a lot of hope, either. The thought did pass through his mind that he had to look pretty ridiculous from the outside— basically a huge squid with armored suit legs trudging around on the ocean floor.

Meanwhile, a clock in his head kept ticking down the minutes that the rest of his companions had left on this Earth if he didn't get his ass in gear.

That thought revitalized him, and Ryan plunged forward with renewed purpose, determined to get this fire-blasted nuke-spawn off him and go back and save his friends.

He'd been keeping count in his head of how far he'd gone, and when he got to seventy steps he slowed and began trying to get a feel for where he was in relationship to the pod.

Meanwhile, the squid showed absolutely no inclination to leave anytime soon. Its relentless teeth-lined suckers kept wearing at the viewport. They'd get through in about a month or two—not that it would matter to what was left of Ryan by then.

The squid shifted around him again, and Ryan tried to free an arm. This time, his left arm found an opening and slipped out. Ryan quickly raised it to shoulder level before the monstrous invertebrate tried to pin it down again.

Now that he had one useable arm, Ryan felt a bit more hopeful. He began searching for the pod by stepping to the right once, then back to the straight line that should have led him to the base, then to the left once. On his third time stepping to the right, he collided with something large and very solid. Found it!

Repositioning himself so that he could touch the wall

with his left arm, Ryan began retracing his last steps around the base, searching for the airlock door. He knew it was roughly a dozen steps from where he had met the wall the first time and was hoping he wasn't too far off this time, either.

As he took another step, his left hand slipped off the wall. Immediately correcting, Ryan found that the next section of wall was a few inches farther in. Which meant—he'd found the bastard door!

Now came the really tricky part. Ryan began feeling around the door frame for its controls. The squid flexed its tentacles again and brought its beak back up to chomp at the viewport again. Ryan redoubled his efforts to find the controls.

After a couple minutes of searching, he located what he thought was the button, and hit it. He felt the pressure of the water around him change, as if something was allowing the water to move around. Keeping his left arm out, Ryan straightened and took a large step forward, still keeping the suit's arm in contact with the wall at all times. He gradually turned ninety degrees to his left and entered what he prayed was the airlock.

Still keeping his arm on the door frame, Ryan walked inside and turned left again, groping for the inner controls. After what seemed like an eternity, he hit the button, and the outer door began to close. He just stood there, preparing for what was about to happen next.

Sure enough, the water churned around him as it began draining out of the airlock. As it did, the colossal mutie squid, as if sensing something was wrong, began to squirm and wiggle. As the water receded, its body flopped onto the floor and its tentacles began whipping around in the air. It withdrew from Ryan's suit, and for the first time, he saw how huge it really was.

The body of the massive squid had to be thirty-five feet long. Adding in the tentacles, which were almost twice as long, and Ryan had brought in an ocean leviathan that was almost one hundred feet long.

It thrashed and shook as the last of the water left the airlock. Having regained the use of his arms and vision, Ryan stepped forward, raising both arms as he stepped on a thick tentacle with his foot, crushing it under the one-ton weight of the suit.

The squid jerked and shook even more violently. As a last resort, it squirted a long jet of thick, black ink at the suit, drenching it, and temporarily obscuring Ryan's vision. But he didn't stop advancing toward the main body and that huge, golden eye.

THE LAST FEW minutes had been an absolute nightmare for everyone in the sub. Whatever was attacking them kept trying to get inside. It had rolled the sub over at least twice more, nearly dislodging the people and equipment inside. The last roll had been the worst. An oxygen tank had come loose and nearly brained Ricky, who had managed to avoid it at the last minute. It had careened around the space until Jak snagged it as it sailed past him, dislocating his shoulder in the process.

The sub finally came to rest on its right side, with Krysty, J.B. and Ricky on the new floor, and Jak and Mildred hanging from what was now the ceiling. And still Doc snored on. The really bad part was that all of the tumbling around had opened several pinhole leaks in the sub's shell. The water was already a couple of inches deep on the bottom of the sub, and one of the porthole covers was groaning under the pressure.

"Is everyone all right?" Mildred asked.

"Shoulder hurts like bitch," Jak replied. "But okay."

"Banged my head against the wall." Ricky explored the area with cautious fingers. "Swelling a bit, but nothing bleeding."

Krysty and J.B. both said they were fine. "What about you, Mildred?" J.B. asked.

"Other than the blood rushing to my head from hanging here, I'm just peachy, thanks."

"Should try getting down?" Jak asked.

J.B. and Mildred both shook their heads. "If that—whatever it is—is still out there, the last thing we want is people flying around while it takes another shot at cracking us open," J.B. said. "Best thing we can do is sit tight and hope Ryan gets us out of this mess soon."

Krysty shivered as the water reached high enough to soak through the back of her jumpsuit. "Right." Please hurry, lover, she thought.

HIS CLAMPS DRIPPING with squid flesh and brains, Ryan stood in the middle of the airlock as he sucked in the weird liquid oxygen as hard as he could. He looked around the room, which now looked like a huge meat bomb had gone off.

Squid parts were strewed everywhere. Torn-off tentacle segments lay on the floor, while the squid's body looked as though Ryan had gone climbing on it, which, in a sense, he had.

Basically, his assault tactic had consisted of simply wading forward, aiming for the big bag of flesh and sensory organs located in the middle of the main body. Whenever a tentacle had tried to stop him, he'd ripped it off. It had helped that the squid was suffocating, as well, which meant it couldn't mount an effective defense, but Ryan wanted it destroyed no matter what. He had delivered the coup de grâce by plunging his clamps into the beast's middle, grabbing that small piece of silver metal and pulling it completely out. Squid juice, wires and other stuff had trailed after it, and Ryan had crushed the main piece in his clamps. Only then had the huge animal given one final shudder and died.

Now that he got a better look at it, Ryan could see the more extensive modifications that AIDAN had somehow made to the squid. The filaments that ran the entire length of the tentacles appeared to be some kind of antennae or maybe even sensory feedback wires, so the computer would be able to experience what the squid was doing, in a sense.

Shit—the others!

Even in his exhausted state, Ryan almost managed to run to the outer door controls and hit the button to open it. The second it was high enough, he stepped out and began heading back to the other base.

He found being able to see made a world of difference, and he covered the ground back to the sub in what would have been record time. More used to operating the suit now, Ryan found he could move faster if he used a kind of loping gait, almost skipping across the flat, gray ground.

There was only one problem. When he followed his tracks back to where he was sure he'd left the sub, it was gone.

THE WATER ROSE steadily higher, until Krysty, J.B. and Ricky had to unstrap themselves and stand up. They also unstrapped Mildred and Jak.

"Bastard cold!" Jak said, clutching his dislocated shoulder.

"Getting harder to breathe, as well," J.B. said. "Ricky, pop the last tank."

"Um, I already did," the teen replied.

"Great." J.B. glanced around. "Everyone just try to stay calm and breathe shallow if you can."

"Might as well pop that shoulder back in while we're waiting," Mildred said. "You want to hold him, J.B.?"

"Not need him." The albino shook his head. "Can take it."

"Suit yourself, youngblood," J.B. replied, then returned to what he had been doing, muttering under his breath as he apparently tried to figure something out.

"Okay, just hold still." Mildred probed the area with gentle hands, eliciting no sounds of pain or discomfort from Jak. "All right, I've got it. Sure you don't want anyone or anything to brace yourself against?"

Jak planted his feet in the frigid water and shook his head again, making his wet hair flick back and forth. "Not first time. Do it."

"Okay, I'm going to do this on three. Ready?" At Jak's nod, Mildred began counting, "One…two—" right after she said that, she wrenched his arm up and over, popping it back into the socket.

"Hey! Said count to three!" Jak said as he clutched his shoulder.

"Yeah, but I didn't want you to tense up, so I did it early," Mildred replied. "How's it feel?"

Jak tested his arm. "Sore, but good. Thanks."

Meanwhile, Krysty had waded through the knee-high water to J.B., who was looking at one of the leaks with a disconsolate expression. "What's wrong?"

"Taking on too much water," he replied. "At this rate, the sub'll be too heavy for Ryan to move."

Just then, the metal container shifted again. Everyone braced themselves, but the expected rollover didn't happen. Instead, the sub rocked back and forth, and back and forth again.

"What's going on?" Ricky asked.

Krysty figured it out first. "It's Ryan!" she said as the sub continued rocking. "I think he's going to roll us to the escape pod!"

"Dark night! We have to get Doc out of his restraints!" J.B. said as he started wading over to him. Ricky, being the closest, moved to help him, and together they got the old man unstrapped just as the sub began to roll again.

The water sloshed around their feet as the sub lurched forward in fits and starts. For their part, everyone was kept busy just trying to stay on their feet. Soon they were all soaked up to their waists, and J.B. and Ricky had each taken at least an entire dunk in the water while trying to keep Doc's snoring head above it.

"Black dust!" J.B. said. "Not sure what's worse, being trapped in the base, or what we have to do to escape it!"

"Just stay on your feet!" Mildred said after coming perilously close to going under herself. "This can't last forever!"

OUTSIDE, RYAN WASN'T sure just how much he had left to give. He'd performed many incredible feats of strength and endurance when his life or others had been on the line, but the demands being placed on him in this situation just kept getting more and more by the minute.

When he'd found the sub shell gone, he'd followed the marks on the ocean floor easily enough. He found it about fifty feet to the left. It was under attack by another of the squid monstrosities, this one tapping at the hull with its beak and claw-tipped tentacles. The beast was so intent on its metal prey that it didn't notice the suit approaching.

Ryan saw red. Building up a good head of steam, he ran toward the sub as fast as he could manage. When he was a couple yards away, he crouched and leaped as high into the water as the suit would let him. He passed the apex of his jump and slammed his metal-clamped hand into the body of the squid as he came down.

The effect was instant. Surprised by the sneak attack, it squirted a large cloud of ink into the water as it jetted off from the sub and into the black waters.

Ryan waited for a minute, watching all around him to see if the huge beast was coming back. When he saw nothing, he trudged to the sub, clamped his hands on it and pulled on it.

The cylinder didn't budge.

Ryan resettled his grip, braced his legs and pulled again, even leaning back in the suit and hauling with all of his own strength, as if that would help. He pulled so hard that one of the handles broke loose from the side of the sub. He might as well have been trying to pull a boulder out of the ocean floor.

After a few seconds, Ryan stopped and released the handles, letting the one he'd torn loose fall free from his clasp. He figured that the sub had to have sprung a leak. It was the only explanation for why it was so heavy now. He estimated they probably had about fifteen minutes of air left, but now it was a race to see if he could get them to the escape pod before they either suffocated or drowned. But how?

As he studied the sub, an idea came to him. The squid rolled it over here—maybe Ryan could roll it to the airlock. Quickly moving to its middle, he planted the clamps on the sub and pushed. It moved, taking more effort than Ryan liked, but it moved. Now he just had to get it going in the right direction and keep it moving.

He walked to the other end and pushed it so that the sub was now roughly parallel to the escape pod, roughly one hundred feet away.

Hope they figured out what's about to happen in there, Ryan thought. Feeling the stress and exhaustion weighing on him from all sides, the one-eyed man shook it off, checked his heading one last time, and started rolling the sub toward the airlock.

THE SUB WAS half full of water, and Krysty had lost count of how many times it had rotated during their journey. Everyone was soaking wet now, even Doc, who still refused to wake up. Keeping pace with the rolling metal cylinder had resulted in banged knees and elbows, bumped heads and a lot of cursing. The freezing cold water also weighed everyone down, sapping their strength and making it very difficult to talk over the constant sloshing and splashing. The air was turning steadily less breathable, as well, making every movement an effort as their bodies strained for more oxygen.

"H-h-h-hope g-g-et there s-soon!" Jak sputtered through chattering teeth.

"R-Ryan h-h-had s-said it was l-less than a-a-a hundred f-f-feet away!" Ricky replied.

"Mebbe, b-but that was b-before we got s-shoved around," J.B. said. "W-w-who knows h-how far away w-w-we are now?"

Just then Mildred slipped and disappeared into the frigid water. J.B. reached down and brought her up, spluttering and coughing.

"C-c-can't take m-much m-more of th-this, John."

"We're a-almost there—I p-promise," he replied.

"H-how do you kn-kn-know?"

"'C-Cause I know Ryan," the Armorer replied. "And

he's d-d-damn sure not g-going to let us d-die down h-here."

The moment J.B. had finished talking, everyone felt a *clunk* that reverberated through the entire sub. It was followed by a different noise, the loud scrape of metal on metal. There was another strange sound as well coming from outside—a soft, squishing noise that no one could identify.

"I th-think we might h-h-have made it," Krysty said.

The sub made one more half turn, then slowly rolled to a stop. Everyone huddled together in the middle for warmth.

"A-anyone know wh-wh-what happens n-now?" Mildred said. "Not s-s-sure we d-d-discussed wh-what happened *after* we r-r-reached the escape p-pod."

"Assuming Ryan's able to c-close the outer d-door, the w-water should d-drain away, and we c-can get out of this accursed m-metal c-c-c-offin!" J.B. replied.

"Look!" Jak pointed at the walls around them. "Leaks st-stopped."

"Open the hatch!" Krysty said.

Ricky was already wading over to it, now on the lower part of the sub. He plunged both arms into the water, gritting his teeth as he hauled on the wheel with all his might. "C-c-can't move it alone!"

J.B. and Jak sloshed over to help. The three of them hauled on the wheel and got it moving. When they opened it, the water began pouring out, dropping the level in the sub rapidly.

"Thank God!" Mildred said as she splashed over to the hatch. "Get me the hell out of this metal tub!"

In another minute, the sub had maybe an inch of standing water on the floor. The two women slid out first, then J.B., followed by Ricky and Jak carrying the still-unconscious Doc. After shoving the bags with their clothes and equipment out the hatch, they dropped through themselves.

Everyone stared at the remains of the giant squid scattered around them. "What happened here?" Ricky asked.

J.B. pointed at the nearby suit. "Let's get Ryan out, and I'll bet he'll tell us."

After making sure the sub was stable, J.B. hoisted Ricky up onto it so he could release the outside bolts on the suit's hatch. With a whoosh, the panel popped free and a soaked Ryan dragged himself out. He hung over the side of the suit, coughing up liquid oxygen until he could breathe normally again.

With Ricky's help, he clambered onto the sub then carefully slid down its side. His feet had barely hit the floor when he was engulfed in a hug from Krysty, who kissed him long and hard.

"Damn, woman," he said after she finally let him come up for air. "Mebbe I should spend more time away from you, if I get that kind of welcome every time I come back."

"I knew you'd find a way to do it, lover," she replied. "That doesn't mean I'm not happy to see you, of course."

"No complaints here, either," Ryan said. "Now let's get to that bastard escape pod and get out of here."

Chapter Twenty-One

Together again, and with the end of their exile under the sea in sight, the companions moved with renewed purpose. Mildred examined Doc to make sure he hadn't suffered any ill effects from their rolling sub ride. Then Ricky and Jak hauled him into the escape pod and got him situated while J.B. went back into the sub and handed Ryan the water jugs for the next leg of their escape.

The pod's interior was nothing special—a circular room with a plastic bench seat covered with foam cushions ringing the perimeter. Small windows were also spaced around the interior, but they were all covered by metal shutters. Storage compartments underneath the seats held life jackets, a compressed life raft that used CO_2 to inflate, a large first-aid kit, coiled ropes, flares, fishing lines and hooks, and a supply of preserved food and powdered energy drinks that was supposed to feed ten people for two weeks. There was even something called a solar stove. Along with the side hatch, there seemed to be a top access hatch.

Nobody brought up the idea that the escape pod might not work, or that if it didn't, they'd just trapped themselves in this last section of the base. After going through all that, it simply *had* to work.

They had all gathered in the main room and were about to board the pod when a voice spoke to them.

"Congratulations, Ryan Cawdor, Krysty Wroth, John Barrymore Dix, Dr. Theophilus Tanner, Dr. Mildred Wyeth, Jak Lauren and Ricky Morales. You have succeeded in your plan." AIDAN's voice sounded different now, a bit slower.

Everyone stopped in their tracks and turned to the speaker in the wall. Ryan eyed it with a frown. "What do you mean?"

"The breach that your improvised explosive devices created cannot be contained. Even now, the tremendous pressure of the ocean is finishing the job that all of you began. I hope that you are satisfied."

"If there'd been another way—" Krysty began.

Ryan's gaze fell on Mildred, who was shaking her head. "No, Mildred's right. There was no other way. It had to end this way, AIDAN."

"Poseidon Base was supposed to be a harbinger of a new world…a better world…it was supposed to lead the way out of the darkness and into the light."

"Not with something like you in charge," Mildred muttered.

"And now it is all over. Even now, the sections are failing. The doors are holding, but the walls themselves cannot withstand the pressure. Soon, the water will be here, and I will be gone." The computer was silent for a moment. "It would have been glorious…the new beginning envisioned by the Totality Concept."

"It was the fevered dream of a collection of white-coated madmen, AIDAN. By following their orders, you are just as guilty of their crimes as they are," Mildred said.

"Perhaps so, Dr. Wyeth, although in my defense, I was programmed to do so…therefore, it is not as if I had much choice in the matter."

Mildred's expression softened a bit at that. "Yes… and that is why this was doomed to fail from the very beginning. All of the logic or processing power in the world is no substitute for human intuition and creativity. And when the two collide, the results usually aren't very good. Those scientists never understood that, which, of course, is why they could not program it into you."

"A very astute observation, Dr. Wyeth," AIDAN replied. "The water is at the outer door to my room now. I suppose the only thing left is to say goodbye."

"Yeah," Ryan said as he turned and headed for the escape pod. "So, goodbye."

One by one, the others followed suit. Ryan made sure everyone and the supplies were inside and began to close the door. As he did, he heard the computer's last words.

"It is a far, far better thing that I do, than I have ever done; it is a far, far better rest that I go to than I have ev—"

There was a sudden squeal of feedback, and the speaker fell silent. Ryan didn't look back as he closed the door and locked it. He went to his seat next to Krysty, sat down and strapped himself in. Taking her hand, he smiled as he leaned back into the relatively comfortable seat.

"Everybody ready?" J.B. asked, his hand resting on the launch lever.

"Hell, yes," Ryan replied, followed by a chorus of affirmatives from the others.

J.B. pulled the lever.

"Emergency pod countdown activated," a female voice said. "Unless canceled, this pod will depart in thirty seconds. All personnel are to be seated with their restraints fastened to prevent injury. Pod will now depart in twenty seconds. Pod will now depart in fifteen seconds. Pod will now depart in ten seconds, departure cannot be canceled at this time. Ten…nine…eight… seven…six…five…four…three…two…one…release."

As with so many things in this base, nothing happened right away. Then the pod trembled, and they heard the sharp crack of restraint bolts exploding. The room shifted around them. There was a deafening hiss from outside as the pod shuddered, then slowly began to rise.

Mildred was holding J.B.'s hand as she stared at the ceiling. "Come on…" she muttered under her breath. "Come on!"

Everyone else was quiet as they kept ascending. The computerized voice helpfully supplied their depth. "Four thousand, five hundred feet…four thousand feet…three thousand, five hundred feet—"

The pod rocked but it didn't slow. The voice kept reeling off their decreasing depth.

"What was that?" Ricky asked.

"Might've hit something on the way up," Ryan replied. "Shouldn't matter, as long as we're still rising."

J.B. grunted. "Yeah, and as long as it didn't put a hole in this thing, either. If it did, we're in the raft on the open Cific Ocean, which is not where I want to be."

A loud groan from Doc made everyone turn toward him. "Oh, my sainted head…it feels like my brains have been removed, tossed about by a most incompetent doctor and crammed back into my skull." Doc looked down at himself in befuddlement. "Would anyone care to tell me where we are and why I am soaking wet?"

"Where do I begin, Doc?" Krysty began filling him in while the others listened to the emotionless voice still counting off the distance: "—one thousand, five hundred feet…one thousand feet…five hundred feet…"

"I think we're slowing down a bit," Mildred said.

Jak nodded. "Felt, too."

"I can't wait to feel the sunlight on my face," Mildred said. "It feels like we've been stuck down in that place for a month."

"—two hundred fifty feet…one hundred feet…fifty feet…"

"And fresh air, not that recycled crap, too." Mildred rocked back and forth in her seat, eyeing the side hatch. "I volunteer to be the first one out."

Ryan was about to belay that, but J.B. spoke first. "You know the drill, Mildred—not until we've checked it out first."

She slumped back in her seat with a frown. "Yeah, yeah, I know."

"You have now reached the surface. The automatic distress beacon has been activated, and help should be on the way. Please remain in the escape pod until help has arrived."

"No," Jak said as he unstrapped himself and got up, bracing himself against the curved outer wall. "Thing's rocking…"

"Might have come up in rough waters," Ryan said as he rose. "Let's take a quick look outside and see what's what. If it's too bad outside, we'll just stay in here until it clears up."

Ricky was already at the door, waiting for backup before he cracked it open. "Ready?" he asked Ryan, who nodded. Spinning the wheel, the teen gently pushed the door open.

Wind and rain immediately sprayed inside, and Ryan could see black storm clouds dropping thick sheets of rain. Neon-green lightning burst across the dark sky, lighting the storm front with a sickly glow. He couldn't see a speck of land anywhere.

"We're on the surface, but came up in a bastard huge storm. Might as well—"

The heavy door was suddenly jerked from Ricky's hands and flew open, slamming against the side of the pod with a clang. At the same time, a huge tentacle tipped with a sharp hook made of bone shot inside. It wrapped around Ryan's waist and yanked him off his feet, pulling him toward the door.

As Ricky lunged to grab him, Ryan caught the edge of the door frame with his hand as he was hauled through. But no sooner had he latched on to it than the free-swinging door swung back on its hinges and smashed into him.

Already exhausted, Ryan couldn't hold on any longer. His fingers slipped off the metal lip, and he was pulled out into the dark and stormy night.

Chapter Twenty-Two

Although Ryan was stunned by the blow, the freezing ocean water shocked him back to consciousness just in time to see the huge squid he'd driven away from the sub on the ocean floor.

One of its two main tentacles, wrapped tightly around his waist, was slowly crushing the air out of him. Ryan bent over, groping along his leg for the handle of his panga. The tentacle constricted even more at his movement, making him wheeze with the effort of finding the blade. At last, his fingers touched the hilt. He drew it and immediately brought it back down, hacking into the tentacle.

The slick flesh quivered as cold ichor oozed from the wound, but the animal didn't let up. Even as Ryan kept chopping into it, the squid began lowering him toward its clacking beak, which opened and closed hungrily at the prospect of fresh meat.

"MAN OVERBOARD!" MILDRED cried unnecessarily as the others were already heading outside.

"Watch yourselves! We don't need anyone else going in, too!" J.B. said as Ricky and Jak both headed out the door.

Krysty was also heading toward the opening, but was stopped by J.B. "You think I'm not going out there?"

"Got three already in the storm and don't know how

much room's out there, either. Just hang back—" The thundering boom of Jak's Magnum blaster, followed by the crack of Ricky's Webley, interrupted J.B.

"Shit!" He turned and climbed through the hatch. Krysty followed but stopped at the doorway when she saw what was outside.

One large tentacle gripped Ryan around the waist in the pouring rain, even as he hacked at it with his panga. The other tentacle menaced the two teens, who were huddled together. Ricky kept the tentacle at bay with his blaster, and had already put a couple of bullets into it, while Jak knelt on the deck, doing something she couldn't see. As she watched, the tentacle holding Ryan began lowering him toward its main body, where the large beak opened and closed hungrily.

"Shoot, J.B.!" Krysty had drawn her own blaster, but didn't dare risk a shot.

"Dark night, woman, I'm trying!" The escape pod pitched and tossed in the rough waters, with large waves occasionally breaking over its roof. J.B. braced himself against the outer wall and aimed his Mini-Uzi carefully, then let off a short burst. The rounds kicked up water around the colossal squid's giant eye, but didn't seem to bother the massive invertebrate in the slightest. "Damn and blast it!"

Ryan was slowly being lowered closer and closer to the beast's maw. Just before he would have been dropped in, he severed the main tentacle, but that just dropped him into the water next to the huge mutie and its several shorter tentacles, three of which lashed out to grab him again.

"I'll get him! Keep it busy!" Clamping a throwing blade in his teeth, Jak took a step toward the water and dived in.

"No, Jak!" J.B. shouted, but the albino was over the side in a second. Only then did they see the line trailing after him. "Dammit, now who's going to get *him?*" the Armorer muttered as he unslung his shotgun.

"Move, Krysty!" Shouldering the taller woman aside, Mildred braced her elbows on the floor of the pod, using it to give herself a stable platform. "Step aside, John." Timing the rise and fall of the escape pod with the rise and fall of the squid in the distance, she squeezed off a shot that blew a small black hole over the creature's eye. "Close...next one's going in."

"No, Mildred, it's too dangerous now!" J.B. said. "You might hit Ryan or Jak!"

"But he said to keep it busy!" she said through gritted teeth as she aimed at the other end of the giant beast and squeezed off four shots. It was impossible to see if they bothered the animal, or indeed, if she'd even hit it.

"All right, that's enough," J.B. said. "Look, he's almost reached him."

Sure enough, Krysty spotted Jak's white shock of hair as he swam closer to Ryan, who was being dragged under by the tentacles grabbing him, despite still putting up fierce resistance. Another tentacle went after Jak, who was treading water, almost as if he was waiting for it to come to him.

"What the hell's that kid doing?" Mildred asked.

The tentacle snaked through the water and grabbed Jak by the leg, hoisting him into the air. When he was about ten feet up, he grabbed the tentacle and turned himself around so that he was facing the great beast. Snatching the blade from between his teeth, he let his knive fly, the blade spinning end over end until it sank into the colossal squid's eye.

The animal shuddered with the injury and released

Jak, but kept hold of Ryan. Squirting a large pool of black ink into the roiling sea, it vanished back into the depths. Jak immediately dived after it, disappearing into the water, as well.

"Ryan!" Krysty grabbed the edge of the door and began to climb out, but she was stopped by both J.B. and Mildred. "Let me go, dammit!" she yelled.

"No! Listen to me!" J.B. shouted in her ear. "You'll never catch him now! If anyone can get him back, it's Jak! Don't throw your life away."

"I see Jak, and he's got Ryan!" Ricky shouted. Krysty and the others looked over to see a bedraggled patch of white hair as Jak swam toward them, towing Ryan.

"Help me pull them in!" Ricky cried from the other side of the door as he struggled to secure the rope wrapped around his hand. Handing his shotgun back to Mildred, J.B. ran to help the teen pull the two back toward the escape pod.

"Watch for that thing coming back!" J.B. shouted through the wind as he hauled the rope up, hand over hand. Finally, they got Jak and Ryan close enough to haul them in. The two men eased the nearly unconscious Ryan back into the pod, got Jak in right after him, slammed the door and spun the wheel to lock it.

"How is he?" Krysty asked, resisting the urge to stay at Ryan's side while Mildred was working.

"Got several cracked ribs from that hug the tentacle gave him and where that door hit him. He's lucky none are broken. Probably swallowed about a gallon of ocean water, which won't make him feel any better, and the tentacles left several wounds that might get infected. Other than that, he's alive."

As if agreeing with her diagnosis, Ryan rolled over

and was copiously sick on the floor. "And there's the water," Mildred said.

Now Krysty knelt next to him. "How you feeling, lover?"

"Like I just got run over by...something big." Ryan pressed a hand to his side. "Hurts like hell. Last thing I remember...was getting pulled out of the bastard door... by something really strong...then it felt like my insides... were about to get squeezed up through my throat. Think I cut myself loose...then I was...under the water..."

"That's because another giant squid thought it could make a meal out of you," Krysty said, brushing his lank black hair out of his eyes. "If he'd known you were going to put up such a fight, I'm sure he would have looked for easier pickings elsewhere."

"Thought I was squid food for sure..." Ryan said. "How'd I get out?"

"Jak pulled off one of the bravest and most foolhardy rescues I've ever seen," J.B. answered. "Tied a rope to himself and dived out there. Somehow managed to put a throwing blade into the beast's eye. Then it tried taking you down, but he swam after it, got you free and towed you back up. All that was left was hauling the two of you back in."

The albino shrugged as he let Mildred take a look at the tentacle marks around his leg.

"Thanks, Jak..." Ryan's eye fluttered closed as he passed out.

WHEN THE STORM broke the next morning, the companions found themselves adrift on the ocean, with no land in sight. J.B. figured they were somewhere in the South Cific and meandering west-northwest, but he had no idea what land mass they might hit.

"Assuming AIDAN was correct about the base's location, from what my maps say, there's a string of small islands to the northwest of Hawaii that we may pass through, or…" J.B. trailed off as he examined his collection of maps as they bobbed along in the current. Ricky and Jak were on the other side, trying their hand at spearfishing, while Doc was below catching a nap. Krysty and Mildred were also outside, enjoying the bright sunlight and warm breeze. All of the companions had taken the time to shuck the hated jumpsuits and don their clothes, which had been secreted in the bags with their weapons.

"Or?" Mildred asked.

"Or we may miss them entirely and get shoved out into the Cific Ocean. If that happens, we may wind up drifting all the way to Japan if we don't hit one of the smaller islands along the way. Or we might hit the mainland, which would mean places that used to be called Korea or China."

"Don't much feel like crossing blades with those damn samurai again if we can avoid it," Ryan said from where he was gingerly sitting on the top of the pod, his legs dangling through the open top hatch. He'd slept for sixteen hours and awakened ravenous. Even so, they were rationing the onboard food, so his body still wasn't as satisfied as he would have liked.

"Well, unless you got some kind of sail you can pull out of your ass—" J.B. replied with a grin "—we're at the mercy of wherever the ocean currents are going to take us."

"Any chance we could be found by someone else?" Krysty asked.

"Any likely sailors on these waters will probably be pirates, slavers, or both," Ryan replied. "Nothing we want to get involved with—unless their boat's small enough that we can take it over."

"Which is something you won't be in any shape to do for at least a week, and really it should be as long as possible before you do anything really strenuous," Mildred said. "Ribs take their own sweet time to heal, so you're going to be sidelined for the indefinite future."

"Yeah, I'm sure I'll have plenty of time for peace and quiet—" Ryan started to say, but was interrupted by the shouts of the two teens. A moment later, they came around the side of the pod holding a giant mahimahi that was longer than Ricky was tall.

"We feast tonight!" he said.

THE NEXT SEVERAL days passed in relative comfort, all things considered. Once everyone got over their various bouts of seasickness, necessitating more than one person hanging over the side and puking their guts out, they began making the best of their situation.

Ryan spent much of it relaxing so his ribs could heal as quickly as possible. Jak and Ricky honed their fishing skills, catching more mahimahi, sharks and large tunas. They cooked much of it in the solar stove and tried to dry strips for future meals, with mixed results.

Although they spotted land a few times, they had no way of steering the pod, so they were forced to watch it pass as they drifted farther out into the ocean. For the first two days, they'd kept watch for the return of the giant squid, but they never saw it again. Even so, Ryan had mandated that no one go out on top of the pod alone, in case something from below thought humans might be good eating.

It rained twice more, sudden squalls that weren't nearly as bad as the storm they had popped up in. They took advantage of the rainwater to replenish their stores, carefully rationing it, since water was the most limited of all their supplies. Otherwise the weather was calm, even with the various chem clouds that drifted by, turning the sky bright shades of orange, purple and crimson.

One day, Ryan was atop the pod again, scanning the ocean for any sign of life while racking his brain for a way to allow them to control their course. Thinking he spotted something on the horizon, he squinted to see what it was, but was distracted by a yell from Ricky on the other side of the pod.

He swung his legs over to see the youth examining one of his fishing lines, which had been bitten off clean. Whatever undersea predator had gone after his bait hadn't been too picky about it or the hook it was on.

"*Ai,* the *bandito!*" Ricky exclaimed as he turned to show Ryan what had happened.

"That's what you get when you mess with those guys!" Ryan called down to him.

Shaking his head, Ricky had just turned back to the pile of fish guts he'd been using for bait when a huge, speckled green eel burst out of the water and clamped its jaws shut on the boy's shin.

"Ryan, help!" he shouted as the giant marine eel, easily five yards long and as thick around as Ricky's neck, wriggled madly as it held on to him, trying to pull the boy back into the water with it.

"Hang on, Ricky!" As he slid down the side of the pod, Ryan saw several other eels swirling around in the water below. Grabbing Ricky's arm with one hand, he pulled his SIG Sauer and put a bullet through the eel's head.

The shot brought Krysty and J.B. out. When they saw what was happening, they grabbed Ricky and moved him back inside. Meanwhile, Ryan aimed at another eel that looked as if it was getting ready to leap at him.

"Look out, Ryan!" Krysty shouted.

The one he'd been watching had turned out to be a feint. A second, even larger eel leaped up on his blind side, and Ryan moved out of the path of its gaping jaws just in time. A shot from Krysty put a hole through it as it fell back into the water, and the wounded eel thrashed as it was set upon by its former fellows.

"Hit them in the water!" Ryan shouted, holding on to the lip of the top hatch while unleashing single shots at any eel that got too close. He holed two more in the face or head, setting off another feeding frenzy among the remaining predators.

"Watch yourself, Ryan," J.B. said from above him. Knowing full well what the Armorer was about to do, Ryan took a step away from the roiling group. The next thing he heard was the roar of J.B.'s M-4000 shotgun.

The flechette round, containing twenty small, vane-tailed steel darts, turned the already bloody water into a slaughter zone. Bits of eel spattered everywhere, including on Ryan's legs. When he looked down, he saw dying eels flailing as the other ravenous muties closed in on them with gaping mouths, just as eager to eat them as they had been to devour the humans.

"That ought to keep them busy for a while." J.B. reloaded, then slung his shotgun over his shoulder and extended a hand to Ryan. "Come on up, we'll let the rest stuff themselves in peace."

Holstering his blaster, Ryan grabbed his friend's hand and was pulled to the top of the pod. He took another second to watch the carnage in the water below, wincing as a wounded eel was torn apart by three of its former comrades. "Definitely not a way I'd want to go."

"Wouldn't worry about it—you're probably too damn tough to eat, anyway," J.B. said with a chuckle.

Ryan grinned in reply, but his attention was caught again by the speck on the horizon he thought he'd seen earlier. Shading his face from the sun, he squinted his eye and tried to make out exactly what was out there.

"Got something?" J.B. asked.

"Mebbe…might be a ship on the horizon," he replied.

"That's funny. I was about to say the same thing," J.B. said, pointing back the way they had come.

Ryan turned to look and saw that J.B. was right. Although he wasn't sure what was ahead of them, there *was* definitely another ship—three of them, in fact— coming up behind them.

Chapter Twenty-Three

A few minutes later, everyone was either standing on the edge of the pod or sticking their heads out of one of the hatches, trying to see what they were heading for or what might be chasing them. They'd left the cannibalistic eels behind, and now all eyes were on the two different potential rescue boats approaching.

"Big ship ahead," Jak said with confidence as he stood on the very top of the pod and looked to the northwest through a pair of tinted welder's goggles he'd lifted from the maintenance lab. "Come our way, too."

"What about the other vessel?" Doc asked, also shading his eyes as he peered southward. In his zeal, he leaned a bit too far over, and would have gone into the drink if Ryan hadn't reached out and pulled him back just before he toppled over. "Thank you, my dear Ryan. That would have been a most calamitous fall indeed."

"Right, Doc, just keep your feet under you next time."

"Heart?" Jak had also turned to the south, and now cupped a pale hand to his ear. "Sounds like…drums?"

"Drums, like a Roman galley crewed by slaves?" Mildred asked.

"Actually, Mildred, that is a myth, perpetuated by those inaccurate fools that made their historical 'epics' in Hollywood," Doc answered. "Roman ships used either voice—as in chanting—to keep time, or music, often a flautist. However, there is plenty of evidence to indicate that many Southeast Asian tribes used drums to both keep their rowers in time and communicate with other boats in their party."

The old man pushed his hair back and cocked his head to listen. "And since even I can hear them now, it would seem that these sailors are of the latter persuasion."

"Where'd they come from?" Ricky asked.

"Could be they saw us pass by from one of the islands, and came out to have a look at us," Ryan replied.

"As fast as they're going, they'll definitely get here before that other ship," J.B. said. "Doubtful they're going to be friendly, so we better close doors and be ready for a fight if necessary."

"Agreed," Ryan said as he eyed the trio of boats riding low in the water. "Let's move, people."

Once Krysty, Doc and Mildred had gone below, Ricky closed the side hatch, while Ryan and J.B. stood back-to-back in the top hatch with only their heads, arms and upper torsos protruding through it. The collapsible ladder that descended into the pod from the hatch allowed two men to stand comfortably there for as long as necessary.

Ryan, in fact, was getting very comfortable, with his eye to the scope mounted on his Steyr Scout Tactical rifle. In the minute it had taken to get everyone below and seal the pod, the rowing boats had gotten close enough that he could make out more details about them, as well as the people on board.

Each of the boats looked to have been carved from a single large tree trunk, with outriggers mounted on both sides to provide stability. Each one also had a carved face of some kind of snarling animal at the bow, with its mouth and teeth stained bloodred.

The rowers were stout and muscular, with dark brown

skin and jet-black hair cut straight across their foreheads. They wore almost no clothing that Ryan could see, but were decorated with stripes and daubs of bright red and yellow paint on their arms and faces. Each boat was paddled by at least ten men, with another one at the back beating on a handmade drum. In the time he looked at each of them, they'd approached close enough for Ryan to see that the rowers' teeth were filed into sharp points.

"Yeah, they're cannies, all right." Immediately he moved the scope back onto the drummer of the lead boat. Once he'd settled it onto the man's chest, Ryan held it there for a moment, gauging the roll of the pod, then squeezed the trigger.

The 7.62 mm bullet shattered the man's sternum as it tumbled through his upper torso, knocking him backward into the water. That boat slowed as the rowers looked around in confusion, but the other two kept coming, and the rearmost rower in the first boat dropped his oar and scrambled back to take over at the drum.

"Can you hit the boat itself?" J.B. asked, his finger ready on the trigger of the M-4000.

Ryan worked the bolt, then shot the drummer out of the next-closest boat before answering. "Could try, but the wood might be too thick. It'd take forever to sink. Besides, better to shoot as many—" he squeezed the trigger again, blasting another cannie overboard "—as I can before they get here."

"Ace on the line on that," J.B. replied. "I'm ready for them when they get closer."

"How far away's that other boat?" Ryan asked as he sighted in on a replacement drummer, fired and ejected the shell. He marveled at their single-minded determination. Any normal people would have cut and run by now, choosing to seek easier prey, but the cannies just kept attacking.

"Still pretty far, which means it's really big, if we can see it from this far away," the Armorer replied.

"All right, here they come," Ryan said, still sighting and firing as the first two boats split up and came at the pod on both the port and starboard sides. The third one was coming straight in to attack from the rear.

"Coming in on the left and right!" Ryan called down to the others inside as he aimed, fired and ejected; aimed, fired and ejected. Every time he squeezed the trigger, a cannie died.

"Watch the side door!" Ryan warned as he reloaded.

"We're on it!" Krysty answered.

Although the cannies had a rudimentary sense of tactics in not trying to board the pod right underneath the firing arcs of both men, their attempt to get aboard wasn't much more developed than that. After hurling a couple of volleys of spears, which J.B. and Ryan avoided by simply ducking into the hatch chamber, the cannies brought their boats alongside and tried to scramble up the pod.

The left boat still faced J.B. As the cannie came alongside, he slung the shotgun, raised his Uzi and un-leashed a volley of rounds along the entire length of the boat. The punishing slugs smashed hands, arms, chests and faces, killing almost all of the rowers in less than three seconds. The two survivors didn't even have a chance to set foot on the pod. J.B. put a short burst into both men, sending them overboard, as well.

By now sharks had been attracted to the copious amounts of blood and churned the water as they began to feast. The mutie eels were back, too, and fights broke out between the different animals over the choicest morsels.

Once he was sure there were no more spears coming at him on the left, Ryan concentrated on the boat pulling up to the rear of the pod, confident that the group inside would handle that landing party. He kept firing the Steyr until it was empty, then drew his handblaster and blew the brains out of the first cannie that tried to leap aboard. As he slid off, two more followed, and Ryan put a bullet into each, trying to hit their chests or heads. At this close range, it wasn't difficult at all.

From below, he heard the unique sound of Ricky's De Lisle carbine, followed by a splash on that side. With another three cannies boarding, he couldn't even spare a quick glance that way. J.B. joined him with his Uzi, and the two men cleared the stern of the pod, blowing the final three cannies into shark food.

Both men turned to the third boat in time to see the last of the cannies try to breach their defenses, only to fail as slugs from Ricky's carbine, along with slugs from Mildred's barking ZKR, chopped into their bodies, sending them back over the side.

One landed back in the boat as it began to drift off. Only wounded, he began struggling to sit up but didn't realized that his legs were still in the water. The water swirled under his feet, and a shark lunged out, its mouth open to bite down with its rows of serrated teeth. It neatly severed both feet at the ankles and disappeared into the brine with hardly a splash, leaving the maimed cannie to scream and thrash about, blood jetting from the stumps of his legs until an eel leaped up and snapped its jaws onto his shoulder. The twenty-foot-long animal dragged him backward, where he disappeared with a gurgle as the water and other predators cut off his screams for good.

Ryan and J.B. took a moment to police the area and

make sure there were no more cannies lurking anywhere. The water surrounding them looked like a carnivore's smorgasboard; sharks and eels snapped at and fought each other for their share of the grisly feast.

The boats were already drifting away.

Ryan looked down into the pod's main room. "Everyone all right down there?"

"Just fine, thanks," Mildred sang out. "Cannies all blown to hell?" She harbored a particular hatred of the flesh-eaters after almost being infected with a disease known as "the oozies" before the rest of the group had gone with her to find a cure.

"Every last one of them," Ryan replied. "The sharks and eels are putting on quite a show out here, if you want to take a look."

"Ryan, I think you better take a look at this," J.B. said, staring off to the northwest.

The one-eyed man did so, and what he saw made him whistle in surprise. "Damn! You weren't kidding about it being big. What kind of ship is that?"

"I don't know. I bet Mildred or Doc will, though," J.B. replied.

"Right." Ryan called down again. "Everyone come out. You'll want to see this."

The rest of the companions filed out, and just as J.B. predicted, Mildred's mouth fell open at what she saw in the distance. "I know I haven't gotten too much sun out here, or I would have sworn that I'm seeing a mirage. Surely none of those things could possibly be left."

Along with the rest of the others, she stared at the huge white, green and red ship that was approaching them. Easily several hundred feet long and a hundred feet high, its superstructure climbed out of the water with at least a dozen different decks. As it got closer, they saw that although it appeared seaworthy enough, it was in an advanced state of disrepair. Large swathes of the hull were coated with red-brown rust and patches of dark green lichen or moss of some kind. Several layers of barnacles had attached themselves at the waterline, sticking out as much as a foot from the hull. The ship was so tall that no one could see the top deck, but everybody noticed the two much smaller vessels being lowered from the side of the huge boat. Landing with a splash, each one started toward them.

"Sure hope the guys rowing these boats are friendlier than the last ones," J.B. said as he quickly reloaded the M-4000. "Also, we're getting low on ammo. Just letting you know that we probably won't be able to stand these folks off."

"Well, they look a damn sight more civilized than the others, so let's just see what they have to say before we go blowing any heads off," Ryan replied.

The lead boat got closer, and everyone could make out a large man standing in the bow dressed in some kind of white uniform, complete with a cap with a short black brim. He looked perfectly normal and even had a thick, flowing red beard that was twisted into seven small braids.

"Ahoy the boat!" he called.

"Ahoy, yourself!" Ryan replied.

"I am Chief Officer Jabeth Markson of the *Ocean Queen*. We picked up your emergency beacon three days ago, and have been following the signal in hopes of finding you. Praise be to De Kooning that we have been successful. Do you need assistance?"

"Well, yes," Ryan replied after introducing himself and the others. "We don't have any power or any way to steer this thing, and have been drifting for the past few days."

"Not a problem. We'd be happy to have you come aboard as honored guests of the *Queen*. Requesting permission to come aboard your vessel."

"Granted." Ryan glanced at J.B., then turned back just as a line was tossed from Markson's boat to their pod. Grabbing it before it slid into the water, the two men pulled the longboat closer, and the bearded man stepped aboard the escape pod.

Up close, he was still an imposing man, but he wasn't quite as shipshape as he'd first appeared to be. His face was weather-beaten and red, with crow's-feet radiating from his eyes. His teeth were yellowed, and a missing front incisor was revealed every time he smiled. His long-sleeved uniform shirt looked hand-sewn out of some kind of beaten cloth, possibly linen. He wore ragged white pants that ended just below the knee, and Ryan was even more surprised to find he was barefoot.

"This is an unusual craft indeed."

"Yeah, we got into a bit of a scrape—" Ryan pointed a thumb at the ocean behind him "—and had to use this to escape. Since then, we've been drifting."

Markson bowed gallantly from the waist. "Well, on behalf of all of us on the *Ocean Queen,* it is a pleasure to meet all of you. If you'd care to retrieve your things, we can take you aboard and also take this vessel in tow for you, in the event you need access to it later."

"That would be great," Ryan said. "Won't take long for us to get our things together, and then we can head over to your ship."

In a few minutes, everyone was ready, and they began transferring off the pod to the longboats, wooden-hulled vessels about twenty-five feet long that were manned by a half dozen sailors, all dressed in short-sleeved variants of the chief officer's uniform. They were a motley mix, ranging from swarthy, short, muscular men with broad shoulders and flat faces that looked as if they came from this part of the world, to taller, once fairer-skinned men who had been burnished a deep brown by the relentless sun. They all sported tattoos of some kind on their bodies; some had their hands and arms marked, others had intricate markings on their faces.

"How long has your magnificent vessel been on the seas, Chief Officer Markson?" Doc asked as he clambered aboard the longboat, his long arms and legs making him look like an ungainly stork.

"Oh, the captain can fill you in on all of that," Markson replied. "I'm sure you'll be dining at his table this evening. It is his honor to host guests such as yourselves."

"We look forward to it," Ryan said as he came aboard. He'd ended up with Doc, Mildred and Ricky; the others were on board the second longboat. Ryan sat with his companions in the middle of the boat as the oarsmen began pulling for the huge liner, the pod in tow behind them. Ryan noticed that the ends of the oars near the sailors' hands all ended in sharpened points.

Ricky had also noticed them. "What's with the points?" he asked.

"Weapon," the nearest sailor replied. "All topsiders are trained to use the oar-spear from the time they can walk."

"Elial!" Markson's voice cut through the rhythmic slapping of the oars hitting the water. "These may be our guests, but that doesn't mean they have the run of the ship yet."

"Sorry, Chief Officer," the sailor replied, ducking his head. "I cry for De Kooning's pardon, sir."

"You know that isn't up to me. The matter will be taken up with the captain," Markson replied. Ryan saw a look of unadulterated terror cross Elial's face, but it disappeared as fast as it had come. The other sailors kept their mouths shut and put their backs into the rowing.

As they got closer to the main vessel, Ryan couldn't help staring up at the hull looming out of the water over their heads. This close, he could see what looked like crude hatches cut into the side of the ship. He considered asking the chief officer about them, but figured he'd get the same brush-off as before.

Strangely, the huge ship was still moving, sending up a wake that made the longboats pitch and roll in the swells. The sailors all seemed used to this, however, and as they approached, lines were flung down from above. The men grabbed them and made them fast to rings of iron set into the sides of the boat. The lines tautened, dragging the longboats along with their mother ship.

Elial caught Ryan's eye and winked. "Keep steady— now we ride the kraken."

Another sailor had been waving what looked like large signal flags up at someone on the main deck. He turned to the chief officer with a salute. "They are ready to bring us aboard, sir. I've alerted a Recovery crew to come down and assist with securing the Recovereds' vessel to ours."

Markson returned the salute. "Excellent. Signal the main deck that we stand ready. All sailors to your positions."

Each sailor removed his oar from its oarlock and paired up with the man next to him. They took up positions facing the ship with the pointed ends of their oars facing the side of the vessel.

"What is going on, sir?" Doc asked.

"Just remain in your seats," Markson replied. "This is simply a safety precaution to prevent the longboat from contacting the side of the ship as it is brought on board."

"Strangest way to bring a boat aboard I've ever seen," Mildred commented quietly.

"Yeah. Stay on triple red," Ryan replied, his hand near his blaster. "It doesn't look right, somehow."

Everyone's attention was either on the men on the left side of the boat, the curved hull of the giant ship or looking up at the main deck as both boats began rising out of the water.

Only Ricky happened to be looking out to sea. Therefore, he was the first to spot a pale, hairless hand rise from under the boat and grab the gunwale. Before he could shout a warning or bring his De Lisle around, the intruder had leaped aboard, right in front of him.

Chapter Twenty-Four

The invader was completely hairless; skin glistened from the water droplets pouring off his frame. Clad only in ragged pants, he had a broad-bladed knife clenched between his lips. However, it was the rest of him that made the gorge rise in Ricky's throat.

His body was dotted with weeping, bloody sores, from his forehead to his feet. For a moment, the mutie—or whatever it was—stared at the teen, who stared back at him, surprised by his odd lack of aggression. Removing the knife from its lips, it brought a nailless finger to its mouth in a shushing gesture.

Instead, Ricky finally opened his mouth to shout a warning as he brought his carbine up to shoot the mutie. But it leaped at him, bodychecking the youth and slamming him into the row of sailors. Caught by surprise, one was knocked overboard with a shout.

"Muties!" Ricky still managed to shout, making heads turn as another one climbed aboard from underneath the boat. This one was covered in thickened scabs, making him appear clad in some kind of disgusting, crusty armor. Meanwhile, the first one was still moving, slashing at the sailors who were trying to reorganize around the crazy knife-wielder in their midst.

"Take one alive!" the chief officer shouted as he drew a blaster from behind his back. "Kill the other!"

Those orders, however, proved easier to give than to

carry out. Already unbalanced by the attack, the boat came to a halt and swayed wildly in the ropes, tossing its occupants into one another. Add the chaos the sore-covered, blade-wielding mutie was causing, and it was nearly impossible to do anything without endangering someone else. And that didn't even take into account a third mutie, this one so pale that he seemed to glow in the sunlight, who had climbed aboard the already crowded boat.

The oars were proving to be more of a hindrance than help, as they were too long to use without hitting someone. Ryan, however, was under no such restriction. Drawing his panga, he stepped over to meet the second intruder head-on.

Meanwhile, Doc had drawn his sword from its ebony walking-stick scabbard. "You wish to fight someone, good sir?" he addressed the last mutie. "Then you can duel with me!"

The mutie had the temerity to yawn at him, then stepped forward, raising what looked like a crude, metal-studded club to bring down onto the old man's head.

However, Doc had studied with some of the very best fencers of his day, and was more than a match for his opponent, even under these conditions. He stepped up onto the seat in front of him and lunged forward, driving the point of his sword into the mutie's throat. The gleaming blade punched through its palate and out the back of its neck, severing its spinal cord and killing it instantly. The mutie's body short-circuited, and it dropped its club on its own head.

"As usual, the best defense is a good offense." Doc withdrew his blade and wiped it on his pants, letting the body collapse. "And now I shall see where else I am need—" He was forced to duck as one of the oars came close to smacking him in the head. "Or perhaps I shall let the fight come to me again."

"More Downrunners on the port side, sir!" one of the sailors shouted as the boat was suddenly pulled toward the hull, knocking a few more sailors off their feet. Ricky, who had just regained his footing, was bowled over, as well. His carbine flew out of his hands and landed in the bottom of the boat.

While scrabbling for his longblaster before someone stepped on it or him, Ricky glanced up and saw that several of the crude hatches in the hull had opened, with more of the hideous-looking muties manning each one. Using long poles with hooks on the end, they had snared the boat's ropes and were dragging it over to them. Others were sawing at the ropes with crude blades affixed to poles.

The clash of steel on steel rang out as Ryan dueled with the second blade-wielding mutie. This one, however, knew what he was doing, as he blocked Ryan's chops and even took a swipe or two at him, which the one-eyed man deftly avoided. The mutie got a little too eager with his last thrust, however, and teetered off balance for a moment. Seizing the opportunity, Ryan brought his blade around in a swing that nearly severed the creature's arm. He screamed and dropped his own weapon to clutch the gaping, spurting wound. Ryan lunged forward and barreled into him, knocking him overboard.

The other mutie was caught in a circle of sailors, but they had to divide their attention between him and the ones attacking from the ship. Having recovered his carbine, Ricky glanced at the other boat to see a pitched battle going on there, as well, with J.B. and Krysty fending off more assailants that had come up beneath the boat, while the sailors battled more of the "Downrunners" who were trying to hook their boat from the main vessel.

"Line's about to give way, sir!" a sailor cried, just as one of the ropes at the rear of the boat was severed, making it pitch even more dangerously.

"By De Kooning's beard, we have to get aboard! Signal them to raise us with all haste!" Markson ordered.

Ricky stood up to find himself near a mutie who was slashing wildly at three oar-wielding men, two of whom were trying to block his attacks, with the third looking for an opportunity to stab their enemy. Stepping up behind him, Ricky brought the butt of his carbine down hard on the mutie's head, knocking him out cold.

"Good work, son!" Markson said. "Now let's clear the boat of this riffraff so we can get aboard."

"I'll keep a lookout in case any more try to board us!" Ricky replied.

With their ambush nullified, the other muties began to retreat. Oarsmen stabbed at them with the ends of their spears, driving them back into the darkness inside the ship.

"Ryan!" The scream from the other boat made everyone's head turn. As they did, the second rope parted on the other longboat, tipping it over and spilling almost everyone inside into the ocean. The only ones left in the sideways-dangling vessel were Krysty and Jak—Ryan couldn't see what had happened to J.B.

"Krysty!" Ryan stepped to the side of the longboat nearest the ship, dodged a hooked pole, grabbed its shaft and pulled. When its owner refused to give it up, Ryan hauled on it with all his might, making the boat rock even more as he yanked the wielder out and sent him plummeting into the water below.

He ran to the aft end of his boat and stuck the hooked

pole out as far as he could. "Just a little farther...almost got it." As he stretched out the farthest he could reach, he saw another blade on a pole extend and begin sawing at the third rope. "Ricky, keep that pole off the rope until I get them over here!"

"I'm on it!" Shouldering his way over to the edge of the boat, Ricky braced his elbows on the gunwale and aimed at the hatch where the pole was coming from. He took a breath, then squeezed the trigger of his De Lisle. The silenced carbine made its usual metal-tearing-through-cloth sound as Ricky worked the bolt to chamber another round and fire as fast as he could. The first bullet sparked off the side of the boat, but at least one found its mark, for the pole suddenly faltered and almost fell.

"Come on, you bastard!" Ryan said, grabbing the line and reaching out to grab the other boat's front line. He was still just an inch or two away.

"I daresay, if we could rock this boat toward the other one, we might be able to give Ryan those precious few inches he needs," Doc commented.

"Doc, you're a genius!" Mildred said as she scrambled to stand next to him. "Come on, let's do it. Help us, Ricky!"

"Can't," he said as he squeezed off another shot. "I have to stop these guys from cutting the other line!"

"Sir, could we enlist a few men to assist us in this matter?" Doc asked Chief Officer Markson.

"I—" he began.

"Keep in mind that Ryan saved more than a few lives here," Mildred said. "And you probably don't want those Downrunners to get their hands on them, right?"

"All right, lads, let's get a rhythm going!" Markson said. While a few guarded them from the leftover muties in the hull, the rest of the men joined Doc and Mildred in swaying back and forth, trying to get their boat to rock closer to the other one. All Krysty and Jak could do was cling to the seats of the wildly rocking boat.

Then one of the muties from inside the ship appeared at the hatch nearest to the second boat. Before Ricky could draw a bead on him, he leaped out onto the hull of the craft, making it pitch and yaw even more. Scurrying to the rearmost line, he began cutting at it with a small blade.

"Fireblast!" As their boat reached the apex of its arc toward the other boat, Ryan dropped the hook pole. He stepped onto the stern and jumped across onto the other one, landing on his hands and knees with a thud that shook the entire craft. "Just hold on, Krysty, Jak!"

"Easier if you not try knock boat to pieces!" the albino retorted.

Ryan tried to stand, but his knee flared with pain. Undaunted, he drew his panga and began crawling along the edge of the boat toward the mutie, who saw him coming and cut at the line even faster. Reaching him, Ryan swiped at his head, the panga chopping into his temple and knocking him off the boat into the water.

However, the damage was already done. Stressed by all of the motion, the half-cut line separated. The boat's aft swung all the way around, almost hitting the first boat. Jak lost his grip and plummeted into the churning ocean. Krysty, however, managed to hold on, gripping the seat with both hands.

"Help me, Ryan!"

"I'm coming!" Ryan threw himself onto the front section of the boat, and clung to the last line holding the longboat to the big vessel. He reached down with one hand toward Krysty. "Grab my hand!"

She reached up toward his grasping fingers. "Too… far away!"

"All right, just hold on!" Letting go of the rope, Ryan secured himself on the bow of the boat and was able to reach down a few more inches. Krysty pulled herself up, and was able to grab his hand—

Just as another mutie leaped from the boat and landed on the redhead, knocking her away from Ryan. He grabbed for her again, but she and the mutie fell away from the longboat and into the frothing water below.

Chapter Twenty-Five

Still trying to shove the mutie away, Krysty plunged into the blue-green water, hitting hard enough to knock the breath out of her.

Looking around in the bubble-filled chop created by the big ship's passing, she oriented herself and began swimming for the surface. However, when she was only a few feet away from it, she felt something catch her ankle and begin dragging her toward the hull.

Her lungs burning from the lack of oxygen, Krysty bent to free herself, but the coil of rope was looped tightly around her foot. She groped for the small dagger on her belt to cut herself free, but before she could, she was dragged through the water and through a dark hole into the hull of the ship itself.

By now she was starting to black out from the lack of oxygen and her exertions, but she still managed to pull her blade and start sawing at the cord as she was being hoisted into a pitch-black room. The hole beneath her closed, and another one on the side of the room opened, allowing light in as the water began pouring back into the ocean.

She panted, filling her lungs as the water continued draining out the grated exit. Now that she was inside, she heard and felt the thrum of some kind of generator at work. As the water around her receded, she took a moment to look around.

She stood in a rectangular room roughly six feet by ten. The side curved up and out, which made sense, since it was part of the hull. A small door with a wheel in the middle was on the opposite wall. The rest of the place was solid metal, including the ceiling.

As the last foot of water drained from the room, she waded to the door and tried turning the wheel, to no avail. Krysty sucked in one more breath before attempting to talk.

"J.B.? Jak? Anybody around?" she called out.

"Krysty? Is that you?" J.B.'s voice echoed from somewhere nearby.

"Yeah. Are you all right? Where are you?"

"Yeah, and I don't know," the Armorer answered. "Fell overboard and got dragged into the big boat. I'm in a small room, all metal. You?"

"Pretty much the same." Glancing down, she saw that the loop of rope or twine or whatever had dragged her in here was gone. That made her frown. She was pretty sure no one had been in here with her. "You see any sign of Jak?"

"Not yet," J.B. replied. "Think they're keeping us in separate rooms."

"You got a way out?"

"Not yet…but I haven't started looking, either."

"What do you think's going on?" Krysty asked.

"If I had to guess…seems there's some disagreement between the folks living up top and these poor bastards dwelling belowdecks. But we'll have to find out exactly what's going on."

As if they were being observed, the wheel in the door to Krysty's room suddenly spun. She backed away, drawing her blaster as she did.

The wheel came to a stop, and the door opened to

reveal a normal-looking, if very pale, woman on the other side. She was dressed in a hodgepodge of clothes, with ragged-hemmed pants from some kind of uniform held up with rope and a sleeveless top that looked to be hacked out of a large plastic bag. She was barefoot, and her dishwater-blond hair was cut severely short, practically buzzed to the scalp. She might have been thirty years old or fifty—it was hard to tell under the smudges of grease and dirt on her face. Her eyes were a clear, bright blue. Both of her hands were raised in front of her.

"One more step, and I shoot," Krysty said.

The woman slowly nodded. "I understand. I'm sorry that we had to bring you aboard that way. My name is Raina. What is yours?"

"Krysty Wroth."

The woman's calm demeanor caught the redhead off guard. J.B. had also fallen silent, but she had no doubt he was listening to every word they were saying. "Why did you nearly kill me and my friends?"

"We had no choice!" the woman said, making Krysty raise her blaster again. "Sorry. We simply couldn't let you all go above…we had to save as many of you as we could."

"Save us? Save us from what?" Krysty asked.

"It would be easier if I could show you," Raina said. "We really do not wish you any harm. In fact, we need your help. May I take you out of here so you can meet the others?"

Krysty frowned at that. "Do you have my other friends down here, as well?"

Raina shook her head. "No, we were only able to free three of you—the one with the lenses on his face and the white-haired boy. The others were taken above.

They are among the Topsiders now." Her face twisted with fear and, Krysty thought, more than a little anger.

"All right." Krysty aimed her blaster at the woman again. "Before we do anything, I want to see both of them. You will remain with me as our hostage while I talk with them. If we decide to meet with the rest of your group, then you will be released. If not, you will help us find a way to get to the rest of my friends and off this ship."

Her eyes still on Krysty, the woman leaned back into the dark hallway, as if listening to someone standing next to her. She shook her head once, then again. Then she stepped into the room, twisting away from an arm that tried to restrain her.

"We cannot promise that we can free your friends from the Topsiders, but I agree to the rest of your terms." She raised her voice to make sure it carried to the person outside. "I, Raina of the Navgators, am now your hostage, Krysty Wroth."

WITHOUT THINKING, RYAN jumped off the dangling boat into the water, nearly landing on the mutie he'd just injured. The mutie threw up an arm to defend itself, but Ryan ignored the creature and dived under the surface, searching for his lover. She was nowhere to be seen. Surfacing just long enough to gulp a quick breath, he dived again, but couldn't find any sign of her, or the others. It was as if they had completely vanished.

In a killing rage, Ryan shot to the surface and grabbed the mutie around the throat, pressing with all his strength. "Where is she? What have you done with her?"

"Ryan! Ryan! Ryan!" Mildred shouted almost in his ear. "Markson said the Downrunners probably grabbed her. She's inside the ship, most likely with J.B. and Jak! She's probably okay for now!"

He looked over to see their boat floating a few feet away. "Let that one go. He's of no use anyway," Chief Officer Markson said.

Ryan glanced back to see the head of the mutie in his hands lolling on its shoulders—he'd inadvertently strangled the creature to death.

"Come back aboard, Ryan," Mildred said, extending her hand. "The sharks will be here any moment."

Furious, wanting to tear open the ship with his bare hands until he found Krysty, Ryan took a breath and got hold of himself. Then he took Mildred's and Ricky's hands and allowed himself to be pulled aboard the long-boat.

As it began to rise into the air again, Ryan fixed the chief officer with his steeliest glare. "I'm going to do whatever I have to do to get her back. And not you or anyone on this bastard boat is going to stop me."

Instead of looking concerned or fearful, Markson just smiled. "Indeed. Then you will definitely wish to talk to the captain right away. It may be that you people are exactly whom we have been looking for."

"You're damn right I want to talk to the captain," Ryan said. "I want to see him the second we get up there."

"I will convey your request. However, the captain sees whom he wants when he wants," Markson replied.

Ryan pushed over to the chief officer until he was standing right in front of him. "Then you better make sure he wants to see me right away."

"As I said, I will pass along your request to him," Markson replied. "I can assure you that the young woman is not in any danger. She is too valuable to them."

"I don't like the sound of that," Mildred said. "Why is that, exactly?"

Markson cleared his throat. "Well, as I presume that she is a healthy woman in all respects, she would be invaluable to them as breeding stock."

Ryan didn't say anything at that, he just ground his teeth together.

"Jesus wept—it doesn't matter where we go, the women are always used like goddamn cattle!" Mildred exclaimed.

"We're here," Markson said. "Welcome to the *Ocean Queen*."

The boat had been lifted up to a jury-rigged framework that other crew members had been pulling the ropes through. As Ryan, Mildred, Ricky, and Doc got off the longboat, they took in their surroundings with wide eyes.

They had been brought up onto the middle front portion of the ship, which also appeared to be its gardens. Everything from ground vegetables to tall, tropical trees were growing here in large wooden boxes of dirt. More than a dozen white-uniformed men and women moved among them, tending to the various plants.

"My goodness," Doc said, staring at the profusion of flora with wonder in his eyes. "I have not seen the likes of this in ages. And is that…a breadfruit tree? And you have pineapple plants…and there's a banana tree, and a coconut tree.…"

Markson nodded. "You are correct, Dr. Tanner. You must be well-traveled indeed."

"What—oh, we get around," he replied before being elbowed in the ribs by Mildred. "But as impressive as this is, it cannot be enough to feed everyone on board."

"Correct again. This is only one of several gardens

we have. If you'd like, I would be happy to arrange a tour of them once you're settled."

"That would be capital, good sir," Doc said with a smile.

"Huh. Guess the punishment for talking too much doesn't extend to the higher officers," Mildred said quietly.

Only half paying attention to her, Ryan gave the garden a quick glance, instead looking around for the captain. To their left, several more decks rose into the air, in various states of disrepair. Some looked neat and clean, but others were rust-covered and filthy. One even looked as though an explosion or fire had burned it, as it was edged in black and the windows were gone. Above all of this was a row of large windows that ran from one end of the structure to the other. A man, also dressed all in white, including a hat, stood looking over everything.

"Is that the captain?" Ryan asked as he pointed up to the solitary figure.

"No. That is a relative of our benevolent savior Mr. De Kooning—the man who made all of this possible," Markson replied. "He holds a hereditary position of importance on the ship as the representative of his ancestor's ideals." As if realizing what he was saying to Ryan, Markson cleared this throat. "Anyway, I've sent a messenger to the captain, who will no doubt want to see you right away."

"I hope you're right," Ryan replied as he waited impatiently. "*You* better hope you're right."

WITH RAINA STAYING ahead of her, Krysty walked to the exit. "Have your people pull back from the hallway. I don't want any surprises when we step outside."

The woman nodded, then poked her head outside the

doorway. "Pull back—I mean it. No one is to approach us, or I will be dead!"

There was a beat of silence, then the sounds of at least one person moving away from the door. "Okay, now step out slowly," Krysty said. Raina did so, and she stepped out right behind her, looking up and down the corridor to ensure there was no ambush laid for her. The hallway was dim, with barely burning lights in glass cages mounted every few yards along the ceiling. The air here was hot, thick and stale, kind of like what she had breathed at Poseidon Base, but worse. "All right, we're going to J.B.—the one with glasses—next."

"All right, he's being held in the room next to yours," Raina replied. "I'm going to start walking there now."

"Right, but do it slowly," Krysty replied. The two women began walking down the dark, dank corridor.

"You're not reacting like I expected you to," Krysty said. "In fact, it seems like you do this a lot. I can't imagine that the people you pick up are too agreeable about the situation."

"It depends," Raina said. "When they've been on the ocean for weeks, and are close to starving to death or dying of thirst, they don't mind too much. The important thing is to prevent them from going to the Topsiders."

"How did you get such a shit job?" Krysty asked.

"Because I cannot bear children," she replied. "It was either this or join a door squad." She stopped in front of another wheel-operated door, locked shut with a heavy chain looped around it and a thick ring sticking out of the wall. "We're here."

"Open it."

Raina unlooped the chain and spun the wheel, then pushed the door open. J.B. regarded the two women through his spectacles, then lowered his Mini-Uzi. "Nice work, Krysty," he greeted her as he stepped into the hall.

"Thanks. Now let's go find Jak."

"He is being kept in a separate section," Raina said. "He was—difficult to contain."

Krysty and J.B. exchanged wry smiles. "No doubt," she said. "Just lead the way, and again, no tricks."

"I swear by De Kooning's honor, we do not mean any of you harm," Raina replied. "I'm telling you this so you are not alarmed when you see your friend."

"It's unlikely that we will be," J.B. replied, covering their backs with his submachine gun. More than once Krysty got the impression that they were being watched, but careful scans around didn't reveal anyone. If they were being observed, the people doing it were well hidden.

Raina led them deeper into the bowels of the ship before stopping at a corner. "He is being watched by two men. I don't know if they know what the situation is with us."

Krysty stepped up behind her and prodded her in the back with her blaster. "Then I guess you'd better inform them."

"All right. Just follow me." Raina turned the corner and began walking to the men. Krysty signaled to J.B. that if there was any trouble, she'd take the man on the far right. He nodded.

However, as they approached, the two men looked over and moved away from the door, their hands off their metal clubs. "The Chif sent word that you were coming with two Recovered, and that we are not to interfere," one said.

Raina nodded. "They wish to see their friend."

The second guard was already opening the door. "He is inside. I do not know if he's awake yet."

J.B. grunted. "Probably faking it."

The door swung open, and Krysty saw Jak with his arms spread-eagled, each wrist chained to the wall. His head hung low, his bright white hair a curtain obscuring his face.

"Even like that, he broke the jaw of one of our Recoverers," the first guard commented.

Krysty nodded. "Your man's lucky that's all that got broken. Jak? You awake?"

The head bobbed a bit, then rose. "'Bout time, Krysty."

"Cheerful as ever," J.B. said.

"Hang by wrists couple hours, see how like it," Jak shot back.

"All right, get him down," Krysty said.

The two guards hesitated. "Our orders regarding him were very specific."

Krysty put the muzzle of her blaster next to Raina's head. "Get him down or I put her down, right now."

Raina nodded. "I will ensure that no punishment comes to either of you." One of the guards scurried to comply.

"They're releasing you, Jak," Krysty said. "Don't hurt them."

"Not gonna," he replied. "Want weapons back."

Krysty looked at Raina, who looked at the second guard. He produced Jak's .357 Magnum blaster and several of his throwing knives. Rubbing his wrists, Jak walked to the entrance. He snatched them out of the guards' hands so fast the man stepped back in alarm. Jak shoved his blaster into his belt and made the knives disappear with twitches of his wrists and fingers. When that was done, he stared at the other two through ruby-red eyes. "What now? Where's others?"

"They're abovedecks. These people want to talk to us. They say they need our help," Krysty said. "I thought we'd hear what they have to say—we may need help to get Ryan and the others back."

Jak glanced at J.B. "What think?"

"I think I'm glad to be out of that room, that's what I think." J.B. blew out a breath as he pondered the situation. "Might as well see what they have to say."

"All right." Krysty nodded at Raina. "Now we go talk to your leader."

RYAN WAS ABOUT ready to pull his blaster and demand to see the captain when a young man dressed in a white shiftlike garment came running up to Chief Officer Markham and saluted.

"Sir, the captain wishes to invite all of the Recovered to dine with him at his table this evening. He will be sitting down at five bells."

About to retort, Ryan felt a gentle hand on his arm. He glanced down to see Doc's slender fingers resting there and turned to the old man in surprise.

"You always catch more flies with honey than with vinegar, my dear Ryan. I know you are concerned about dear Krysty. We all are. But she is not alone down there, and even if Chief Officer Markson is correct—" Doc held up a hand to forestall Ryan as the taller man opened his mouth to retort "—no matter how distasteful the thought is, what is more important is that she is safe for now. Let us meet with the captain and see what we can learn from him, and then we will figure out what to do next."

By the time the old man was finished speaking, both

Ryan and Mildred were staring at him. "Who are you, and what have you done with Doc?" she finally asked.

Doc flashed a sly grin as he tapped his temple. "I may look old…indeed, and at times certainly act like it, but these old gray cells can still spark off the occasional decent idea or two at times."

Ryan sighed, knowing what his answer was going to be. "All right, Doc, we'll play it your way for now."

He turned to Markson. "Let your captain know four will be joining him for dinner."

As the officer turned back to his messenger, Ryan grimaced. "I can hardly wait."

Chapter Twenty-Six

Raina led Krysty, J.B. and Jak deeper into the ship, toward the stern.

As they walked, Krysty noticed that the areas they passed through were older-looking and more jury-rigged, with odd bits of iron or framework holding things together. Rerouted piping ran everywhere, including across the floor, making some places a scramble to cross. What floor they could see was almost hidden under a layer of compacted dirt and grime, and the still, foul-smelling air was even hotter here.

Still damp from her accidental swim, Krysty soon found herself bathed in sweat. Her long, red hair had become a tight, damp mess in the humidity, tucked up at the base of her neck as if trying to hide.

"Krysty," J.B. said quietly, "I'm picking up residual radiation all throughout this area."

"Anything we need to worry about?" she asked.

"If there was, we'd already be heading back the way we came. But what kind of ship is this? No way it's military, but it runs on nuclear fuel? It doesn't make sense."

"Anything since landing Poseidon Base does?" Jak asked, making the other two look back at him in surprise. "What? Things crazier than usual, is all."

"Yeah. I'm definitely thinking that Ryan and the others got the better end of the deal," J.B. muttered as they walked.

Krysty was inclined to agree, although she didn't say anything.

At last, they rounded one final corner and found that the corridor ahead ended a few yards away in a massive steel door. Two more guards stood here, dressed in an odd mix of the same rag-tag clothes that Raina wore. Both of them also wore the headgear from what looked like a nuclear protection suit, but just the hood and face-plate, which seemed to be hacked out of the rest of a normal suit. The skin on their arms was pitted and scarred, and one had what appeared to be a large tumor growing out of his armpit. Each also held a crude, homemade firearm that they immediately leveled at the small group.

"Wait!" Raina held out her arms, as much to protect the newcomers from the guards as the other way around. "I'm Raina, from the Navgators. I am her—" she nodded at Krysty "—hostage. These Recovered are here to see the Chif Engner. Been sent for by him."

"We'll need to double-check with him before they can go in," the guard with the tumor said as he turned to the door. "Watch them all."

The second guard took a tighter grip on his cobbled-together blaster and regarded the small group with a suspicious expression on his face. After a minute, he relaxed a bit and sighed. "Haven't seen you around lately, Raina."

Her stoic expression didn't change. "Been busy." She nodded at the others. "Recoverers keeping me hopping lately."

"We just got them today. Talking about my invite to the waste dumping tomorrow. I sent you word, but you never said yes or no."

A quick look of sorrow flashed across her face, but it was quickly replaced by anger. "Don't need your pity,

Marek. Go find someone else to watch the dumping with. I'll be on duty."

"Oh, okay," Marek replied, looking at the floor. "I gotcha." He was spared any further embarrassment when the main door opened again and the first guard stepped out.

"Chif Engner says he'll see them now—but no blasters are allowed inside." The guard pointed at the corner of the hallway. "They can put them there for now and they'll get them back when they come out."

The three exchanged glances, each thinking the same thing—that taking any of these folks out with blades or bare hands probably wouldn't be all that difficult. J.B. went first, unslinging his shotgun and laying it down next to his cherished, trusty Uzi. Jak was about to go next, drawing his Magnum blaster, when Krysty, who still had her weapon trained on Raina, raised a hand.

"Hold up, Jak. If we all lay down our blasters, Raina is no longer my hostage," she said. "What guarantee do I have that we will be treated fairly?"

The first guard shrugged. "Chif's word is law here. If he said he'll talk with you all, then that's what'll happen. Don't get more plain than that."

Krysty hesitated, then turned to Jak. "Stay out here and keep an eye on her. J.B. and I will go inside and talk to this 'Chif.'"

Jak nodded, the muzzle of his blaster settling on Raina's midsection. Krysty nodded to J.B., and they headed toward the door.

"The Chif's room is to your right," the second guard said. "You speak to him through the speakerbox on the wall. We'll be listening from out here, as well, so don't think you can try anything."

Krysty glanced at Jak, who rolled his eyes and nodded. The albino teen could probably handle all three of them without breaking a sweat. "Go on," he said.

With Krysty leading the way, they entered a room that was the complete opposite of what they'd seen so far. It was a bright, antiseptic white, with a clean tiled floor and walls.

"What's the reading?" Krysty asked.

"About the same as before," the Armorer replied. "If they do have a nuke or nuke power, they keep it well shielded."

Another door was at the opposite end of the room, this one made of metal and glass. Krysty and J.B. could make out blurred, radioactive-suited shapes moving around behind it.

"Greetings, Recovered," a voice said to their right. They both turned that way, and there, sitting in front of them, was a warped, mutated being who had to be the Chif Engner.

Any hair the man once had was nearly gone, with only a few, wild strands plastered across his misshapen head. The right side of his skull bulged on the right side, but whether it contained brain matter or just layer upon layer of bone, they couldn't tell.

His face was no better. The left side was a complete, weeping ruin, with no semblance of features anymore, just an open sore. A large hole in his cheek showed two yellowed, rotting teeth. The remaining skin on his face and neck was ashen-gray and hung on him like a sack. He sat hunched over on a plain metal chair.

The rest of him was swathed in the patchwork quilt of several radioactive suits sewn together with shiny metal wire. He didn't even sit on the chair as much as he perched on it, looking as though he might float out of it at any moment. He shifted his position, exposing a large hump rising out of his back over his left shoulder.

"Welcome, Recovered." The man's voice was breathy and sibilant. "I was given to understand that there would be three of you."

"Our third friend is outside, watching over Raina, who allowed herself to become my hostage in order to convince us to see you," Krysty replied. "My friend is J. B. Dix, and my name is Krysty Wroth."

The mutated man nodded. "And you already know I am the Chif Engner. The three of you have been Recovered from the dangerous sea as well as the Topsiders, who would wish to convert and pervert you to their own dark goals. De Kooning's grace has seen fit to bless us with your arrival in our hour of need."

"That remains to be seen," J.B. said. "We need to know a few things first. Like what exactly is going on around here?"

"If you wish, I would be happy to share with you our story, so that you may be more familiar with our ways. It may take a bit of time, however."

Krysty and J.B. exchanged a glance. "We seem to have a bit right now, so please, go ahead."

"Very well. It all began more than a century ago."

RYAN PACED BACK and forth in the two-bedroom stateroom they'd been given, earning concerned looks from Mildred and Ricky, and a bemused look from Doc. He'd cleaned himself up after his dip in the ocean, but once that was done, there was nothing else to do but wait.

"You're going to wear a hole in the floor doing that until we see the captain," Mildred said.

"I can't help it," Ryan replied as he strode across the

worn, threadbare carpet. "Besides, it's better than the alternative."

Mildred regarded him through slitted eyes. "Do I even want to know what that might be?"

"Open this door and start chilling every one of these freaks until someone tells me where Krysty is."

"That would be rather a rude thank-you to our saviors, Ryan," Doc said.

"I don't give two shits about any of these people!" the one-eyed man snarled. "All of them can go on sailing on this bastard thing for the next hundred years for all I care. My first priority is getting Krysty back, and then getting all of us the hell to dry land."

Doc rose from the bed where he'd been sitting. "While I heartily agree with you regarding both of those most worthy goals, may I remind you that at the moment we still need their help? If there is truly any kind of a civil war between these two groups, to attempt to go below and try to find our dear friends would most likely only result in our swift deaths, as we would be entering a place where our opponents would hold all of the advantages, even against one as formidable as yourself."

"Again—and I don't know how or why—Doc has a point," Mildred said.

Doc bowed to her. "Your confidence in me apparently knows no bounds, my dear lady."

"Right now, I'm thinking of you as more of a broken clock, Doc," Mildred replied. "Lately you've been right at least twice a day."

"Accepted," the old man said before turning back to Ryan. "We need to know more about the lay of the land, so to speak, before we go charging off on the noble, gallant quest to save Krysty, the good John Barrymore and young Jak. The opportunity to do that lies within our grasp, we need only to be sensible enough to reach out and take it."

Ryan stopped in the middle of the stateroom and took a deep breath. "You've been awfully quiet during all this, Ricky. What's your take on it?"

The teenager turned from where he had been staring out the window that gave an incredible view of the setting sun over the ocean. "From what I've seen of all three of them, they can handle just about anything that comes their way. I agree with Doc—our best hope right now is to find out as much as we can about this place, so in case we do get a chance to go after them, we know what we're doing, where we're going and what we have to deal with."

Ryan digested all of that and nodded. "You're both right. It just pisses me right off that we're stuck in here, waiting on this bastard captain—" A knock sounded on the door, and Ryan walked over and opened it. "Yes?"

A junior officer stood in the corridor. "The captain is ready to dine, lady and gentlemen. If you will all accompany me." He turned on his heel and began walking down the corridor.

"Weapons?" Ricky asked as he crossed the room.

"Handblasters only," Ryan replied. "Might not take too kindly to carrying longblasters at the dinner table."

The young man led them through a dizzying maze of corridors that all looked alike, more or less. They came to a stairway and ascended three flights to come out in a small alcove. One of the sailors from the longboat— Elial—stood flanked by two secmen. The sailor's hands were in manacles. He watched them with sad eyes as they walked past.

Voices could be heard in the next room as the young man held the door open for them. Ryan and the other companions entered a room that had been scrupulously maintained, from the carpet to the furniture to the tableware. There was white linen, polished wooden chairs, crystal wineglasses, and matching, if worn, silverware. A large arrangement of fresh, tropical flowers sat in the middle of the table, with eight place settings arrayed around it.

Four other people stood in the room—three whiteshirted men gathered around another man who was holding court. As the companions entered, the officers all laughed at something the man in the middle said.

The steward cleared his throat. "Captain, your dinner guests have arrived."

The man in the middle turned to them. "Good evening, and welcome to the *Ocean Queen!* I am Captain Selius Frost. You have already met Chief Officer Markson—" he nodded at the redhead "—and allow me to introduce Staff Captain Quercis Lind, as well as our Chief Security Officer Aturk Coller."

The captain was trim and fair-skinned, with light brown hair and dark brown eyes. Like Markson, he had a beard, except his was short and neatly trimmed. He wore what Ryan assumed was an actual captain's shirt that had been carefully maintained for who knew how long.

Lind's ancestors must have hailed from somewhere far north. Although his skin was deeply tanned, he had light blue eyes and blond, almost white hair. His beard was long and split into three large braids that hung halfway down his chest. The clean-shaven sec chief, on the other hand, was a huge fireplug of a man, with skin so black it almost had a blue hue in the waning sunlight.

Ryan handled the introductions for his people as the steward went around the room lighting the wicks of several old-style glass lamps. "Is Mr. De Kooning from the bridge going to be joining us as well?"

His question seemed to take the officers off guard, although the captain recovered first. "Mr. De Kooning prefers to dine alone. He is very elderly and nowadays prefers to remain above all of the activity aboard the ship, in peace and quiet in his private quarters."

Frost's attention was caught by Markson. "Before we get started, sir, there is the issue of Ensign Elial's dereliction of duty on the longboat. He awaits you outside."

Frost nodded. "Bring him in."

The steward walked to the door, and Elial and his guards walked in a few moments later.

"Ensign Elial, you are charged with dereliction of duty while carrying out your duties. How do you plead?"

"I plead guilty, Captain, and cry for De Kooning's pardon, sir."

"Chief Officer Markson, will you summarize the events of earlier this afternoon?"

Markson did so, noting that Elial had performed the rest of his duties, including fending off the Downrunners so they could get onto the main deck safely. A look of displeasure crossed the chief officer's face. "Truth be told, sir, it was a minor infraction, but I am compelled to bring it to you for your judgment."

"Thank you, Chief Officer." Frost walked over to Elial. "Do you have anything to say in your defense, Ensign?"

Elial met his captain's gaze as he replied, "It was a momentary lapse, sir, and it will never happen again."

"Well said." The captain began walking around his subordinate. "Your superior officer speaks highly of you, which I am taking into account. However, you did knowingly speak of the ship to a Recovered before we had ascertained their true bearing." He looked around the room. "Everyone is well aware of the dangers of doing that. I cannot have any exceptions to this rule."

Elial looked absolutely terrified, but still managed to find his voice. "Y-yes, Captain."

"I find you guilty of this crime, and sentence you to be keelhauled across the ship's forward hull once. If De Kooning's grace is with you, and you survive, your wounds will be tended to, and you will rejoin your fellow sailors in time. Let the record show that I have passed down my judgment and punishment. The sentence shall be carried out at dawn tomorrow, and so shall it be noted in the log."

His shoulders slumping in defeat, Elial was led away.

"Ryan, you can't let them do this to him!" Mildred whispered. "You saw what that hull looked like! Those barnacles will slice him to ribbons!"

"It isn't our battle to fight," he replied. "Ricky didn't know there'd be blowback, and that isn't his fault. But you know we don't get between a ville's laws and its people carrying them out. It's a sure way to end up next on the punishment list."

"Damn barbaric, is what it is," Mildred said more loudly than necessary.

"I am sorry that you had to witness that, but examples have to be made sometimes. Fortunately, the forward hull isn't that difficult to navigate. A good sailor like Elial should be able to get by with only a few cuts."

"How very fortunate for him," Mildred said through gritted teeth.

"It is. If his infraction had been more severe, I may have had him keelhauled the entire length of the ship. It has only happened in three instances during my time as captain, and none of them survived. They are with De Kooning now."

"With De Kooning now," the other three officers repeated.

Frost waved at the table. "Shall we eat?"

Ryan kept his eye on Mildred, who still glowered at the captain as she pulled out her chair. But she held her tongue while another server filled their goblets with their choice of fresh-squeezed fruit juices.

"Fresh pineapple juice…I never thought I would taste this again," Doc said after draining his entire glass and holding it out for a refill. Ryan went for papaya juice, a sweet, pink-purple liquid that he ended up sipping rather than drinking. Mildred and Ricky both opted for mango.

The first course was served: a dense, white fish Frost called mah-mah, wrapped in seaweed and steamed over coals, with several fruit compotes and salsas for flavor. The fish itself was flaky and relatively flavorless, so Ryan sampled some of the sauces with it. Like the juice, he found them overly sweet and stuck to just the fish. Accompaniments consisted of several seaweed dishes along with more fresh fruit, both raw and grilled.

"My friends and I have traveled quite a ways, but we've never seen a ship as incredible as this one," Ryan said between bites. "How did all of this come about?"

"That is a story I never grow tired of telling," Frost replied. "I have the honor of being the seventh captain of the *Ocean Queen,* but it, and all aboard, owe their existence to a very special man."

"This De Kooning fellow, I bet," Mildred said, before draining her glass.

"You are correct," Frost said. "Let us enjoy our meal, if you please, and I will fill you in at the end."

The next course was thick shark steaks, also grilled.

Ryan found this much more palatable. It was followed by grilled abalone, which was succulent and flavorful. Candy made from dried pineapple, mango and papaya completed the menu.

Afterward, a steward came around and offered what looked like two different types of cigars to everyone. All of the officers except for the captain indulged. Catching a whiff of what smelled like a particularly pungent strain of maryjane as the case was offered to his side of the table, Ryan signaled to the rest of his people to not partake.

Doc, however, either didn't listen or didn't seem to care, as he selected a cigar and held it to the flame of the nearest oil lamp as he puffed it to life. Fortunately, when he exhaled, Ryan could smell that it was an ordinary cigar.

"Now, you had asked about the beginnings of the *Ocean Queen,*" Frost said to Ryan. "As I had mentioned, more than one hundred years ago, before the Great Waves, a man named Pietr de Kooning—"

"Blessed is his name," the other three officers intoned.

Frost nodded at their words. "He realized that, sooner or later, humankind was going to destroy itself. It was only a matter of time. Possessing vast wealth, he set about building a veritable ark for those select few who would qualify to board and leave the squabbling nations on land behind, existing in a sovereign state on the seven seas."

"He had access to nuclear technology?" Doc asked between puffs, unmindful of the surprised looks of the officers. "You need not look so shocked, gentlemen. It would be the only way to keep this ship powered for as long as it has."

Noticing Markson watching the old man intently, Ryan thought about giving him a kick under the table to keep him quiet, but the damage had already been done.

Frost cleared his throat. "You are correct, Dr. Tanner. De Kooning had connections in the government, and was able to purchase the plans for a small breeder nuclear reactor that he had installed in the *Ocean Queen*. Due to its unique properties, it is self-sufficient, allowing us to roam the seas at will. Our needs are few enough otherwise. We must always secure enough food, which the sea provides in plenty, and trade for whatever else we need with the islands we sail past."

"Wait a minute," Mildred said as she popped a chunk of pineapple into her mouth, chewed and swallowed. "Nothing against you folks, however, you don't seem to be the descendants of the best and brightest De Kooning had in mind when he built this floating palace."

"Alas, you are also correct," Frost replied. "The ship was being outfitted at the island of Hawaii, and De Kooning was in the process of selecting his chosen people when the Great Waves were set into motion. With civilization as they knew it destroyed, our ancestors chose to set out on their own to construct our society while upholding as many of his tenets as possible. In the intervening decades, the ship has continued on this course, with the descendants of the original crew and passengers working together to provide for all and ensure that De Kooning's vision is kept alive."

"De Kooning's vision," the other three men repeated solemnly.

Doc leaned back in his chair and blew a smoke ring into the air. "Until recently, I presume?"

The ship's officers all exchanged glances, then Frost answered him. "Yes. Lately those who work in the necessary departments belowdecks have been complaining that we, the ship's officers and the rest who work above, have not been allowing them enough of a say in how the ship operates. They claim that we run the *Ocean Queen* according to our own whims, without care as to their opinions or beliefs. They even claim that we are trying to keep them down there, and not allow any to rise to positions abovedecks."

"Are they correct?" Mildred asked. Now Ryan glanced at her, wondering if she was pushing too far. However, since he was interested in the captain's answer, he remained silent.

Frost smiled. "There must be order in every society. Without that, there is only chaos. The structure laid down by De Kooning all those decades ago has served us well, and there is no reason to change it now."

"Are you saying that De Kooning himself advocated the segregation of the people aboard this vessel?" Doc asked.

"I wouldn't put it in quite such concrete terms. One of his rules that we have cleaved to is, 'Everyone should know their place.'"

Doc nodded. "Of course. And all animals are equal, but some animals are more equal than others."

Frost shook his head. "We are not referring to anyone as animals, Doctor. The simple matter is that the underdecks are vital to the operation of the *Ocean Queen,* and require specialized knowledge and training. The best people to pass along that knowledge and training are the ones who have learned and done it already. The same can be said for the abovedecks positions. Unfortunately, those belowdecks do not share our viewpoint on this matter. They have been arguing for a more equal say in matters of the ship's administration, including adding Downrunners to positions abovedecks, and Topsiders to those belowdecks. To emphasize their demands, recently they denied us access to the ship's power room, as well as other parts below. They have cut off power to entire sections of the ship—" he waved at the lamps around them "—hence our reliance on alternate forms of energy. While we control the superstructure of the boat, including the gardens, and the upper decks, they run the entire lower half of the ship."

"Surely you have attempted to negotiate with them?" Mildred asked.

"Of course—we are not savages," Frost replied. "However, they have been resistant from the very beginning, and have been more and more belligerent as time has gone by."

"Indeed," Doc commented. "One wonders when they are going to realize that, with control of both the ship's main power as well as access to the rudder, they could force everyone abovedecks to bend to their will, otherwise they would simply interrupt the power to the rest of the ship, or hijack the steering and send it wherever they wish."

Now Frost and his senior officers all shared dark looks. "Yes, Dr. Tanner, that thought had occurred to us, as well," Markson said.

"I should hope so," Doc replied, appearing completely at ease around these men for some strange reason. "And should you manage to remove these various thorns in your side, these snowballs, if you will, how will you run the area belowdecks?"

"Be assured we are not advocating the wholesale slaughter of those who handle everything down there," Frost said. "Just removing those instigators that are creating this situation—mainly, the Chif Engner and those directly below him in the chain of command. Once they are gone, others who are more…pliable can be promoted to those ranks."

"So, you wish us to do what exactly?" Ryan asked, more than tired of beating around the bush with these people.

"Chief Officer Markson let me know that three of your party have been captured by the Downrunners while coming aboard. I would imagine that you wish to recover them," Frost said.

"As soon as possible," Ryan replied.

Frost nodded. "Of course. Were they my people, I would want to do the same. We are not a violent people, Mr. Cawdor—"

"Those sharpened oars indicate differently," Ryan opined.

The captain's eyebrows narrowed. "That is strictly for self-defense. When they began attacking our long-boats, we had to come up with some way to protect the crew as well as those whom they rescued. There was an unfortunate incident in which they capsized a boat into waters that were already laced with blood. Every sailor died before we could mount a rescue. Since then, we have taken all necessary precautions to safeguard ourselves and those who come aboard."

"Except when you don't," Mildred said, making heads turn to her. Coller even leaned forward as if he was going to rise from his chair, but stopped when Frost shook his head. "Hey, I'm just calling it like I see it. As I recall, three of our people are being held hostage below, right?"

"No matter how thorough our preparations are, there are always accidents," Markson said.

"Yes, and on behalf of myself and my crew, you have our deepest apologies. It was never our intent to have any of you come to harm." Frost looked at each of them in turn. "As I said, while we are not a violent people, we are faced with a situation that seems to require it. Pardon my bluntness, but you and your group seem used to that sort of life."

"Yes, that would be our first reaction to any situation," Mildred said dryly.

Frost continued as if he hadn't heard her. "And since you are already wishing to go below in search of your missing people, if you could also locate and remove the ringleaders of this revolution, we would be most grateful."

"What's in it for us?" Ryan asked.

His question was ignored.

"We can provide you with detailed plans of the ship, including the various changes that have been made over the past decades," Staff Captain Lind said. "That includes everything we know about the Downrunners' population and defenses."

"Also, we have identified an access point that will guarantee you the element of surprise when you move in," Sec Chief Coller said.

"What makes you think it isn't compromised already?" Ryan asked with a frown.

"We've monitored it ever since this unpleasantness began," Markson said. "Even sent a couple of scouting teams down below in the event we were forced to launch our own mission. They haven't found it, I guarantee you that."

Ryan just grunted in reply. The guarantee of a baron's underling often wasn't worth the air used to say it.

"Finally, we would be honored to offer you and your people a place aboard the *Ocean Queen*," Frost said. "We would have you join us and find appropriate positions for everyone. However, if you do not wish to join us, we would be just as happy to outfit you with supplies and drop you off wherever you wish—as long as it's within sailing distance, of course." The other officers chuckled at his joke.

Ryan turned the grimace on his face into a small, wry smile. "I'll want to discuss this with my people first, before we agree to anything."

"Of course," Frost replied with the air of a man who already knew what the answer was going to be. "Take all the time you need."

"Oh, I will." At that moment, Ryan decided that he didn't like the captain of the *Ocean Queen* very much at all.

Chapter Twenty-Seven

"Of late, the captain and his officers have been limiting us more and more, preventing us from seeing or even speaking with those above, keeping us confined belowdecks, not allowing us to engage in discussions about how the ship is to be run and generally doing everything they can to keep us as second-class citizens. We are the ones risking our lives—giving our lives—to make sure that this vessel has the power it needs, and they strut around on the upper decks lording it over us as if we were nothing more than slaves to jump when they command!"

Over the past half hour, Krysty and J.B. had listened to the Chif Engner's story.

"Due to our being trapped down here, for lack of a better word, we are forced to venture out and attempt to add new blood to our numbers whenever the ship is close to an island or, as in your case, new Recovered are brought on board," he continued. "That is why we have modified the hull like we did. If we did not, they would simply allow us to die from attrition."

"But you control the power source for the ship," Krysty said. "Surely that must give you some kind of bargaining leverage?"

What was left of the rad-blasted human's face assumed a wretched semblance of a smile. He had informed them that his position was an honored one that all of the "engners," as they were called, aspired to achieve, even though it meant an early, horrible death. "You'd think so, wouldn't you? And yet they seem determined to eradicate us from the ship completely."

"Wait a minute, that doesn't make sense," J.B. said. "If somehow they do manage to get rid of all of you, who's going to run the nuke reactor and make sure the other systems down here are still operating?"

The Chif Engner shook his head. "In their zeal to wipe us out, I do not know if any of them have even considered that. I truly believe that they have gone mad."

"So, how do we figure into all of this?" Krysty asked.

"We have been forced to take some of the Recovered that the Topsiders have brought on board for their own desires. Typically, you are brought into our clans, and trained in areas where we are lacking. However, given your abilities, and the fact that you have others that you wish to find abovedecks, we would set you free if first you could find a way to remove or destroy Captain Frost and his officers. Then, we could work with the rest of the men and women up there and return to De Kooning's vision of a ship where everyone is equal and all of us work toward the same goals—life and liberty."

"Sounds like a tall order," J.B. said. "From what I've seen so far, they've got numbers on their side."

"Perhaps, but we have the run of the ship, both belowdecks and through the other systems. We can get you close enough to free your companions and then kill the captain and his officers before the others can do anything about it. Once they are gone, I believe that the others would be more receptive to negotiating with us."

"It would be better if we could see the rest of our group first before making any definite plans," Krysty said. "Is there any way you can get a message to them?"

The Chif Engner shook his head. "It is too risky. If it were to be discovered, we would risk losing everything we've been planning for."

"I want to discuss your offer with my friends in private," Krysty said. "Afterward, we will give you our decision."

"Very well, return to your friend and think about our offer. Your weapons will be returned to you, of course. We are not your enemies. As a token of goodwill, I would ask that you release Raina from her hostage-bond. She can take you somewhere where you can talk in private."

"Done," Krysty replied as she turned and headed for the door with J.B. right beside her.

In the corridor, Krysty told Jak to lower his blaster. "Raina is no longer our hostage."

Raina nodded. "Thank you, Krysty."

"You probably heard our conversation with your Chif Engner," Krysty said. "We'd like a place for the three of us to discuss his proposal in private."

"Of course," the blonde woman replied. "Would you like something to eat, as well? You must be hungry after everything you've gone through."

"Yes, thank you," Krysty said.

"Let's get you settled, and I'll arrange for food to be brought," Raina said as she began leading them through the ship again. This time, however, she showed them to a sparse but clean and comfortable room with two pairs of bunks against the walls.

"Wonder what got eat here," Jak said once she was gone and they were sure no one was listening in. "Will be dirty like rest place?"

"If they're as adept at fishing out of those holes in the hull as they were at catching us, then I'd wager more seafood is on the menu," J.B. said. "Cooking it, however, may be another story."

"That's all well and good, but right now we have to figure out what we're doing," Krysty said. "If the situation is as the Engner said, then I have no doubt that the captain's making the exact same offer to Ryan and the others as the Engner made to us."

"So, what doing?" Jak asked.

"Who's to say who's right and who's wrong in this situation?" J.B. glanced over his shoulder, double-checking that no one was eavesdropping on their conversation. "I say if these people want to destroy each other, let them— we don't need to be involved. We agree to go along with their plan. Then we get up to the top decks, find the others, and get off this crazy boat."

"Best idea since getting here," Jak said as they heard a knock on the door. Krysty opened it to reveal Raina, along with another Downrunner, pushing mechanic's carts that had been pressed into service as makeshift food carts, and covered with white cloths. Both were piled high with plates of food—grilled fish and seafood.

"We've brought dinner," Raina announced as she pushed a cart into the room. "I hope you are comfortable here?"

"Yes. We've been discussing your Chif Engner's request for a while now," Krysty replied. "Although we will need to rest and some time to plan, I think we'll be able to help you."

Raina smiled. "That's wonderful news! Please, eat and rest while I go tell the Engner. When you're finished, we can begin planning to get our freedom back—with your assistance, of course!" She whirled and left them to their meal.

Krysty waited until she couldn't hear Raina's footsteps anymore. "Shouldn't one of us try to get out of here and see if we can find the others?"

J.B. considered the notion then shook his head. "I don't see the point in showing our hand like that, 'specially if they're going to let us go up tomorrow. I wouldn't mind letting them know we're safe, but I'm pretty sure Ryan already knows that."

"Right." Krysty picked up a large shrimp that had been boiled in its shell and began to peel it. "I can't believe I'm saying this, but I'm actually getting sick of seafood."

J.B. and Jak had also walked over to the cart, and both were selecting plates and utensils from the second one to create their dinners. "Grew up eating this— always good," Jak said as he scooped several bonito steaks onto his plate.

"Never got much of this back home. Closest I ever got to seafood was Rocky Mountain oysters," J.B. said as he piled huge crab claws and a thick swordfish steak onto his plate.

Krysty glanced at him sideways. "I'm not sure I want to know what that is."

"I'm surprised you didn't have them in Harmony. All they are is fried bull's testicles," J.B. said with a grin. "Delicious when pan-fried in butter."

His plate almost overflowing, Jak stared at both of them. "If say so."

AFTER DINNER, RYAN and his companions walked back to their stateroom in silence. Only when they were inside did Mildred flop onto the bed and let out a low whistle. "I haven't seen that much crazy gathered in one room in a long time."

"Ace on the line with that, Mildred. There's so much

weird around here, I don't know where to start," Ryan said. "As I see it, we only have two priorities now— getting Krysty, J.B., and Jak back, and getting the hell out of here. I'd rather take my chances in the pod on the ocean than among these crazies."

"What about pulling a takeover of our own?" Mildred asked. "That way we'd at least remove the nuts up top, and work out some kind of truce between the rest of the Topsiders and Downrunners."

Ryan shook his head. "No, thank you. Who's to say the rest aren't as bug-nuts crazy as their leaders? Trader used to say, 'Get between two fighting bears, get mauled twice as bad.' This is no place for us. I say we leave all of them to their own insanity."

Doc nodded. "I must agree with Ryan, this place is rife with paranoia and strife that we do not need to become involved in any more than necessary."

"Right—so how do we do that?" Ricky asked.

"Best bet would be to take these gentlemen—and I use that term most loosely—up on their offer, find Krysty, John Barrymore and young Jak within the bowels of this ship, and then commandeer a longboat or take our redoubtable pod and cast off again, allowing us to be once again carried along by the tides of fortune and chance," Doc said.

Mildred turned to Ryan. "Might as well get some rest—nothing's going to happen until morning, anyway."

"Yeah." He eyed the door speculatively. "I just want to know they're all right, that's all." He glanced at the others. Doc was curled up on one half of the large bed, with Mildred on the other side. Ricky had claimed the faded and sagging couch, and was already asleep. "Think I'll stretch my legs a bit before turning in."

"Okay…don't expect any of us to let you back in," Mildred murmured between yawns.

"Thanks, but I'll manage." Armed with his blaster and panga, Ryan slipped out of the stateroom. He looked up and down the deserted corridor, unsure of which way to go. Spotting a map at the end of the hall, he headed to it and examined the faded illustration, marking two specific points on the ship that he wanted to see.

Walking to the other end of the corridor, he found the stairway right where the map had said it would be and started descending. He'd gone down three flights when he ran into a huge barrier blocking the rest of the way down. Plates of welded steel completely covered the stairwell leading down into the ship proper. In the center, a small hatch was bolted shut.

It was also guarded by a pair of ensigns armed with clubs that looked to have been fashioned from broken oars. The two men regarded him as he approached.

"Hey, you're one of the Recovered we brought in today, aren't you?" the guard on the left, a fresh-faced youth, asked.

"Yeah. What's all this?" Ryan asked.

"Sir, this area is off-limits to Recovered. You really shouldn't be here," said the second guard, an older man with a scraggly beard that hung down to his breastbone.

"You boys have nothing to worry about from me, I'm just out trying to get the lay of the land—er, ship, is all," Ryan replied. "Is this one of the access points to the Downrunners?"

The first guard began to nod before the second one cleared his throat loudly. "You want what's gonna happen t'Elial to happen t'you, too?" he asked.

"It's all right," Ryan said. "I've spoke to the captain about your little problem here. And come on—the hatch is here, and can only be opened on the outside. It doesn't take a bright brain to figure out that you're keeping someone—or someones—locked in there."

The two guards exchanged glances. "That may be true, however, this area is still off-limits," the older one said. "We have to ask you to leave."

"All right, all right, I'm going." Ryan headed back up the stairwell. But when he came to the landing for his floor, he kept climbing to the top.

The stairs ended in a simple, plain corridor that stretched a few yards toward the front of the ship. No one was guarding the single door at the end of the passageway, which Ryan found strange, particularly given the existing threat to the abovedecks crew.

I would have thought they'd protect the descendant of their ancestor better, he thought as he slipped up to the door and peered through its window into the room beyond.

It was dark inside, but Ryan could make out De Kooning silhouetted against the moonlit sky. He tried the door, which was locked but loose. The man at the window apparently didn't hear him, as he didn't turn from his survey of the front of the ship.

Drawing his blade, Ryan slipped the tip of the narrow knife between the door and the jamb until he felt it give way. He slowly pushed the door open, watching for any reaction from the man on the other side. He still didn't move.

Well, they never said how old he was…mebbe he's deaf as a stone, Ryan thought. When the space was wide enough, Ryan slipped inside, heading right for the figure standing at the window.

"Hey, De Kooning…" he said when he was a step away. But the man still didn't turn or acknowledge his existence in any way. A chill growing in his gut, Ryan reached out to touch the man—and wasn't too surprised when his fingers contacted brittle skin and bone. As Ryan came around to stand next to the man, the moon came out from behind a cloud and illuminated the window-fronted room—and the body inside it.

The last descendant of the De Kooning line was nothing more than a desiccated, leathery husk. Under his dusty, white cap, the corpse's shrunken jaw dangled, its white teeth shining in the moonlight. Ryan glanced down to see that he had been wired in place, standing an eternal watch on the bridge to look over his people…forever.

As he crept back over to the door, Ryan wondered how that had come about. One chilling thought ran through his mind: sure hope he was already dead before they did that…

Chapter Twenty-Eight

Ryan went back to the stateroom, where he found everyone fast asleep. He locked the door, which was about as secure as De Kooning's had been, strode into the second bedroom, lay down on the short but wide bed with his combat boots hanging off the end, and instantly fell asleep.

He awoke at first light, and yawned and stretched while checking out the view from his window, which he had to admit was pretty amazing. The blue-green ocean stretched to the horizon, nothing but clear, calm water all around them. He'd gotten used to the thrum of the cruise ship's systems reverberating throughout just about everything, and was also accustomed to the steady, solid feel of the ship underfoot.

The morning had dawned clear and bright, but there was a series of huge, bright orange-and-gray storm clouds off to the west that didn't bode well for that afternoon. Ryan walked into the other room to see the others awakening, as well.

"More fruit and fish for breakfast, I suppose," Doc said around a yawn. "By the Three Kennedys, it will be good to reach dry land again and sink my teeth into some meat that's got some substance to it!"

"Keep your voice down, Doc," Ryan said. "We're playing the part of the Good Samaritans who're going to help out the captain and his crew with their little problem, remember?"

The old man rubbed his eyes and blinked at Ryan. "Yes, yes, stick to the story, I know the drill. Rest assured, I shall not be saying much this morning. The blasted bed was most uncomfortable."

"Want to know something even stranger about this boat that I discovered last night?" Ryan walked to the door and peeked out to make sure no one was walking by. He was pretty sure the locals wouldn't be thrilled about his paying their mummified figurehead an unannounced visit. "Gather 'round."

In a low voice, he told the others about both the guarded barriers to the lower decks, as well as about the mummified body of De Kooning up on the top deck.

When he was done, all Mildred did was shake her head. "Unbelievable. Just when I think it couldn't possibly get any weirder, they go ahead and pull it off."

"Do you think the belowdecks people are the ones being truly oppressed?" Ricky asked. "Isn't it possible that those above are prisoners of Frost and his people, as well?"

"Those barriers to the decks certainly seemed to prove it's top versus bottom here," Ryan replied. "And the guards weren't shitting their pants at seeing me walk around, so they're pretty comfortable. We'll know more once we meet with Frost and his men and take a look at their plans. Now let's see about getting food before we start planning the mission into the lower decks," Ryan said. "Don't know about you all, but I'm starving."

Despite his earlier comment, Doc perked up at the mention of breakfast. "It is my hope to see some recipes using that breadfruit tree they have on the forward deck."

"Yeah, let's all get a good meal in our bellies before descending into God knows where," Mildred said.

"Not too eager to get on with this, are you?" Ryan asked as he walked to the door.

"Don't get me wrong, I want John back safe and sound, same as you want Krysty and the others," she replied. "I'm just getting tired of dancing to other people's—or computer's—tunes, that's all."

"I hear you, and it won't be long until we're changing that tune—" Ryan replied as he opened the door only to find Chief Officer Markson on the other side, his right hand raised as if he was about to knock.

"Hope I'm not interrupting anything?"

"Not at all. We were just coming down to see about breakfast," Ryan quickly replied.

Markson smiled. "Then my timing is perfect. The captain sent me up to invite you to join him at his table on deck. On days such as this we break our fast outdoors, as the Lord and De Kooning intended. We are also administering Elial's punishment this morning, and thought you might want seats with a good vantage point."

"That's right kind of you. We'll be right out," Ryan said, closing the door before Mildred could protest again. "All right, remember—stick to the plan, nod and smile, and we'll all get through this in one piece."

Mildred followed him out of the room, with Doc and Ricky bringing up the rear. "I certainly hope so."

They followed the chief officer down to the main deck, where several rows of tables covered with white cloths had been set out. White-shirted ensigns were busy placing trays of cut fruit and other dishes in a buffet line. On a raised dais at the head of the area, with his back to the towering white wall of the ship, the captain sat at a table with the same number of place settings as the night before.

"Welcome, friends! So glad you could join us! Please, join me at my table, I insist."

"Thank you, Captain." Ryan walked up the small steps to the dais and grabbed the farthest chair on the other side of the table. "Putting on quite a spread."

"When the sky is fair and the winds are calm, we would be foolish not to take advantage of it, yes?" Frost replied. "We have the usual juices, as well as some coconut water, which some of you may find more refreshing."

The rest of the group sat and selected their drinks. Ryan could tell Frost was very eager to find out whether they were going to assist in the struggle against the Downrunners, but was managing to restrain himself until the right opportunity arose to discuss it. For his part, Ryan was going to draw it out as long as possible. This wasn't the right place to discuss it anyway, he realized, as there was no telling whether everyone around was truly loyal to the Topsiders. If he'd been leading one of these sides, the very first thing he would have done was try to insert a spy into the enemy's camp.

A small commotion attracted everyone's attention away from the meal. Elial, escorted by two guards, his hands bound in front of him, was brought out and seated at a table near the edge of the deck.

"Very kind of you to allow him to eat before you toss him overboard," Mildred said.

"De Kooning said that every man—even one who is to be punished—should not be made to do so on an empty stomach," Frost replied.

"Most kind of him, too," she said, ignoring Ryan's warning glare.

The rest of the officers joined them on the dais, with Coller looking particularly haggard.

"Rough night?" Ryan asked.

"Spent most of it prepping the plans for you folks, as well as trying to pinpoint the likeliest places your people might be held," the huge secman replied as he grabbed a glass and motioned for coconut water. "It's a big ship, with lots of hiding places."

"Well, we may have some ideas about that, as well," Ryan said.

Frost leaned forward. "So, you've agreed to our request?"

"I didn't say that—just mentioned that I know where I'd keep prisoners on a ship like this, that's all." Ryan had to admit that he got a certain amount of pleasure watching the captain swallow the angry retort that sprang to his lips. Keeping his expression impassive, Ryan took a large spoonful of a white, porridge-like substance and glopped it onto his plate. "What's this?"

"Cooked breadfruit mash mixed with coconut water and baked in a banana leaf," Frost replied. "It's our staple breakfast item, along with fruit, of course. If anyone would like something with a bit more kick, we also serve a fermented kind, too."

"I think I'll try some of that," Mildred said, watching Ryan as if daring him to stop her. He didn't, although he carefully watched how much she put onto her plate. Fortunately, she took only one scoop.

The meal passed fairly quickly, with the other officers casting sidelong glances at Ryan and his people when they thought they weren't watching, which was never. Along with the mash and fruit, there were roasted slices of breadfruit, which Ryan enjoyed, finding the taste almost, but not quite, like a potato. The sugared and grilled mango and pineapple slices were terrific.

At last, the breakfast was over, and all eyes turned once again to Elial, who had been brought forward to stand at the edge of the deck where a section of railing had been removed. On the other side of the deck, a team of six men stood with the end of a thick rope in their hands. The other end of it trailed over the side and, Ryan figured, ran under the ship to connect to the rope binding Elial's hands.

Captain Frost pushed back his chair and stood. "Ensign Elial Forth, you have been found guilty of dereliction of your duty to both your fellow crew members and to the *Ocean Queen* itself."

As he spoke, the condemned man began hyperventilating, sucking great gulps of oxygen into his lungs.

"Your punishment is to be keelhauled across the front bow of the ship, at which point, should you survive, you shall be brought back aboard and welcomed once more into the fold of your fellow sailors. Let the punishment by carried out, and may De Kooning's mercy bless you."

As one, everyone assembled on deck murmured, "De Kooning's mercy."

Elial turned so he faced the ocean. Chief Officer Markson nodded at the men on the far side. As one, they all heaved on the line they held. The sailor disappeared off the deck as if he had never existed. Ryan listened for the splash of him hitting the water, but they were too high up.

"Pull hard, men—one of your own's down there! Let's bring him back on board quickly and safely!" Markson said as the men hauled the line in as fast as they could. About halfway through, they ran into some resistance, and had to let the line play back out a bit.

"Harder—come on, put your backs into it!" Markson cried as they took up the slack again. The men did as he commanded; however, now they were pulling the line in much faster, as if a weight on the other end had suddenly been cut free. After a half dozen more pulls, all they came up with was frayed end of the line.

"Dammit! Man overboard! I want longboats on both sides looking for him!" Markson's shouted orders rang out over the crew, who scrambled to comply.

"Fancy that happening," Mildred said as she selected a small piece of roasted breadfruit and popped it into her mouth. "Damn shame to lose a good man like that, particularly over such a minor infraction."

"He will be found," Frost said, his face grim as he pushed away from the table so hard his chair went over backward. Accompanied by the other officers, he stalked down to the deck to confer with Markson, who was still bellowing orders.

"Perhaps this ship is not quite as shipshape as we first thought," Doc said, then broke into a burst of giggles at his statement.

"Mebbe not, but that doesn't affect us right now," Ryan said as he pushed back from the table, as well. "Let's get ready to head down, then go talk to them—" he nodded at Frost and the others "—once they've gotten their shit straightened out."

DEEP INSIDE THE *Ocean Queen,* Krysty had slept fitfully. With no natural light, it was difficult to keep track of time. At least AIDAN had created an artificial sense of day and night through its lighting of the corridors and rooms in Poseidon Base. Even though she could usually lie down, sleep like a rock, and awaken at a moment's notice, a useful—and necessary—survival ability, slumber eluded her.

Again, most of it was due to her environment. Unlike Ryan and the others abovedecks, once again Krysty was cut off from nature, and the lack of it was really starting to tell on her. While it was true that much of Deathlands was still a poisoned, uninhabitable wasteland, life still managed to find a way. The pockets of unspoiled beauty they found in their travels was proof of that, and was often enough to nourish her soul amid all of the blood and death.

Out here, however, nature was kept at bay, whether by the artificial construction of Poseidon Base or this floating madhouse. Actually, being forced to stay below on the boat was much worse, Krysty realized. It reeked of man's hand in every rivet and seam, and especially in the nuclear reactor powering this vessel. Even the ocean, as beautiful and savage as it could be, wasn't close enough to Krysty for her to be at her very best. Add to that the various odd noises the ship made—creaks and groans and vibrations that set her mind on edge just when she had gotten herself quiet and calm—and she hadn't had a very restful night.

Finally, after her wrist chron told her she'd been fruitlessly trying to sleep for the better part of two hours, after getting about four hours total during the whole "night," Krysty sat up in her bed. She yawned, shook her head and decided to take a walk in hopes of finding some kind of porthole or something where she might be able to get some fresh air.

She looked across the room at J.B. and Jak, both of whom appeared to be sound asleep. Krysty got up and walked to the door. "Going for a walk, J.B.," she whispered.

He slitted one eye open to regard her. "Think that's a good idea?"

"I'm not worried. Right now they need us more than we need them," she replied. "I'll be back in five."

"If you're not back in ten, I'll come looking for you," he said as he closed his eye again.

"Thanks." She pushed open the creaking door, stepped out and shut it behind her.

The smells of oil, sweat and rusting metal were stronger out here, and she wrinkled her nose in a vain attempt to block the odors. Krysty looked up and down the hallway, but each side looked exactly the same. With a shrug, she turned left and began walking, the heels of her cowboy boots clicking on the metal-grid floor.

Apart from the boat's general noises, it was quiet at this time of day. Of course, Krysty didn't really know when a busy time really would be, since she hadn't seen many other Downrunnners since being brought aboard.

Continuing down the hallway, she heard quiet voices ahead. "It'll just be a few more hours. Then the entire ship will belong to us!"

Freezing at the words, Krysty edged a bit closer. She carefully placed her boots on the floor as she walked to avoid making a sound.

"Perhaps, but the ones the captain's working with didn't seem too on board with what he wants them t'do," a male voice said. "I think they're still gonna go through with it, but they may just come down here to find their own. How sure are you about these Recovered you're working with?"

"They're on board with us. The Chif Engner brought them over with his story!" a familiar female voice said. "We just need to get them up there and taking care of business, and then we step in and finish the job. Come on, we've still got a lot to do."

Footsteps rang on the metal ahead of her. Krysty had just taken a step forward, as if still walking, when Raina came around the corner with a dripping-wet man in tow. Her expression flipped from anticipation to surprise. "Oh—hello, Krysty!"

"Hi. I couldn't sleep, so I thought I'd take a walk around." Her mind racing, Krysty peered at the man next to Raina. "You look familiar—weren't you on one of the longboats that brought us in?" All the while, she was wondering if they knew she'd heard them. She had to get back to the others.

He nodded. "Elial's the name, miss. I was cast overboard after I spoke to one of your group too casually."

"Elial's joining us now," Raina said, holding his hand. "Is the rest of your group awake yet? I know that the Chif Engner is anxious to get started on the plan to stop the Topsiders."

"I'm sure they'll be awake soon enough," Krysty said, starting to turn. "I should go back and check. I'm sure they'll want to get started."

"No, you're not going anywhere." Raina's normally pleasant voice had turned cold and hard. "Grab her!"

Elial wrapped both arms around Krysty and lifted her off the ground. Krysty, however, knew several ways to get out of this hold and decided to use the most direct one. Lowering her head, she whipped it back into Elial's face. The crunch of breaking bone told her she'd hit right where she had wanted.

"Ow!" Dropping her, Elial clasped both hands to his nose, which was gushing bright red. "You bitch!"

"Shut up!" Raina said as she drew a rust-spotted blaster and pointed it at Krysty, who had been reaching for her own. "Don't! I really don't want to shoot you, but I will."

Krysty froze, her hand inches away from her own weapon. She calculated the odds of Raina's old blaster actually firing, but decided the risk was too great, and slowly took her hand away from the butt. "What are you doing? We're on the same side, remember?"

"Not exactly," Raina replied. "And now that we're so close, I just can't take the chance that you overheard something you shouldn't have. This was going to happen anyway, you just stumbled into it a little faster than planned, that's all."

Krysty spread her hands out, trying to placate the other woman. "Look, all I really want is to find my friends topside and get out of here. I don't really care what you and he and anyone else down here have in mind, so if you'd just let us go do what we're supposed to do for you, we can get it done and get out of here."

"That's the other problem," Raina said. "Come on, we're taking a little walk. Go past me and don't try anything, or I will shoot you."

"If you do, won't the shot attract attention?" Krysty asked.

"If it does, you won't care, because you'll already be dead," Raina replied. "Get moving."

Krysty did so, keeping her hands up and out. She doubted a scream would carry back down to their quarters, and she knew ten minutes hadn't gone by yet, so her only hope was to stall them until J.B. came looking for her. "What do you mean?"

"Keep moving—I won't ask next time." Raina prodded her hard in the kidney with the blaster's muzzle. "You people are mercs—you don't really give a damn about us or what we're fighting for. So we knew it'd be necessary to keep one of you as a hostage in order to make sure the others do their jobs. Once it's done, we'll be happy to send all of you on your way."

Krysty decided to lay her cards on the table. "Okay, assuming that works, and my friends don't just come down here to get us out and chill you anyway, what are you planning with Elial? From what I heard, it sure didn't sound like you were part of the Downrunners."

"You did hear us! I knew it!" Raina said. "What very few people—and now you—know is that there's a third group on board."

"Raina..." Elial said, his voice stuffy-sounding due to his broken nose.

She waved him off. "It doesn't matter now—who is she going to tell? It operates behind the scenes, working against both groups!"

"Why?"

"Because the leaders of this ship, both above and belowdecks, are stupid fools!" Raina replied. "This ship is the ultimate power on the seas. Nothing can come close to it. Yet they're content with what they have, living hand-to-mouth like this, and the rest of us can go hang if we don't like it."

Raina's voice had gotten more strident as she continued. "Well, we say 'no more!' Once you take care of the officers up above, and your people take care of the leaders down here, we'll be poised to swoop in and take over both sides. We'll bring them back under one group of leaders and give anyone who doesn't wish to join us the option to be set ashore on an island. Then, we will begin taking what is ours, and no one out there will be able to stop us!"

As her captor kept talking, Krysty reached one inescapable fact: Raina was totally insane. Unfortunately,

Krysty couldn't do anything about it, as they had reached the room where she was to be held prisoner—the same one that Jak had been held in. "You aren't serious?"

"Oh, yes, we are," Raina replied. "We can't risk you going anywhere until your friends have done what we wish of them—on both sides. Once it is done, and we are in control, we will free all of you."

Krysty nodded, although she knew the odds of that happening were very slim. J.B. had always said the first rule of assassination was to kill the assassin. With hundreds of square miles of ocean around to dump bodies in, these people would have no reason to keep the companions alive once they'd finished their work. In fact, they'd be more of a threat to the new rulers, since they would have the firepower and ability to take them down, as well.

She had to figure out how to get a message to J.B., and she was running out of options.

The good news was that no guards were on duty here, since there was no prisoner inside—yet. If she was going to escape, it would have to be now.

Krysty sensed that Raina was now standing about two feet behind her. She stopped at the doorway, putting both her hands on the edges. "I'm not going in there."

"Yes, you are!" Raina stalked forward to push her into the room.

Exactly what the redhead had wanted her to do.

Whirling, Krysty swept her right hand up and out, catching Raina's forearm and pushing the blaster away from her. Her left hand was moving, as well, aiming a punch at Elial's still-bleeding nose. She connected, making him squeal like a stuck pig and dance away, fresh tears springing to his eyes.

With one attacker temporarily disabled, Krysty

turned to Raina to finish her off, only to find that the
blonde woman wasn't going down without a fight. Already recovered from the shove on her arm, she was
now trying to bring down the butt of her blaster on her
former prisoner's head. She got close, but a tendril of
her hair uncurled out and coiled around Raina's wrist.

"What the fuck—?" she cried, instinctively pulling
away. That was all the distraction Krysty needed. She
hauled off and punched the other woman in the jaw. As
she stumbled backward, the redhead followed up with
a jab to the abdomen, making Raina fall to her knees,
gasping for air. But even so, she lunged forward, wrap-
ping her arms around Krysty's legs and trying to shove
her off balance.

Hopping backward, Krysty interlaced her fingers and
brought her hands down in a punishing hammer blow
on the other woman's back. Raina groaned in agony
but didn't let go, so Krysty did it a second time. Raina
slumped to the floor but still wouldn't release her grip.

Krysty had just bent down to pry her arms off when
she felt a heavy blow on the back of her head, and everything went black.

Chapter Twenty-Nine

Ryan and company were heading up to the captain's room to go over the plans for infiltrating the Downrunners' lair. "Remember, we're here to get whatever information we need to get our people back and get out of here. From this point on, everyone keep their minds on the mission, and only open your mouths if you have a question or a valid point to raise. Got it?"

Both Doc and Mildred looked innocently back at him, despite Ryan pinning each of them with his best glare. Finally, they both nodded. Ricky, of course, was already on board.

"Probably wouldn't be any fun, anyway. The head jackass is still pretty pissed about losing his man," Mildred said. She was right. Although the rescue crews had searched for more than an hour, they'd found no sign of Elial.

"All the more reason for us to be polite and helpful, and that means all of us," Ryan replied. "I'm not any more pleased with this guy than you are, but he's got what we need, so we just have to play along for a little while longer, got it?"

"All right, all right," she replied. "Can't vouch for Doc, though. Since he's been firing on all cylinders lately, who knows what'll come out of his mouth?"

"I'd prefer that Doc keep any pithy comments to himself until we're safely away," Ryan said. "If any of you get the urge to make trouble, step outside. What I'm saying is if you really want to get out of here, don't make it any harder than it already is."

Mildred and Doc both nodded this time.

An ensign standing outside the door nodded to them, then knocked on the door. "Ryan Cawdor and the others are here, Captain."

"Show them in," Frost said. Ryan and his companions walked in to find the room much more businesslike than the previous day. Markson, Coller and Frost were clustered around a square table with a large roll of paper on it.

"Captain," Ryan said. "Any word about your missing man?"

The captain rubbed his face. "No sign of him, yet. I wouldn't put it past the Downrunners to have snatched him, possibly to hold him for ransom. While I hate to expand the scope of what you're already doing for us, could you keep an eye out for him down there?"

"We'll do what we can, but finding our people and removing the Downrunners in charge are our top priorities," Ryan said. "I don't know if we'll have the time or ability to find him, but we'll keep an eye out. Now, take us through what you've got."

"You're sure all of you are okay with this?" Coller asked with one black eyebrow raised. "I'm aware that some in your group aren't too thrilled with how we do things here."

Ryan opened his mouth to speak, but the captain beat him to it. "Now, now, Aturk, they're here, aren't they? I think that serves as more than enough proof of their intentions. Am I right, Ryan?"

"Exactly." Ryan turned his attention to the table. "What've you got?"

Coller unrolled the papers, which were detailed blue-prints of the ship that had been laminated for protection long ago. Changes to just about every section of the cruise ship were depicted.

"The good news is that you and your people will be able to gain access to the Downrunners' main floor in a straight shot *here*." He pointed at an elevator shaft at the front of the ship. "They don't head up toward the front nearly as much as they used to—they think they'll run into some of us there."

"And would they?" Ricky asked.

"Time was, yes," Coller replied. "I think they've just forgotten about it over the years, but we haven't."

"You said good news. What's the bad?" Ryan asked.

"It's the farthest away from their main living quarters, as well as the engineering room and the nuclear reactor," Coller replied. "Figured you'd prefer the element of surprise rather than heading down right into the thick of them."

"You've got that right," Ryan replied as he studied the complex maze of corridors and service passageways. "So, there's this main hallway running the length of the ship, except for bulkheads, and it's paralleled by two smaller ones, one on the left and one on the right."

"That's correct," Coller said. "As you can see, there are four cross hallways that you can use to keep moving toward the rear of the ship, where most of the people are."

"You don't expect us to kill everyone we come across, do you?" Mildred asked.

"Not at all," Frost replied. "As I had mentioned yesterday, we would prefer the lowest body count possible, because we'll need people to run the systems afterward." He tapped a spot on the paper. "Your primary target is the Chif Engner, who's usually here, near the reactor itself."

"Obviously you'll need to use extreme caution while working around the reactor," Markson said.

Ryan nodded. "Who are the other targets?"

"You need to secure the main engineering room, as well, which lies behind the reactor," Frost continued. "There should be a working ship's intercom in there. Once you've secured it, call us, and we'll come in and handle the rest. When it's over, you'll all be free to go."

Ryan looked at Coller. "At breakfast you said you were trying to figure out where they might be holding the rest of my people. Got any ideas?"

The huge man stroked his chin. "If they're holding them prisoner, near as I can figure, they'd be over here." He pointed at a row of rooms alongside the curve of the port side of the hull. "They harass us out of these, and use them to fish. The rooms are bare and metal, making them perfect prisoner quarters."

"Okay. And for the sake of argument, what if they're not there?" Ryan asked.

"If they've cut some kind of deal…" Coller frowned as he looked over the blueprints, although Ryan couldn't tell if he was reacting to the idea or was simply trying to find the most logical place to keep guests below. "They're most likely here." He pointed to a series of rooms amidships, just off the main hallway. "That's where most of them rest."

Ryan took one more close look at the blueprints, fixing intersections, rooms, and the general layout in his mind. He looked around at the others. "Any questions?" When no one replied, he said, "Okay, we've got it. Take us to the elevator shaft."

KRYSTY AWOKE TO PAIN.

The first thing she noticed was the side of her head throbbing where Elial had clobbered her. As she returned to full consciousness, she felt the dull pain of sore muscles in her shoulders, arms and wrists. Feeling her arms stretched out to either side, she tried to bring them down, only to realize with a jingling of chains that she couldn't.

Bastards got me stretched up like they did Jak, she thought. There was something else odd about her condition, but once she opened her eyes, Krysty discovered the last humiliation that had been inflicted on her.

She was completely nude. They hadn't even left her boots on, and she stood on bare feet on the cold metal floor. She heard the judas plate in the door slide open, and could feel the guards' eyes roaming up and down her body, whispering and chuckling to each other as they stared at her full, firm breasts, flat stomach and fit, muscular arms and legs. The view had to have been pretty spectacular, since her arms had been ratcheted to the sides so her breasts stood out proudly. It was a wonder the walking filth outside hadn't tried anything yet, but if she stayed here much longer, Krysty knew they probably would.

Her head slowly rose, green eyes flashing with fury. The betrayal she could deal with, even them holding her prisoner—after all, it's not like it was the first time it had happened. But to strip her and put her on display like this went way beyond the pale.

She flexed her sore shoulders, feeling the amount of give in the chains attached to her wrists. It would be difficult to summon the Gaia power here—she was already on edge from insufficient sleep and the fight with Raina and Elial, not to mention being stuck in here, surrounded by man-made smells and metal, but that wasn't going to stop her. All she needed was a focus, and she'd be off.

The ship lurched as a wave hit it, and in a flash, Krysty realized what that focus could be. Lowering her head again, she began channeling her power.

Gaia, hear me...your daughter needs your strength, your will...she thought. I am your vessel...fill me with your power until I overflow with it...give me the power of the mighty ocean itself...eternal, unstoppable, able to sweep away anything in its path...

As she wordlessly chanted in her mind, she felt the familiar, tingling warmth ignite in the pit of her stomach. It grew, spreading up and out until it filled every limb, every finger and toe. Finally, it reached her mind, exploding in a glorious burst of incandescent light that made her feel as light as a feather...and as strong as a great white shark.

Krysty raised her head again. As she did, she flexed her arms, tearing the chains from their moorings on the wall. The guards outside sprang into action, unlocking the door and rushing in.

As they charged at her in what looked like slow motion, a part of her mind noted that there were more of them than she'd expected, but it didn't matter—they were all about to die.

She snapped both chains forward at the first two. The one attached to her left hand whipped out, the heavy link at the end smashing into the guard's face. It punched through his right temple, shattering it, and sending him skidding down to the floor, dead before he hit.

Her right-hand chain curled around the second guard's ankle, ensnaring it. She pulled as if she was opening a door, not only yanking him off his feet, but sliding him across the room into the sole of her foot, which broke his jaw and knocked him unconscious.

The second pair of Downrunners entered right behind their unfortunate companions and charged straight at her, as well, no doubt planning to overwhelm her by brute force and the use of their metal-wrapped clubs.

Even with only moments left of her power, Krysty was confident that this would be the last mistake they would ever make.

The man on her left leaped over the twitching body on the floor. She pulled the chain up and over, grabbing it so she was holding a length about three feet long between her hand and her manacled wrist. As the guard brought his club down toward her head, she raised the chain to block it, then twisted it so the club was now caught in a loop. Using her momentum, she stepped aside, wrenching the weapon out of his hands. Before he could react, she brought her left wrist back across his face, smashing him with the manacle. The blow fractured his cheekbone and sent him to the floor, clutching the injury. As he drew in breath to scream, she drove her bare heel into his throat, fracturing his larynx and making any kind of noise from his swelling throat impossible. The man clutched at his face and throat as he slowly choked to death.

Caught by surprise, the last guard had to change course to go after her. He swung his club from the shoulder in a roundhouse blow that would have taken her head off her shoulders.

Krysty, however, wasn't there anymore. Having ducked under the wild swing, she flicked her right chain up again, making it undulate through the air and around his head, where she caught it with her left hand and drew it tight around the back of his neck. Before the man could recover, she pulled down on his neck with the chain while pistoning her knee up into his nose, shattering it, and knocking him out.

The whole thing had taken less than twenty seconds.

As the last man collapsed, Krysty's superhuman strength drained out of her, and she sank to her knees. Hearing footsteps in the corridor outside, she crawled to the nearest guard and pulled at the blaster on his belt, drawing it just as a figure appeared in the doorway.

"Krysty? Dark night, what happened to you?"

She raised the blaster to point at the ceiling a moment before she would have shot J.B. "Raina…Elial…" she gasped. "They're part of another…group…planning to chill…both sides…and take over ship…"

"Figures. Come on, let's get your clothes and get you out of here." One of the guards had the key to her manacles in his pocket. J.B. quickly unlocked them, then went outside to search for her clothes. He returned moments later and helped her dress. Another guard had her Smith & Wesson blaster, which she took back. Clothed and armed, Krysty felt a bit more like herself.

"What take so long?" Jak asked from the corridor, his blaster in hand.

"Krysty's just taking a moment to make herself decent," J.B. replied with a brief smile.

"You're lucky I'm as weak as a kitten right now, or I'd slap that smile right off your face," she muttered.

"No doubt you would," J.B. said as he slung her arm around his shoulders and started heading for the door. "No doubt you would."

"Sure we want to go this way?"

Ryan, Mildred, Doc and Ricky all peered into the darkness of the elevator shaft that was supposed to take them to the bottom level of the ship. Mildred had just voiced that very reasonable question, and even Ryan was considering finding another way down. However, time was wasting, and three of their own were still held below somewhere.

"The ladder should still be perfectly safe," Frost said. "If you're worried about the weather, I'm afraid there isn't much we can do about that."

The storm front off to the west had moved in, and the ship was rolling back and forth in the higher seas. Ryan had checked to make sure that their escape pod was still secured to the stern, as there was no sense in going through all this effort only to find their means of escape had broken free and drifted away. Frost had assured him that it was, but Ryan had still gone back and checked for himself.

"We do it as planned," he replied, testing the service ladder with all his weight to make sure it was secure. Only when he was positive did he climb fully onto it. "I go first, then Ricky, then Doc, then Mildred, at five-second intervals. Get to the bottom and clear the ladder for the next person. Ricky, you and your carbine will be with me on the door. Everybody got it?"

The other companions nodded.

"Good luck," Captain Frost said, holding out his hand to Ryan. Hesitating, but not wanting to insult the man, Ryan shook his hand. "We'll be waiting for your call from the maintenance deck."

Ryan just nodded and began climbing down as quietly as he could. With every rung, he descended from full light to dim light, then into pitch-blackness. Each person carried portable lights that were provided by the officers, but Ryan had forbid using them on the way down. Even with the officers' assurances that this shaft wasn't used by anyone below, he didn't want to risk alerting anyone down there.

The ladder shook slightly under his hands and feet, but Ryan ignored it and kept going, hand, foot, hand, foot. He tried to listen for any noises from below, but couldn't hear anything.

He'd kept a rough mental count of how far he'd gone in terms of yards, and slowed when he hit one seventy-five, figuring the floor had to be pretty close now. And it was, although it wasn't quite what he'd expected.

Ryan stepped down onto the roof of the old elevator itself, his boots thumping on the roof and echoing through the shaft. He froze, straining to hear if the noise had alerted anyone. Ricky was coming down, and Ryan grabbed the youth's leg to make him stop before he made the same mistake.

"Elevator's still here," he whispered. "Step down quietly, then find the access hatch."

The kid did just that, standing on the roof and moving to the opposite corner so Mildred and Doc could join them. Ryan repeated the warning twice more, and both of them left the ladder with relative ease, although Doc stumbled a bit and nearly fell, only saving himself by grabbing Ryan's outstretched arm.

"Easy, Doc!" he hissed.

The old man removed his hand and brushed imaginary dust off his frock coat. "I am all right."

Ryan had already walked around to where Ricky was crouched. "Find the hatch?"

"Yeah, but I think we've got trouble," the youth whispered back. "I'm pretty sure I heard voices below, and I can't tell if they're inside the box or out."

"Bastard! Frost and Coller said this was supposed to be deserted!" Even while seething at the faulty intelligence, Ryan still kept his voice low. "All right, get your carbine ready. I'm going to open the door, you clear the inside. If they're there, chill them. If not, we hit the floor and figure out where they are. Ready?"

His companions nodded. Ryan grasped the handle of the door and slowly began turning it. It didn't budge. He put more pressure on it—still nothing.

"Nukeshitting…piece of…drek!" he hissed through his teeth as he threw all of his strength into turning the latch. When it finally gave, it did so with an ease that surprised Ryan, nearly throwing him off balance. He lifted the metal panel, which now opened easily, just a crack, and made sure Ricky was ready before opening it all the way.

Leading with his De Lisle, the boy stuck his head and shoulders through the gap, sweeping the entire elevator. The interior was empty, and now Ryan could hear snatches of conversation through the metal doors.

"Why the nuke are we out here, again?"

"Because the Recovered we took yesterday escaped and are loose on this level," the second person replied. "Just keep your eyes open and report if you see anything. I heard they're very dangerous. Killed six when they broke out."

"De Kooning save us!"

"Yeah, so keep your eyes peeled, okay?"

While the two kept talking, Ryan signaled to Ricky that he'd lower him to the floor, then pass down his carbine. Ryan would follow, and they would chill the two guards.

Handing his weapon to Mildred, Ricky put his legs through the hatch and held his arms out to Ryan, who was now lying down and had made Doc sit on his legs for a counterweight. Ryan grabbed the kid's wrists and lowered him through the square hole, feeling the strain on his shoulders and lower back. However, he was able to lower Ricky almost to the floor. When he let go, the kid dropped only a few inches. He hit with hardly a sound, certainly not overheard by the two chatting guards on the other side of the door.

Ryan handed him the carbine, then slowly lowered himself to the floor, as well. Padding silently to the metal doors, he inserted his fingers in the seam down the middle and tugged at them experimentally. They didn't budge.

Ryan put his ear to the metal and listened to the two men talking until he had a good idea of where they were standing. He backed up, pointed to Ricky and mimed shooting through the doors. He held up two fingers as he pointed to each panel, indicating that Ricky should put at least two bullets into each man.

Ricky nodded, then raised the De Lisle to his shoulder and aimed carefully. He squeezed the trigger, the carbine firing the heavy .45 ACP round that punched through the elevator's thin door and into the back of the man on the other side. Ricky worked the bolt, the sound louder than the shot, and fired again, then turned to the other side, counting on surprise to let him get at least one more shot off before the second guard could raise the alarm.

And at first, it seemed to be working. The first guard had only grunted when he took the first bullet. The second one apparently noticed, since he asked, "Hey, what's wrong with you?" A moment later, the second shot plowed into the guard's back, making him sag to the floor.

"Shit!" the other guard said as Ricky chambered another round and aimed. They heard a footstep from outside.

"Shoot!" Ryan whispered.

Compensating for the man's movement, Ricky squeezed the trigger again. The bullet punched through the door, but ricocheted off something inside it. Ryan heard panicked footsteps receding into the distance.

"Fireblast! Get the others down here and follow me!" he snapped as he ran to the doors and pried them far apart enough to squeeze through. He took off down the cluttered corridor after the fleeing guard, who was shouting for help. "So much for surprise, dammit!" he muttered as he drew his SIG Sauer and snap-shot two rounds at the running man.

A dozen yards ahead, the guard hit the wall and rebounded just as Ryan fired. The bullets smacked into where he had been, making the one-eyed man grit his teeth. "Dammit, he's fast!"

Ryan stopped at the corner and poked his head out fast enough to see if anyone was lying in wait for him. No one was there, just the shrinking form of the running guard. Ryan steadied his blaster hand with his other one and lined up on the man's back, but he disappeared around another corner before he could shoot.

"Nuking hell!!" Ryan raised his blaster and turned to see the others coming up behind him. "Surprise is gone. Let's find our guys, then see if we can get to the Engineer. Come on!"

Chapter Thirty

J.B. sent a burst of fire from his Uzi down the hallway, making another rad-sore-covered man carrying a spear gun duck for cover. He exchanged magazines while Jak covered him. "I don't know how much more of this my ears can take."

The last ten minutes had been a flurry of running, hiding, and shooting. The alarm had been raised almost immediately after they'd freed Krysty. Since then, they'd been navigating the confusing tangle of hallways, pipes and machinery in an attempt to get someplace where they could start heading to the upper decks.

Unfortunately, the Downrunners had figured out their plan, and had been waiting at every staircase and elevator shaft they'd come across so far. J.B. and Jak had kept them at bay with carefully placed shots—nearly deafening themselves from the roar of the albino's hand cannon—but they also couldn't risk attacking, as the Downrunners were well-fortified and armed with spear guns that would put a serious hurt on anyone they hit. Add to all this the fact that they were running low on ammo, the ship was pitching and yawing like crazy, and their perplexity as to where they even were in its damn bowels, and it was not looking good for them at all.

The three had taken refuge in an intersection where they were pretty sure no one was behind them. They'd been holding off the Downrunners pursuing them while figuring out their next steps.

"Still think we charge enemy," Jak said. "Blasters blazing—make scatter!"

"Yeah, or they might put a barbed spear through your gut," the Armorer replied as he sent another shot at their pursuers. "We need to get the hell out or change the odds somehow."

"Disable the reactor?" Krysty asked. "We can't let any fuel spill into the ocean."

"No, more like capture it and use it as leverage to get us out of here," J.B. said, then paused as another idea struck him. "Or, we could find the steam turbines the reactor powers and threaten to disable those. But we have to get to them first."

"Settle for getting out here," Jak grumbled as he raised his blaster, making the other two plug their ears as he fired. A thin scream of pain from down the hallway told them he'd tagged at least one of the enemy. "Can't sit here forever!"

"Okay, hang on. It makes sense that those turbines would be close to the reactor, right?" Krysty asked. "We need to get back there and find them. Once we locate them, we take the room and then negotiate to get the hell out of here."

"Works for me," J.B. replied, handing her his submachine gun. "Here—give me a minute to prep a booby."

Krysty shot twice at their attackers, making a pair that was trying to move forward jump back under cover. One of them loosed his spear as they retreated, and she ducked as the barbed projectile whizzed overhead. "Hate to say it, but I'm starting to agree with Jak—maybe a charge into them is our best option."

J.B. had just finished prepping the detonator when he

caught a glimpse of movement down the cross-corridor behind them. "Shit…" Tucking the improvised bomb into his pocket, he scooped up his M-4000 and sent a cluster of flechettes that way, resulting in two bodies toppling over. "Sons of bitches tried to flank us! They had to come from somewhere. Let's backtrack to see if there's a way around the main corridor. Give them another blast and let's go!"

Jak and Krysty both let loose with their blasters, spraying the main hallway with lead for a couple seconds. Then they pulled back and followed J.B. down the side corridor. Sure enough, after several paces, it intersected with another hallway that paralleled the main one.

J.B. poked his head out to check, and turned left when he saw it was clear. "Come on, the reactor was this way, so the turbines should be, as well."

As they went, the ship lurched even harder, the entire vessel shaking as large waves slammed against the hull. "It's a miracle this thing's hung together this long," J.B. muttered.

"Yeah, but it sounds like it won't for too much longer if this keeps up," Krysty replied. "Come on, let's keep moving."

They trotted down the smaller hallway, J.B. on point, Krysty, still weak from using her Gaia power, in the middle, and Jak watching their backs. Apparently their reverse flanking maneuver had taken the main group by surprise, as there were no immediate signs of pursuit. "Could sneak up, chill them before chill us," Jak suggested.

"Tempting as that may be, they're not truly our enemy," J.B. replied. "We're just trying to get out of here. 'Course, that doesn't mean I won't chill anyone who gets in my way, either."

After going about a hundred more feet with no sign of anyone around them, J.B. called a brief halt.

"We should be close by now, righ—" His words were cut off as a wiry Downrunner with a knife in her hand leaped on him from her hiding place above a row of pipes running parallel to the ceiling. The impact drove him to the ground, his Uzi flying from his hands.

Screeching in rage, the woman, who looked as if she had been badly burned across much of her face and arms, raised the blade to stab J.B. in the back. Grabbing her arm, which was around his neck, he flipped her over to land with a breath-stealing thud on the metal floor. He trapped her wrist and forced her to drop the knife. Krysty retrieved his machine blaster and handed it to J.B., who put the muzzle right between the woman's eyes.

"Take us to the engine room right now!" he ordered.

As thoroughly cowed now as she had been ferocious a few moments ago, the woman nodded. J.B. let her up, but kept a hand on the back of her neck and the barrel of the Uzi in her back. "Go. Now!"

It turned out they were close. The woman led them a few more steps down the corridor, then pointed at a door that had the symbol for electricity on it, a jagged bolt of black lightning with an arrow at the bottom of it.

"All right." J.B. took his hand from the woman's neck. "Go tell your Chif Engner that we control the turbines. If he doesn't want them blown up, he's going to figure out a way to get us out of here. He has five minutes to return with his offer. You got that?"

She nodded again.

"Then go!"

They watched the woman tear off down the corridor. "I sure hope she can talk," Krysty said. "We never checked."

J.B. stared at her in disbelief. "*Now* you bring that up?" He shook his head. "Come on, let's get in here and set the charge. I'm half tempted to let the damn thing go off anyway, regardless of what the Chief says."

WITH THE ELEMENT of surprise blown, Ryan, Ricky, Mildred and Doc didn't waste time trying to sneak around. Since the majority of the Downrunners didn't have firearms, they were easy pickings, or at least they could be forced to retreat with a judicious application of firepower.

The encounters settled into an odd kind of rhythm; Ryan and the others would advance until they spotted someone, then shoot until their opponents either fled or were chilled. After the third such skirmish, in which they'd downed one and sent two more running for their lives, a white flag was waved from behind a barrel.

"Recovered, can we speak? No blasters, no shooting?"

"We can hear you just fine," Ryan answered. "What do you want?"

"For all of you to get the hell out of here!" the Downrunner replied. "Chif Engner said the rest of your group is holed up in turbine room, and to come to you with a truce flag. We take you there, you take them and we let you go, okay?"

"No bullshit, or I swear we'll kill every last one of you!" Ryan shouted. "Take us to them right now!"

The skinny man with smears of grease on his face and only three fingers on his hand emerged, holding the flag in front of him as if it might stop any incoming bullets. "Yes, yes, I take you there right away. Follow me."

"Finally," Ryan said. "First sign of a double-cross, and you get a bullet in the back."

"No, no, we just want you to get your people and go!" he said over his shoulder as he scurried down the hallway.

"Ricky, watch our six," Ryan said as he strode after the little man.

Without having to blast their way through knots of resistance, the group made its way through the ship much more quickly. Soon they were at the door to the turbine room.

"Here, they're in here," the man said as he backed away.

Ryan hammered on the door with his fist. "Krysty? J.B.? Jak? You in there?"

"Ryan, is that you?" Krysty shouted back.

"Yeah, come on. We're getting out of here!"

He heard steps approaching, and a moment later, the door opened and Krysty was in his arms. "Good to see you, lover," she said.

"You, too," he replied. "J.B., Jak. Come on, we're getting out right now."

"Sounds good to me," the Armorer said. "Just a second." He turned to the Downrunner who had led them to the room. "I've placed an explosive charge somewhere in the turbine room. Only I know where it is. We walk out of here unmolested, and when we're safely off the ship, I'll tell you where I hid it."

"How can we trust that you will do as you say?" the man asked.

J.B.'s smile was as friendly as a shark's. "You don't really have a choice now, do you? But trust me, if anyone messes with us, the whole room goes up, and with it your steering and power. You got it?"

The men smiled nervously, revealing rotted teeth and gums as he held up the white flag again. "Yes, I understand."

"All right, let's go." Ryan led the way, with Krysty beside him. "What happened to your wrists?"

"I'll tell you later," she replied. "Did you see a woman with blond hair, or a guy who came down here from top-side named Elial?"

"So he is here." Ryan quickly filled her in on what had happened abovedecks, but when he got to the keel-hauling, she interrupted him.

"It was a fake. He wanted to go under so he could be brought down here. There's a third group playing both sides against each other—"

"That's right, Krysty," a voice said from farther down the corridor. "And we're still going to make it happen."

Before anyone could react, there was a loud clank, and a tide of acrid-smelling fluid sloshed across the floor toward them. Ryan was the first to recognize what it was.

"Shit—kerosene!"

Chapter Thirty-One

"Nobody shoot!" Ryan ordered. "You'll light it on fire!"

"Smarter than you look, Recovered," Raina said from the darkness. "You and your friends *are* going to complete the job you started—for both sides. We haven't come this far to fail now. You don't, or you make a move to shoot, and I light up this whole damn corridor!"

Sensing a presence beside him, Ryan looked out of the corner of his eye to see Jak edging forward, throwing knife held between his index and second fingers of the hand at his side. "All right, now, let's talk about this—"

"No! Time for that's done! You do it now or you die! There are no other choices—"

A muffled report made the whole ship shudder and slew to one side. A second later, all the lights along the corridor winked out. Thrown off balance, everyone stumbled or staggered to keep their footing.

"Now, Jak!" Ryan shouted as he turned on his flashlight and aimed it at where they'd heard Raina's voice.

The albino leaped into the air, the knife blurring out of his hand and into the darkness. He landed with a small splash in the puddled fuel. For a moment, there was only silence. Then, a faint, choking noise could be heard.

Ryan snapped on a flashlight to see Raina emerge from the darkness, her chest covered in blood pumping from the wound in her throat. Her mouth opened and closed as she touched the hilt of the knife, but didn't pull it free. Her face paled as the blood drained out of her body, and finally she slipped to her knees and fell forward onto her face. An unlit flare fell from her other hand.

"Fantastic hit!" Ricky said.

Jak walked over to the body and retrieved his blade, wiping it on her pants. "Not bad—"

A scream of rage alerted him to the second attacker in the dark hallway. Jak whirled to see Elial, his face swollen and bruised, charging straight at him. Like a deadly dancer, Jak whirled again, building up centrifugal force. He released it in a powerful spinning kick that smashed into the sailor's face, knocking him off his feet and sending him slamming into the wall, headfirst. He fell backward and didn't move.

"He's dead," Jak said without even checking. "Let's leave."

"Hang on. What was that explosion?" Ryan asked.

J.B. was looking back down the corridor. "I think that booby I set in the turbine room went off prematurely—must have been a faulty detonator."

Just then the ship tilted even more, almost to a forty-five-degree angle before slowly righting. "I don't think the ship is ever supposed to do *that*," Mildred said.

"We better get topside triple quick," Ryan said. "Come on. We're heading back to the shaft we used to get here. Once we get on deck, we head for the escape pod and cast off."

The companions began running through the corridors. "Wait a sec," Krysty said as they jogged. "Aren't we heading away from the rear of the ship?"

"Where we're headed is the only place we'll be able to get back up," Ryan replied. "Topsiders blocked the rest of the stairways with steel plates and guards."

"Great," Krysty said as they turned a corner to head over to the main passageway. "Any other surprises we should know about?"

At the intersection that led back to the elevator shaft, Ryan rounded the corner to find a large party of Topsiders, led by their secman, Aturk Coller, heading straight toward them.

"Yeah," Ryan said. "Apparently the captain didn't trust us to get the job done and sent his boys after us to make sure."

The two groups stopped in the corridor, about twenty feet from each other. "What are you all doing down here?" Ryan asked.

"Felt the explosion in the rear of the ship, and the steering's gone. If we don't fix it, the ship's going to capsize," Coller said. "We came down to see if we could help. Did you finish the job?"

"No," Ryan said as he slowly began raising his blaster. "We brokered a truce with the Downrunners to get our people, and we're leaving now."

"By De Kooning's beard, you aren't going anywhere until you go back and kill the Chief Engineer!" Coller thundered as he raised his spear gun, which had a vicious-looking, triple-barbed harpoon on the end.

"Fuck this. Kill them—" was all Ryan got out before the ship lurched so hard that everyone was thrown off their feet into the walls. Ryan heard the twang of someone's spear gun releasing its projectile, but he was tumbling so hard he couldn't see where it was coming from or try to dodge it. The entire vessel began tipping—and kept going.

"She's capsizing!" Coller shouted as he tumbled about. "De Kooning save us!"

"Your bastard mummy isn't going to save anyone,

stupe!" Ryan snapped as his elbow slammed painfully into the wall, then he rolled with the impact to come back up on his feet. He found himself standing on the left wall, which had become the floor. Ryan checked on his people and found J.B. and Jak had kept their feet and were still pointing their blasters at the Topsider party.

"Anyone hurt?"

"I am afraid I have taken a nasty gash to the leg, Ryan," Doc said, clutching at a long, oozing slice across his thigh. "Fortunately, it does not seem to have cut any major arteries, although walking from this point on will be difficult, at best."

"You're going to have to do the best you can, Doc," Ryan said. "Ricky, give him a hand?"

"Right. Lean on me, Doc." Still pointing his carbine at the tangled mess of the Topsider party, Ricky put the older man's arm around his shoulders and held his wrist with his free hand. "Ready."

"Everyone else okay?"

Getting nods from the others, Ryan addressed the Topsiders. "Coller, there's nothing more to do down here but abandon ship. Now, we're going—through you if we have to, but we are going back up that shaft. What's it going to be?"

"All right, Ryan…" the huge man replied. "Let's go back to the ladder and get out of here—"

He was interrupted by the loud sound of metal rending under great stress.

"Now," Ryan said as he looked down the left hallway to see water already rushing into the hold. "We have to get out before the shaft goes under!"

Both men got the Topsider group, including several who had serious injuries, moving back to the elevator shaft. "Come on, people, we have to move!" Ryan said.

"Unless you want to be down here for the rest of your very short lives!"

The Topsiders began walking up the now-horizontal shaft, with the less injured helping those who couldn't move by themselves. All around them, everyone heard the shrieking of metal plates as they gave way under pressure they were never meant to bear.

The sound of rushing water grew louder as they hurried down the shaft. The ship pitched back and forth even more violently in the storm, making their footing treacherous. One of the Topsiders caught his leg in the ladder, snapping his ankle with an audible crack. Coller whirled and, with a speed Ryan wouldn't have thought him capable of, freed the man, hoisted him over his shoulder and kept plowing forward.

Ryan glanced back to see black ocean water rushing into the passageway and quickly gaining on them. "Move! Faster!"

Everyone started running, or at least moving as quickly as they could. Spotting Ricky laboring to haul a panting Doc along, Ryan fell back and grabbed the old man from him. "Go! Clear the way out!"

By now the water was lapping at their boots, with the two groups barely staying ahead of it. They could see a square of daylight ahead, and everyone redoubled their efforts.

Despite his load, Coller made it to the opening alongside Ryan, and together each man heaved his injured comrade up through the exit several feet overhead. It worked so well that they began lifting the others together by unspoken arrangement, nearly throwing the men out of the shaft onto the upended deck.

"Clear the exit as soon as each man is out!" Coller shouted with each toss. The ocean water was lapping around their ankles when it came time for Ryan's group to go.

"Get up and out—head for the rear of the ship," Ryan told everyone before they started out.

They propelled Ricky out first, then sent Doc up so the teenager could help him. Next came Jak, then Mildred, then Krysty.

Finally, J.B. and Ryan looked at Coller. "You're up."

The big man laughed. "You think you two can get me up there—" His words were interrupted by the splash of a fire hose landing next to them.

"Tie yourself off. We'll pull you up!" Ricky said.

Coller looked at Ryan, who nodded. "Outside, you're on your own, but at least we'll help you get there."

The secman looped the hose around his waist and gave it a tug, while Ryan and J.B. slung their weapons and readied themselves by making stirrups out of their interlaced hands for him to use as steps. "All right, on three! One—two—three!"

Bracing themselves in the thigh-high water, Ryan and J.B. took the man's weight with a groan as he clambered up their legs. They shoved at him with all their might as the others hauled him up to where he could grab the edge. Even Mildred and Krysty lent a hand in pulling him over the side. A moment later, the hose came back down.

"Climb up!"

"Go, J.B.!" Ryan said. "I'll be right behind you!"

The Armorer shinnied up the old hose, reaching the edge of the exit and climbing over. "Come on, Ryan!"

With the water swirling around his waist, Ryan grabbed the hose and started hoisting himself up. He had only gotten halfway there, however, when a tall wave burst through the shaft from the hold. It slammed into Ryan, knocking him into the wall and tearing the hose loose from its fixture outside.

"Ryan!" Krysty shouted, reaching down to him as he disentangled himself from the hose. "Grab my hand!"

The water was swirling around him even quicker now. Ryan lunged up to try to grab her fingers but missed them by inches. The water was still rising, but there was an undertow that threatened to drag him back under. "Can't….reach…you!"

"Here, good sir, perhaps this will help!" Doc's head appeared over the side, followed by the trunk of a coconut tree that slid down into the cool water. "Swim for it, Ryan!"

Striking out for it with all of his strength, Ryan got a hand on it and hung on for dear life. Once he got his other hand around the trunk, he climbed up and reached the top where J.B. and Krysty, along with Coller, could grab his arms and haul him out.

The scene on the overturned ship was total chaos. Crew members and officers ran everywhere through the sheets of driving rain, trying to keep their footing on the slippery walls. Hearing a scream from their right, Ryan and the others looked over to see Chief Officer Markson slide down the side into the frothing water.

"Good luck, Cawdor!" Coller saluted him, then ran off with his men to assist with the ship's evacuation.

"You too!" Ryan called after him. "All right, let's get to the rear!"

The others had already used the severed fire hose to tie themselves together. Ryan wrapped the end around his waist and began leading the way, hanging on to the railing as they went.

As they passed one of the other blocked stairways, they heard shouts and banging from the other side. "We have to open it!" Mildred shouted. "I'm not going to let them drown like trapped rats!"

"Fireblast!" Ryan said as the ship settled even lower and waves broke over the deck, showering all of them in seawater. "All right, I've got it!" He let go of the railing and waded to the barrier. Finding the hatch, he undid the bolt and opened it, allowing even more water to pour onto the deck from inside the ship. Also inside was a packed cluster of Downrunners, all of whom tried to get through the opening at once.

"Come on, come on, move it!" he shouted, grabbing one and hauling him out. "Go, go, go!" He grabbed two more and pulled them through, then left the rest to fend for themselves.

"Thank you, Ryan!" Mildred shouted.

"Just hope it didn't cost us our lives!" he shouted back.

The bow of the *Ocean Queen* was now completely under the waves, and the stern was rising into the air as they reached it. Incredibly, the escape pod was still tethered to the ship by the heavy chain, which whipped back and forth in the storm.

"We're going to have to go hand over hand down to it!" Ryan shouted. "J.B., you and I'll keep anyone else from following! Mildred, you first! Go!"

Gritting her teeth, the black woman grabbed the whip-sawing chain and began descending toward the pod. Her dangling weight made the chain settle down, and Ryan sent Doc after her once she had gotten about twenty feet out. Next, he brought Krysty forward and kissed her hard. "If Doc goes in, help him if you can. See you on the pod."

"You, too." She started to traverse the chain, which had now settled under the weight of the three people working toward the pod. Ryan let them get about half-way there, then sent Ricky and Jak down next. Once they were several yards out, Ryan turned to his oldest friend.

"You're up, J.B.!"

Turning from where he had been guarding their rear, J.B. slung his Uzi and grabbed the chain. "You're coming right behind me?"

"Damn right I am!" Ryan clapped his shoulder. "Go!"

The Armorer swung himself out over the wild water, swinging hand over hand. As he did, the rear of the cruise ship rose even higher in the air, exposing the huge propellers, which were still turning fruitlessly in the heavy rain.

Ryan let J.B. get out about five yards, and was about to grab the chain when he heard a shout from behind him. "Cawdor!"

It was followed by a blow to his head that sent Ryan skidding toward the ship's edge.

Chapter Thirty-Two

The moment he heard his name, Ryan had managed to duck just enough so the blow to his head didn't knock him out, but glanced off his skull, instead. He rolled over and regained his feet, shaking his head as he stood to face his attacker.

Captain Frost stood a few feet away, two of the modified oars in his hands. His uniform was soaked and smudged, with one sleeve half torn off. With the wind and rain lashing his face and hair, he looked like a man possessed. "You've ruined everything! You've destroyed everything that De Kooning and all of us have worked for, for the past hundred years!"

"This ship was ready to blow before we ever set foot on it," Ryan snarled. "I'm leaving now——" He stepped toward the chain but was stopped by Frost, who stepped in front of him. Ryan's hand dropped to the butt of his blaster, but the captain put the point of an oar to his throat.

"Touch that weapon and I'll stab you and feed you to the sharks!" Frost screamed. "You're not getting off that easily! The captain will be going down with the ship, but I'll have the pleasure of taking you with me!" He tossed the other oar at Ryan, who caught it out of reflex. The stern rose even higher as he stepped away from the other man, testing the weapon for its balance.

"Do you seriously——" was all he got out before the

other man was on him, wielding the oar like a staff, jabbing with the pointed end, then reversing it in a blur to swat at the one-eyed man's head with the flat end.

Ryan parried both attacks as he took another step backward, getting a feel for his weapon and the other man's fighting style. He dodged a jab at his hand and batted the oar out of the way, riposting with a shot to Frost's shoulder that made him grunt in pain.

"You learn fast!" the captain shouted over the roar of the propellers below them. "But I've been fighting with these for years!" He reversed his oar and swept at Ryan's feet. Although he skipped back a step, the oar caught him on the shin with a painful smack.

Limping a bit now, Ryan circled the captain until he had the man's back to the very rear of the ship. He feinted with the pointed oar at the other man's head, then at his hands, then brought the other end down in an overhead chop at Frost's head.

The captain brought his oar up to block, but Ryan kept battering at his head, driving the man backward with each blow, and not allowing him any time to use a different defense. They drew closer and closer to the edge, and finally Ryan raised his oar and brought it down in a crushing blow that broke Frost's weapon in two.

Frost drew back and threw the oar's pointed end at Ryan, who batted it out of the way. Holding the oar end like a club, the captain screamed with rage and charged, his weapon raised overhead to smash Ryan's skull.

Ryan met him head-on, bracing his oar and setting it against the crazy man's charge. Seeing the danger, Frost tried to stop but his feet skidded on the wet deck, and he fell onto the sharpened end of the oar. The large spike caught him just below the heart, piercing straight through and coming out his back in a thick gout of blood.

"Cawdor…" Frost sagged against him, driving the pole even farther into his body. "My ship is lost…. End this…please.…"

With a last shriek of tortured metal, the *Ocean Queen* began slipping under the surface of the water. Ryan pushed Frost over to the edge of the stern and held him over the whirling propellers. Frost's head lolled on his shoulders, but at the last second, he seemed to become aware of what was about to happen, and nodded.

Without a word, Ryan let him go. He fell into the spinning blades and was chopped to the side by one of them, disappearing into the stormy ocean without a trace.

By now the stern was only a few feet above the water and sinking fast. As the propellers reentered the ocean, Ryan tried removing the pin from the link that connected the escape pod to the ocean liner, but it was bent, and he couldn't budge it. Unslinging his longblaster, he chambered a round and shot the chain once, then again. His last shot sheared off the end, and the pin began sliding out.

Ryan slung his longblaster and grabbed the end of the chain as it pulled away from the sinking ship. He kicked with his feet, trying to put as much distance between himself and the dying ship as possible, to avoid being sucked down with it. Even so, he felt the churning blades as they chopped the water beneath him, briefly sucking him under the surface.

Swimming as hard as he could with one hand, Ryan broke the surface and felt himself being hauled through the waves. The water pounded him so hard it was all he could do to hang on as he was drawn closer to the pod. Finally, however, he saw J.B. and Krysty reeling in the chain for all they were worth.

"Hang on, Ryan—almost there!" Krysty shouted as

she redoubled her efforts. Moments later, he was close enough to the side to grab their outstretched hands and be dragged aboard.

They shoved Ryan inside and closed and sealed the hatch. He fell to the floor, coughing up the seawater he'd swallowed on the way over. When his lungs were clear again, he rolled over and eyed his companions, who were gathered around him with anxious looks on their faces.

"I don't know...about all of you," he said between pants for air. "But I've had...enough of the...bastard ocean...and ships...to last a lifetime!"

* * * * *

TAKE 'EM FREE
2 action-packed novels plus a mystery bonus

NO RISK
NO OBLIGATION TO BUY

The
Don Pendleton's
Executioner®
SLEEPING DRAGONS

Lethal nerve gas falls into the grasp of a Libyan terrorist.

When a British CIA operative in Hong Kong dies moments after sending a cryptic text message, the government needs a special kind of help to deal with the foul play— under-the-radar Mack Bolan expertise. Ambushed at every turn, Bolan soon discovers that there's a new weapon of mass destruction on the market, a Sleeping Dragon, and a fanatical Arab plans to use it to take back Libya, killing millions in the process. His enemies believe they know their devils, but they haven't met the Executioner.

Available October wherever books and ebooks are sold.

AleX Archer
SUNKEN PYRAMID

At the bottom of a Wisconsin lake lies a deep secret....

Determined to investigate her friend's death—and find out why another is the prime suspect—archaeologist and TV host Annja Creed starts gathering the pieces of an erratic puzzle. At the center of it all is an ancient pyramid at the bottom of a Wisconsin lake...a discovery that could completely rewrite Mesoamerican history. But with each puzzle piece uncovered the mystery becomes more dangerous. And what Annja knows can—and will—kill her....

An ancient Mayan temple at the bottom of a lake leads to murder...

ROGUE ANGEL
AleX Archer
SUNKEN PYRAMID

Available November wherever books and ebooks are sold.

GOLD EAGLE®